BENEATH A HUNTER'S SKY

Short Fiction

**by
John
Bascom**

Canniche Cove Publishing
Gladwin, Michigan

Beneath a Hunter's Sky

Copyright © 2015 John G. Bascom

All rights reserved; permission required to reproduce in whole or any part

Canniche Cove Publishing
4472 Queens Way
Gladwin, Michigan 48624
www.cannichecove.com

Large Format Edition 2015
Printed in the United States of America

Text editing and proofreading by Sharon Honeycutt and Catherine McQueen; interior image editing assistance by Stacy Kitchen; cover design by John Bascom

Library of Congress Cataloguing-in-Publication Data in process and will be provided upon request when available

ISBN   -13: 978-0-9831892-4-4
       -10: 0-9831892-4-2

Beneath a

Hunter's Sky

<u>Stories</u>

<u>Stories</u>

<u>Stories</u>

This book is dedicated to all those who have

walked with me beneath a hunter's sky

Author's Note

I first heard of a *hunter's sky* on safari one very hot afternoon in Zimbabwe. It was late in the dry season and the temperatures were insufferably high, well over one hundred degrees. The sky was cloudless and the air dry. It hadn't rained for months. On this kind of day, my PH explained, a beige haze hung overhead even in the absence of any measurable humidity, filtering the sun and making it appear a sort of burnt, rusty orange. Heat waves shimmered over the dry riverbeds and just above the leafless mopane and acacia trees. Water sources largely go dry that late in the season. On such a day as this one, he explained, game would be heat-driven to bed down in shade during the height of the afternoon. With all quiet and the animals alert as they all are when resting, it would be unlikely we could approach. But as soon as the sun dropped near the horizon and the temps backed off, he went on, they would be compelled to slake their mounting thirst at the nearest surviving little spring or seep. And if a hunter knew the location of those few remaining watering spots, there they might be readily intercepted in the classic fair chase, track, or spot-and-stalk style of the wooded Zambezi Valley. It worked perfectly for us.

Later, back home, I had a chance to think about the hunter's sky. I was reminded of the different types of skies that characterized so many of my hunts throughout my lifetime, and especially of the people I hunted with beneath them. I vividly recalled taking ring-necks in Michigan's thumb in early November with my young daughters, Beth and Lynn, then nine and eight, beneath a high, chilly late autumn overcast, a harbinger of winter. The best pheasants of the year could always be had on a day like that. Charlie, my Brittany

Spaniel—it's a point of great pride and satisfaction that I trained him myself—quartering naturally but responding to whistle and hand when directed, steady to wing and shot, retrieving the killed birds and cripples to hand. A stiff fall breeze making the scent spread. Then walking back to the car, Beth carrying the dead roosters by their feet, dangling them upside down, Lynn not wanting to touch them, Charlie tired and panting at heel without being commanded. How I value the memories of those long ago hours with Beth and Lynn, now adults with children of their own. And how I miss those days afield with Charlie.

As I complete this volume at age seventy-one, I cannot help but reflect on how lucky I've been. There have certainly been ups and downs throughout the years, successes and failures, mostly good health with an occasional bout of illness. But overall my life has been blessed, far more than I deserve. And it has been made all the richer by days spent on water and in the field. There is something about getting close to nature as a hunter or fisherman that cannot be achieved any other way. And at least for me, it seems to ground one with a connection to our roots as once primitive humans, to our mortality, and to the wonders and beauty of the natural world. I know there are those who care little for taking fish and game, and I don't resent them in the least. But for me, it is hard to accept how my life would have been diminished absent the outdoors and the people who shared it with me.

When I recall my experiences of a lifetime with gun or rod, it is mostly about the people. Cliff Higgins, now long dead, after ruffed grouse in the Pigeon River State Forest of upper Michigan on a beautiful sunny, crisp mid-October day, the hardwoods in glorious color, hunting over his German drahthaar, two pats flushing, me hitting the one on the right and Cliff taking the other. Cliff talking about his lifelong ambition of a true double, taking two with successive shots while they are flying at the same time, a thing he never did achieve although he never stopped trying.

Or John Verdon casting on the sand flats for tarpon in behind Ambergris Caye, John the much better fly fisherman, casting long and accurately at the little swift shadow fifty yards out where the blue-green seawater turned beige above the shallow sand. The tarpon leaping for the fly, breaking water strong, making long runs and multiple jumps until it spit the hook from its hard mouth, its silvered flanks flashing, the black Belizean guide bouncing from foot to foot on the poling platform from excitement, losing the fish not detracting from the thrill or memory of the experience. And then Drake and Jim and Pat and Tom deer hunting or walleye fishing up in Canada, me completing *The Fishing Five*. Memories that could not be replaced for all the money in the world.

I've attempted to capture in this collection some of the feelings experienced and lessons learned in the outdoors, rather than simply recording the plain details of my outings. That would be far too dull. As such, by and large these stories are not simple recounts of actual adventures. It's true enough several of the stories are in the style of memoirs—*Molly & Me, Chewore Safari Journal, The Fight of the Century*. But others are traditional works of pure fiction written to create the drama, suspense, sense of danger or conflict, fear, elation and sadness, humor and a range of other emotions that are best developed through tales of the outdoors or adventure. Some are intended to teach—I'd like to think there are lessons in all—but every story is designed to entertain.

This book is therefore dedicated to all, past and future, who enrich my life by walking with me afield. I hope readers will enjoy these stories and in so doing, share in the wonders I have experienced by joining me *Beneath a Hunter's Sky*.

John Bascom, June 2015

IN AFRICA
A story in four parts

Part 1 AFTERMATH

The Bushmen here have a saying, *Africa is a harlot who can take you to unimaginable ecstasy, then dump you like a piece of garbage.* This particular afternoon she blasted me with the hot, hard wind blowing off the Kalahari from Namibia, burning my exposed face with the endless supply of loose grit and sand from the unpaved street I walked along in the little Botswana desert town of Ghanzi.

I stopped in front of the small church, a few spots of faded white paint visible here or there where the wind had not sanded everything to graying boards. The three splitting, wooden-plank stairs flexed as I climbed them and entered through the open doors hanging crooked on bent hinges. A holy-water fount nailed on the wall just inside the doorway was a cut-down tin can with a discolored slurry in the bottom. Metallic-green blowflies lining the inside rose in a buzzing swarm as I placed my finger in the half-inch-deep semi-liquid and then made the sign of the cross.

A large, rusty scrap-metal cross with a crudely carved ironwood image of the crucified Christ hung on the wall behind the makeshift altar. To the left along the sidewall stood what I had come for: a tall, two-chambered booth of sorts. The bare wood confessional was without exterior windows. A plaque turned green-side-out above the narrow door on the

9

priest's side told me what I needed to know. He was waiting within.

The divider slid open only a moment after I had entered the adjoining curtained doorway for the penitents and knelt. I could sense more than see the priest's form in the dark interior of his compartment through the veil of mosquito netting over the small portal between us.

"In nomine Patris, et Filii, et Spiritus Sancti," he said, and I imagined the movement of his hand in front of the dark opening as he made the Catholic sign of the cross before me.

"Bless me Father; I have sinned. It has been..." I hesitated then began again, *"many, many years—several decades—since my last confession."*

"Yes, my son," the priest said, sensing my reluctance. *"You may confess your sins. Continue."* He spoke in the careful, precise, softly accented English of an educated professional who conducts his business in the language, even if it is not his first tongue.

Still I hesitated.

"Go on," he said. *"Have you lied, cheated in business?"* he prompted. *"Engaged in adultery? Have you beaten a woman or child? You are safe to confess here."*

"I am not here to confess the sins you named, Father."

"What then?" said the priest.

I hesitated again. "I...I killed M'bogo." The words caught in my throat.

"You killed M'bogo?" The priest's voice betrayed his surprise and confusion. "The Black Death?"

"Yes, Father. I did it only this afternoon."

"The sin you wish to confess is the slaying of Nyati?" he said incredulously.

10

"Yes, Confessor," I whispered.

"Was he drinking at the waterhole?" the priest asked. "Sleeping in the tall grass?"

"None of those," I said. "He was a big bull, very close, looking at me. I had stalked him a long way and was facing him."

"Were you careless, did you wound him badly causing prolonged and needless suffering? By the grace of God, did you run? Such things would be a sin."

"No, Father."

"What then is the sin in killing M'bogo? It is, after all, a badge of courage, to our people the fulfillment of a lifelong quest."

"I should explain, Father."

Part 2 SIMBA

Hunting Africa had long been my dream. I had carefully researched the options for years before selecting professional hunter Peter Ladnek and his exclusive half-million-acre safari concession leased from the Botswana government near the Namibia border. Peter had earned a reputation as an experienced and productive PH.

I was after an African lion with the chance of picking up a nice Cape buffalo and some plains antelope in the process—impala, kudu, or sable.

"Botswana is one of Africa's best secrets," Peter had told me over the phone. "It doesn't receive nearly the pressure of Zimbabwe, Tanzania, or the other concessions you may have heard of. But it has a concentration of some of the largest bull elephants on the continent and its lions are legendary. The government reopened lion hunting just this year, so you may be in luck. And the buffs are underrated. Not in the numbers you see elsewhere, but because they're not a priority with hunters here, the herds aren't hit aggressively. Takes a bit more work but it can definitely be worth it."

I booked a fourteen-day safari late in the dry season. Our camp was a tented affair well north of the Kalahari Desert and some miles south of the Okavango Delta. The central groupings in camp included separate housekeeping tents for Peter and me, cooking and dining tents, and a big, open-sided canvas awning set up on long poles for relaxing in the evening. A large fire pit with improvised stone benches and a few camp chairs sat in front of the awning. The compound for the assorted Bushmen and Bantu trackers, skinners, gun bearers, porters, and the general camp odd-job boys was about fifty yards away.

"We've seen good sign everywhere," Peter said on my first evening in camp as we sat by a blazing campfire near dusk. The bush sounds were thrilling to me. Jackals yapped from the dark followed by that eerie, rising *wooo-WHOOP* of the hyenas. At one point a leopard complained of something in the night, its odd growl sounding as if someone were sawing wood in the darkness.

"Of course, the damned elephants are everywhere," Peter continued. "Need to be careful we don't get stepped on. There is fresh lion and buff sign crossing some of the back-trails. Tomorrow we'll have a drive and see if we can't pick up something good to follow."

My heart raced with excitement.

"Everything here is spot or track-and-stalk, except night hunting hyena from a baited hide," Peter went on. "We'll drive the trails, and if we see tracks of something interesting, we'll get out and follow for a bit. Then there are always the dry riverbeds. The bush is thicker along the banks and all sorts of game go there. To dig for water, visit the odd mineral lick, or wallow in the mud holes in the case of buffalo and elephants. Maybe you can pick up a nice warthog on a floodplain there. They're always something a bit different to break the monotony."

"What'll we go after first?"

"Lion are chanciest," Peter said, "and your main interest. We'll go after a good male if we can find one and get that behind us. It may take a while. We've seen some big tracks in early scouting, but the truly good ones are few and far between. There's always the element of fortune to deal with, more so with lion than other game, it seems. Once we have a good cat in the bag, we'll switch over to your buff. Or if it's going badly on lion, we'll give them a rest, try and find you a nice bull buffalo, then return to old Simba a bit later. Let our luck reset. Plains game we can take last, or simply when the off chance presents itself."

At first there was endless walking, tracking, stalking, stopping, listening, and watching between seeing anything we were after. And then the animals often spooked and disappeared, or turned out to be females and juveniles, simply not up to hunting standards. The whole process then began anew. It was sometimes long, exhausting, and frustrating. Still, just being in Africa was mesmerizing.

We had been finding and following lion tracks for several days without reward. We had seen a few elephants in groups, including some nice bulls, and had stalked up on a pride of lions composed of females, half-grown cubs, and a few adolescent males. Nothing we wanted. The concession was vast, extending over a dozen miles in each direction from our base camp. There was a lot of territory to be covered, and I sensed even Peter was getting a little discouraged.

It must have been seven or eight days into the safari on a scorching sunny afternoon. Our Basarwa Bushman tracker, Enteie, banged on the roof of our modified Land Rover bush-lorry. Everyone piled off to bend over the large sets of lion tracks he had spotted in the road. Peter had told me by the fire one evening, according to a Shona tribal legend, there are three times when a man fears the first lion he is hunting. "When he sees its track, when he hears its roar, and when he faces the beast." I had seen a few smaller lion tracks earlier in the hunt, but these huge and fresh prints brought the legend to mind again. A chill ran down my spine.

"Two very big lions crossed here—recently," Peter told me when he had stood erect again.

That much I could see for myself.

"Undoubtedly big males from the size and depth of their tracks," he continued. "Sometimes older adolescent males are expelled from their pride when they first become sexually aggressive. They often roam and hunt together for a few years until they're large and strong enough to defeat a dominant male and take over a different pride. Nature's way of preventing inbreeding, you know. These big ones may be just about ready to do exactly that. We have a good chance to stalk up on them from the looks of it."

I almost leaped into the lorry to grab my .375 H&H magnum bolt action. "Let's go!" I realized I was shouting with a mix of excitement and a dose of fear.

As usual Enteie tracked in the lead, followed by Peter with me close behind and Enteie's thirteen-year-old son taking the rear as our bearer. The son shared his father's muscular if small frame, good-looking light cocoa skin, and curly dark hair with a hint of rust color. All typical of the distinctive Kalahari San people here.

The trail wound through the now familiar open areas of waist-high brown grass dotted with acacia trees, thorny bushes, and mopani scrub. We pushed on for several hours until the lion tracks joined the prints of a group of buffalo.

"It seems as if our lions are on a hunting trip of their own," Peter told me. "They're trailing these buffalos. We may find them on a kill. We could be close."

Everyone became visibly more cautious as we pressed on.

About two miles farther into the thin bushveld, Enteie stopped suddenly in front of us, raising his open hand to his shoulder in a gesture that caused everyone to halt. He studied the earth closely, then motioned us forward. Even I could clearly see the jumble of lion and buffalo tracks mixed over a fairly large area. Splashes of blood and clumps of dark, coarse hair lay in various places. Enteie took his time examining an increasingly broad area before he returned and spoke to Peter in a local Setswana dialect that was a mystery to me.

"Looks as if our lion pride-mates caught up with something here," Peter said. "They obviously attacked a buffalo, a huge one from the looks of the tracks, but couldn't bring it down. Maybe a straggler that was weak or lame. Seems as if quite the scuffle went on for some time. It looks like our lions lost this round since the buffalo and cat tracks go off in different directions and there're no drag marks of a carcass."

"What now?" I said, feeling a combination of fear and anticipation.

"This is all very fresh, I'd say less than an hour ago. After the exhaustion of the fight, these lions may lay up for a while until this evening when it cools. Let's push on carefully and see if we can get up on them."

After another twenty minutes of tracking I heard it. A low growl almost like a long moan. Everyone froze. It sounded close. *The second time a man fears his lion*, the legend had said, and for me it was true.

We crouched and crept forward until the growl seemed impossibly close. Then Enteie raised his hand, we stopped, and Enteie moved back to Peter and me.

"He's in that thicket up there," Peter said. "Follow me up and be ready. I'll tell you when to shoot."

I pushed the safety off and followed Peter forward, his double-barrel .458 Lott at the ready. Almost immediately the foliage ahead began to move and the biggest lion I had ever imagined burst from the brush, running directly toward us. His massive black mane surrounded a huge head at the front of a long, heavy body. He stopped only sixty yards out as suddenly as he had appeared, glaring directly at us. The lion's muscles were visibly tensed, his weight forward on his forelegs, and his eyes fixed on me like a tomcat ready to pounce on a mouse. The third part of the legend, but I had no time to feel fear.

I swiftly raised the .375 to my shoulder, put the cross hairs of the 2.5X scope on the center of his chest, and quickly but smoothly squeezed off a round. Peter told me later he had hissed, "Shoot!" but I heard neither him nor the report of my rifle.

The big cat lurched backward and sank to his front knees before promptly standing then moving toward us again in a purposeful trot. I worked the bolt, chambering another round, and snugged the already raised rifle to my shoulder once more just as the lion quartered slightly to our left as if trying to flank us. I could see blood on his chest an instant before I fired the second round at his exposed shoulder. The impact was audible, the puff of dust from his hide visible as the round struck behind the shoulder on his ribcage. *Need to lead a little when they're moving,* I recall thinking. Still, a clean lung shot, just a little back from the shoulder I had intended to shatter to drop him in his tracks. He took another few steps as I reworked the bolt, then settled slowly to the earth resting on his side like a napping kitten. His legs were still kicking the air when I put the third shot between his shoulder blades, angling straight through toward the bottom of his chest. He didn't move again. Peter never had to fire.

We had all started to breathe again when we heard it once more—the long, low moaning growl. Peter and I looked at each other. "Seems the brother is still with us," Peter said.

I reloaded and again we crept forward. We had filled our only license, so our purpose was to fix the big cat's position and drive him away. After a few yards Peter stopped.

"There he is, under that acacia," he said.

About eighty yards ahead, the lion was lying on his side. A small amount of blood stained his exposed belly, but not enough to be noticed by Enteie while tracking. The moaning growls continued. It was clear he wasn't getting up.

"He's been gored badly," Peter said. "Looks like this pair tangled with a nyati that was more than they could handle. There's nothing for us to do. The law is clear—with our tag filled, we cannot kill another lion, even if he's sick or injured. Let's back out and return to the truck. By the time we get it back in here, this fellow will be finished. Africa can be a bitch at times."

The dying lion put a temporary damper on our kill, but still there was backslapping, handshaking, and staff celebration back at camp later. My lion was received by the Africans with great jubilation as some kind of an extraordinary achievement.

"He really is a fine cat," Peter said, sipping straight whiskey by the fire that evening. "You know he went a bit above four-hundred-fifty pounds, don't you?"

"He looked a ton when I first saw him," I laughed. "The men seem excited enough. Have you gotten bigger ones here?"

"It's not just the size, but how it's done. It was quite dramatic. And your shooting was brilliant. It all adds to the moment, you see. This kind of day keeps us professional hunters coming back."

"I simply reacted. I didn't do anything special."

"He was coming for us, you understand. You can tell by their posture, their look. His was quite the bad attitude. Your first frontal chest shot took the starch from him a bit, then when he came again, he couldn't muster the full-out charge. But it was clear enough what was on his mind. Any of your three shots were kills. It just takes some time with these big fellows."

The staff was singing and dancing off to the side of our fire. "M'windaji yetu kuuawa tuzo kuu," they chanted while clapping and bouncing.

"They're singing your praises, you know," Peter said to me. "*M'windaji*—the great hunter."

I couldn't supress a broad grin as I looked down at the ground. I'd never experienced anything like this before. "What's the rest of the chant?" I asked, trying to deflect the discussion from me in my embarrasment .

"Kuu tuzo," Peter said. "The 'grand prize' in Bantu Swahili. The ultimate trophy. Your lion has made quite the impression with them."

"Kuu tuzo," I repeated.

"Too bad your wife couldn't have made the trip with you, been here to experience all this. Many of our hunters bring someone."

"Yes. She wanted some time apart, though. Things have been a little rough between us lately. I'm not sure where it all will go."

"I'm sorry," Peter said. "Keeping the fairer gender happy can be quite the challenge, I know. Mine is my third wife. It's hard—we hunters being away half the year. And the life here is difficult, especially for our women. I'm hoping I do a better job on the relationship side of things. I keep thinking this may be my final real chance to build something lasting. It goes to one's core, really, doesn't it?"

"It's more important to us than they think," I said, revealing myself in a way I hadn't believed possible. I had been sipping whiskey all evening as well and was feeling the effects. "Bethany, I call her Bitsie, is my second. It seems we clash on everything anymore, though. It wasn't like that at first. Money, social activities, lifestle, friends. How to spend our liesure time. And especially family issues. Everything's a battle. She's a headstrong one. We've completely stopped talking. I felt coming to Africa would give us a break. Give me a chance to think things through and find the right answers."

"Everyone on safari, it seems, is running after something, or away from it," Peter said. "Usually himself."

We each were silent for a long time, self-conscious about the direction our conversation had taken. Finally I said, "What's the plan for tomorrow?"

"Those buffalo tracks showed some remarkable bulls in the herd. I thought we'd double back to the area where we took your lion today, eh, and see if we can't cut the herd's track again."

"I'm excited and a little nervous, too," I said.

"A wounded bull can be very cross. Just do as I say and remain calm no matter what. Everything will be fine." Peter looked at me to gauge my reaction. "You do know," he said, "if a wounded nyati comes for you, you can kill him well enough but you can't stop him. They've even been known to circle back and lie in wait. That's why the first shot has to be good— and why I'm behind you with my double."

I was absolutely silent.

"No troubles, though," he said. "There's a dry river near where we last saw the buff tracks, with a few odd seeps still a bit wet. With those lions out of the way, they'll have bedded for the night near water and won't have moved off very far by morning. We'll get an early start and see if we can't find a really good m'bogo, a big bull. See if we can put a hide in the salt."

"You stood your ground, then," the priest said. "With the lion."

"Yes, Father." I could tell by the timber of his voice, his manner of speaking—the suggestion of his form and the

movements I could sense through the window between us as my eyes adjusted to the dark—he was a very young priest. Less than thirty, I thought, some fifteen or more years younger than me.

"We Bantu have a song. It serves as our code for life, a shared belief system more than a simple song." He recited a portion of the song as if it were a poem:

Hatima ya mwanadamu si kutimia
Mpaka yeye kinafikia mambo matatu
Peke kukabiliana na unaua mnyama mauti
Huwafufua m'toto
Anakamilisha mwanamke

"And its meaning?" I asked.

"It does not translate precisely into English. It can be understood as 'A man's destiny is incomplete until he alone confronts and slays the feared beast, raises a child, and fulfills a woman.' "

"What has this to do with my confession , Father?"

"Have you committed the sin of rejecting your destiny?" the priest asked.

"I'm not sure I understand."

"As you have now explained, you clearly fulfilled facing and killing the most fearsome of beasts. You stood singularly to meet its charge even if others observered. That is permissable. You have met this requirement. But have you raised a child?"

"I have no children, Confessor. Neither by my present nor former wife."

"We Bantu understand 'raising a child' to include what you English would call mentoring, or even saving a child's life. In our tradition an uncle or aunt, perhaps a grandparent, is often responsible for providing care, support, or protection for a child. Have you done such things?"

"I'm not sure. It gets complicated, Father. Let me continue my confession to the slaying of M'bogo."

Part 3 M'BOGO

We left camp early in the predawn darkness, traveling slowly for more than an hour over the rough two-tracks barely scratched on the Botswana landscape. Peter was driving and pulled off the trail about two miles from the place where we took my lion. As the glow of the dawn just became visible on the horizon, we started our trek into the mixed African savannah and bush.

We threaded our way through the countryside for what seemed to be days but in reality was only hours, seeing little but old buffalo spoor, several elephant cows with their calves in a dry riverbed, and a troop of baboons barking angrily. We stopped in the shade of a huge, spreading baobab tree for water and a sack lunch Enteie's young son, our porter, had brought along. The ever-present Botswana dry-country sun had climbed high into the sky and the heat was bearing down on us.

After finishing lunch, we pressed on at a brisk pace for some time until Enteie, in the lead as always, began motioning urgently. We moved up to where he was examining plenty of moist dung piles and a whole parade of obviously fresh tracks.

Peter conferred with him for a moment and then said, "Very fresh. They've moved through here quite recently, within the hour I'd say. Let's be careful now."

Again we moved forward, this time more cautiously. Everyone's eyes were darting around, on the alert for any odd shape, movement, or sound. It was only a few minutes before we all spotted them at about the same moment. A herd of sixty or more animals moving leisurely through the grass and bush just ahead of us. No more than two hundred yards away.

From our position among a clump of thorntrees, we had a pretty good view of the group. Peter put his binoculars to his eyes and studied the massive black forms carefully. Then he motioned me back a few yards to talk while Enteie and his son stayed forward to keep an eye on the animals.

"We're in luck," he whispered excitedly. "There's a fine bull in there. Big-bodied with symmetrical horns easily over forty inches. They've got great drop, spread, and curl," he said, refering to the size and shape of the horns. "And the boss is massive," he added, describing the thick, bony covering of the forehead where the two horns joined together. "A big herd bull, only just now past his prime. He's near the right side. Move up a little and have a look."

I moved forward again, observing the herd with my naked eye and also glassing with my field binoculars. I spotted the trophy bull right away. Then I noticed one even more impressive, more or less by himself off to the far left of the group. "What about the one over there?" I said, pointing. "The brownish one. He's even bigger."

"A big old dagga-boy," said Peter. "A bull well past his prime that's a hanger-on so to speak. I'm afraid he's in advanced decline. The fit breeding bulls beat them up when they get old and weak. Drive them from the herd and don't allow them to mate. They leave and rejoin periodically until they're booted by the young bulls again."

"His color is different," I said. "More like a reddish-brown."

"When they're that old they're vulnerable to parasites," Peter said. "Dagga-boys off on their own wallow whenever they can. Keeps a coating of mud, dirt, and dust on the hide to hold the ticks and flies at bay. That's what 'dagga-boy' means in Bantu—the dirty one. They urinate and defecate in those wallows. Makes them smell like hell. Do you see all the oxpeckers on him, the little birds that hop around on his nose,

24

forehead, and ears mostly? They pick off all the insects, a real lunch wagon for the oxpeckers. They're thick on these dagga-boys."

"His head is massive, though," I said. "And his body is huge."

"Quite the lover and fighter in his day, I'm sure. It's certain he sired many of the juveniles in this and the other herds around here. But take a close look at those horns. They've started to deteriorate, from old age and parasite infestation. The horn is broken off the one side, and there are areas of cavities and craters in the bosses and along the inner parts of the other. When both horns are broken, we call them 'scrum caps.' The remaining short horn fragments fit tight to the side of their head, like a rugby player's helmet. This one is like that on only the one side. A half scrum cap," he smiled.

"Still, there's something noble about him," I said.

"His better days are behind him. It's well enough to take an old trophy animal beyond breeding age, but this aging gentleman has been savaged by Mother Nature. On his last leg. He's junk, a 'management' bull. The government issues extra permits for animals like him to thin the herd and keep it healthy."

"It looks like he's injured, too," I said. There were scars all over his head and body. Some looked fresh, moist with seepage.

Peter took a closer look with his field glasses. "He's almost certainly been attacked by lions. Quite recently. Maybe that scrap with the two bad boys we bumped into yesterday. His nose has been bitten, and there seem to be claw marks on his hind quarters and neck. A younger bull might survive that kind of ballyhoo, but I'm not sure about this old fellow."

Peter seemed to sense my hesitation. "That mature, fit herd bull is the one you want hanging in your study," he said. "He's had his chance, passed on his genes and will be yet another dagga-boy all too soon. I'll see that broken-down scrum cap is collected for hyena bait by another party later, one that has extra licenses."

Peter was right enough, of course. But sometimes you follow your gut rather than your head. "I'm taking the dagga-boy," I said. And that decision would change everything.

"You're the client," he said resignedly. "We'll need to get closer. Stay low and be absolutely quiet. I'll tell you when to shoot. If the whole herd comes, back slowly away and I'll handle it or give you instructions. Let's go."

Enteie and his son faded behind us as Peter and I moved closer. About fifty yards from the edge of the herd—from the monstrous, old, ravaged m'bogo—Peter stopped. The wind was in our face. The herd was oblivious.

"Wait until he's broadside. Take him in the center of the shoulder when I give the word. What kind of round is chambered?" Peter asked.

"A 270-grain expandable now and 300-grain solids in the magazine under it," I said.

"Quietly eject the softpoint," Peter whispered, "and load the big solid. We'll need to crush plenty of bone on this big boy with our first shot.

I did as Peter asked and slowly worked the bolt. The sound must have been just enough for the m'bogo to hear, because he abruptly stopped grazing, raised his head, and stared directly at me. He was perfectly broadside.

"Take him NOW," Peter said in a hoarse whisper. Just as I fired, the old bull lurched forward, the herd wheeling in unison. I saw a shower of dust, mud, and dried dung chips explode from the bull's ribcage where the bullet struck. "Hit

26

him again!" Peter shouted as the buffalos thundered down toward a dry riverbed bordered with an area of unusually dense brush. "Hold up—hold up—hold up!" Peter yelled. The dagga-boy had merged into the compressed, stampeding herd and no longer offered a shot. They disappeared over the riverbank.

"I saw him move just as you fired," Peter said. "He simply bolted at the last instant. Bad luck. But you smacked him neat enough in the boiler room. A good lung shot."

I felt pretty good about the shot. It was the same bullet placement as with my lion the day before, and I saw what it had done to him.

"Let's have a rest for a few minutes to let him lie down," Peter said. "These boys can absorb a lot of punishment, but they're not Superman. Eventually he'll bleed out. No point in riling him up before he's finished."

After about fifteen minutes Peter got up and said, "I think we're okay to go now."

Enteie tracked in the lead, followed by Peter with his double elephant gun and me close behind. Enteie's boy, our bearer, took up the rear with an extra, loaded gun for Peter and plenty of ammo. Enteie quickly pointed to blood spoor as we worked carefully toward the river's edge. We stopped close to the dry riverbed and just next to the dense area of jesse bush. It extended far to our right and all the way forward over the bank. The willows were thick and leafless back from the river's edge, but were choked with green where we stood closer to the river, betraying the trace of water it must have held. We couldn't see into the riverbed or the brush either, for that matter.

I was standing with the tangled thicket to my right when it happened. Enteie's boy, our bearer, had moved up directly next to me on my left, then Enteie to the boy's left, and finally Peter. All in a row. I was aware of an odd, total silence.

First came the quick flush of the oxpecker from the jesse, only a few feet to my right. Then the massive, rusty brown-black form of M'bogo rose from his knees in the heavy green tangle, simultaneously driving toward me. In my mind everything unfolded in surreal slow motion. I felt his breath, the fine mist of lung blood enveloping my face as the wounded animal grunted under the great effort of his charge.

As if in a single, perfectly choreographed dance, I wheeled and pushed the safety forward on my rifle. I realized at the same instant I was between the others and the buffalo. I thought of jumping to the side, but even if there had been time, I somehow understood Peter would not raise his rifle with me between him and the bull. Even if I cleared his line of fire, with the speed of this dagga-boy's rush, there would be no chance to get a round off. The dying bull would slam full-force into Enteie's child and the rest of them. I had the only possible shot. "You can kill a buff, but you can't stop him," I recalled Peter saying.

I fired from just above my hip far less than a second before the impact. I could see the muzzle flash on the buffalo's shoulder, a shot I instinctively understood would most certainly crush a shoulder blade and angle back and down through muscle and organs. His massive boss struck me cleanly in the chest, and I was wrenched up and onto the one side of his head that held the slab of broken-off horn as he simultaneously hooked and lifted. I realized I was airborne from the attack, but the shortened, downward-cast horn fragment did not have the shape to succesfully gore me. As I spun through the air, I recall thinking, "Hold onto the gun— hold onto the gun."

I crashed down on the animal's back as he kicked and spun. I quickly found myself on the ground under his head and between his front legs. In the instant it took for the m'bogo to comprehend my location, I somehow worked the bolt once more. Just as I fired for the last time, he bore down on my body with his good horn and forehead, twisting and thrusting. The crushing sensation on my chest and abdomen was intense. With me lying on the ground, my last, desperate shot drove into his underside angled upward toward the base of his tail. The big dagga-boy slumped heavily to the ground, the side of his bloodied head on my stomach. I realized he was finished just before I heard the twin roars of Peter's rifle. The whole episode might have taken four or five seconds.

"Then you chose to kill the dagga-boy rather than the kuu tuzo, the magnificient trophy bull?" the priest said.

"Yes."

"And you stood to face M'bogo alone to save the child?"

"And the others. It happened without thinking."

"My son," said the young priest, "by the Lord's providence did you select the old dagga-boy so that your destiny might be fulfilled. It could not be otherwise."

"But why here, now?" I asked.

"There is a final verse to the Bantu song, to our creed. It concludes, 'Mtu lazima kupata na kutimiza hatima yake, Katika nchi ya mababu zetu.' A man must find and fulfill his destiny, In the land of our ancestors."

"But Father, this is not the land of my ancestors."

"The prayer says, 'the land of our ancestors.' " He emphasized the word "our." "We all trace back to African forefathers. That is well established. But the words 'Katika nchi ya mababu zetu—the land of our ancestors,' are understood to mean, not the listener's home, but simply in Africa, the land of the Bantu and San people. Here, where fate has now brought you. Perhaps to face your destiny."

"I see," I said.

"In the meaning of our legend, you have fulfilled the requirements of singularly confronting and slaying the beast, twice over. And now saving a child. I hear no sin, my son."

I fell silent again.

"What brought you here, then, to our small church?" the priest said at last.

"After the attack I was badly hurt. I don't remember everything. I'd been battered and slammed around violently. Lost consciousness for a time, I think. They brought me to the nearest medical clinic, here. Then I began to think I was wrong to kill the noble old M'bogo who had endured so much. Who had served his herd, defeated the lions, who deserved his remaining years in Africa. That I should have have taken the younger bull who had not yet earned his place of esteem. I began to think I had brought bad fortune on myself and the others through my blasphemy. That I had affronted God's plan. Sinned."

"In Africa we understand it is a sign of respect to hunt a magnificent animal," the priest said. "It is no sin to fairly and honestly slay the most noble prey. It has been our way for all of creation. Nature demands those who have fulfilled their purpose must leave to make way for others. You were right to kill the old dagga-boy. The sin that led you here must be something else. Continue on then, my child."

"I knew of this church since I had passed through this town after our charter flight landed at your airstip on my arrival in Botswana. After I was checked over by the nurse, I simply left and walked over here to make my confession. It seemed like the thing I needed to do."

"I understand," the priest said.

He seemed to pause in thought. "The final piece of our code? Have you then fulfilled a woman?"

30

"How do you mean?"

"We understand it to include providing her with a child, unconditional love, support, forgiveness, devotion. Placing her above others, above yourself. Merging your life with hers."

"I've been married twice," I told the priest. "As I said, I have no children. It was my choice. I simply felt it wouldn't be wise. There have been many problems between us, she—my wife now—at fault as much or more so than I."

"Our code makes the obligation that of the man, not the woman," the priest said.

"It's difficult, Father. We've turned out to be very different people than either of us understood when we married. God knows I've tried."

"You were wise to come here, my child. I understand now. You have turned your back on the final requirement. Your sin has been great in scorning your destiny. Your confession is complete."

"May I have your absolution, My Father?"

"Have you repented your sin?" the priest asked. "Are you resolved to sin no more? Will you make amends for your crime against God? Only if you so resolve can you be absolved."

"I...I think so, Father," I said. "Yes."

"Then say a prayer of contrition."

"I confess to almighty God..." I began, "... I have sinned exceedingly in thought, word and deed..."

"Deus, Pater misericordiárum—God the Father of mercies," the priest recited, "through the death and resurrection of your Son, You have reconciled the world to Yourself and sent the Holy Spirit among us for the forgiveness of sins. Through the ministry of the church, may God grant you pardon and peace."

31

"Mea culpa, mea culpa, mea maxima culpa..." I prayed. "I beseech blessed Mary ever Virgin and all the saints, to pray for me to the Lord our God."

"Your sins are forgiven," the priest said. "Go in peace, and sin no more."

"Father," I said, "what if I am unable to make amends through events beyond my control? May I still be forgiven?"

I watched as the priest pulled aside the mosquito netting separating us. He reached his hand through the opening. I could feel the warm, thick balm he had placed on his thumb tracing the figure of a small cross on my forehead. "In the name of the Father, and the Son, and the Holy Spirit," he said. "By this laying of hands may the power of evil be overcome. By this holy anointing and by His most tender mercy may the Lord forgive you all the evil you have done. May your purified soul be accepted by God."

I heard the divider between our compartments close. I leaned back in exhaustion, slowly taking in and exhaling a deep breath. I could see from the gap at the edge of the curtain the intense afternoon desert sun had moved to a position where it flooded through the single plain window on the opposite wall of the church and engulfed the interior with blinding white light. Still, I could faintly detect that people had entered the church and filled the pews. I experienced the puzzling, impossible illusion that the faces were those of friends, relatives—people from my past, some long gone. I relaxed my body and decided to close my eyes for a moment before leaving the confessional.

Part 4 REDEMPTION

When I opened my eyes again, Peter was standing by the mosquito netting surrounding my hospital bed. "Welcome back," he said.

"Hi, Peter," I said slowly and softly, feeling as if I were enveloped in a thick mist.   Then I was aware of an uncomfortable oxygen cannula clipped between my nostrils and an IV needle in my arm connected to an array of liquid-filled plastic bags. Sensors were stuck to my chest. "How long have I been here?"

"Going on two days. You gave everyone quite the fright. A bit more exciting than simply putting down your charging lion. You really do have the flair for the dramatic."

"How is everyone?" I asked. My memory was foggy and I wanted reassurance no one else had been hurt.

"All fine... except you. You were the only one in the fray. Enteie and his son got the hell out of the way in a flash. I simply couldn't shoot with you bouncing all over that buff until you were clear. By then he was down anyway and pretty much dead. I put two into him for insurance. He doubled back on us through the thicket, you know. While we were waiting. Then laid down until we walked by."

"I remember everything until after you shot. After that it's mostly a haze."

"You were out cold most of the time. A few delerious moments of semiconsciousness. We had to bring the lorry in and get you here to Ghanzi. Only medical clinic in the area, such as it is. I'm sure you don't remember, but you were pretty bad off. Lots of bleeding, broken bones. We thought you were gone more than once. That old dagga-boy you were so keen on

33

gored you with his one intact horn all the way through your belly to the backside."

"Jesus!" I said. Even with the cocktail of drugs flowing into the IV, I was aware of intense pain.

"There were no doctors here, just the nurse. And no plane to evacuate you. When they sent a plane from Johannesburg they put a couple surgeons on it because you wouldn't have lasted the flight out. Couldn't believe you were still alive when they first saw you. They performed emergency surgery here at this broken down little bush clinic. A first, they tell me."

"Thanks," I said. "I'm grateful. I'll thank the doctors and staff when I have the chance." My head was slowly beginning to clear.

"Now that you're stable and awake, they said they'll be taking you to Cape Town in a small medivac jet. That's where I'm from. World-class docs and facilities there. You're a lucky man."

"How long have you been here?"

"Stayed with you since we brought you in. You were here a few hours before the plane arrived, then they took you straight off into surgery. By the way, you're a little lighter now. Minus one spleen. They had to stitch a few blood vessels and intestines back together. You've been on massive antibiotics since surgery. Last thing was to tape your broken ribs and sternum. Must hurt like the devil, eh?"

"It's not too bad," I lied. I knew enough to realize there was morphine in my IV, too.

"It was all touch and go here at first. They brought a young Bantu priest, a nice fellow, over from the local church. You were out like a light. Just so you know, he gave you the Catholic last rites."

"Yes," I said. "I know. Extreme Unction."

"Annointed your head with some kind of holy oil. Said something in Latin or whatever. All that's beyond me."

"I haven't practiced the faith for years, but still I appreciate it," I said. "Must thank him as well if I have the chance."

"And in case you're interested... your dagga-boy? He weighed in at nearly a ton and a quarter. If his horn hadn't been broken, he would have gone forty-eight inches. He would have stood as the Botswana official record, another kuu tuzo," he laughed. "For the '*M'windaji*'—the great hunter."

"Wait'll next year," I smiled. I was coming out of it enough to kid with him a little.

"There's someone else here who's been with you the last few hours, too. She traveled thirty-six hours straight as soon as I called to tell her. Just stepped out for the first time a second ago. I'll get her. And by the way, don't let her get away. She's a pretty one."

Bitsie walked through the door and over to the bed. She pulled the netting aside, put her hand on my arm, and kissed my forehead. "And how's my hunter this morning?" she said softly.

"Oh my God, I'm so glad to see you." I could feel my eyes moisten with tears although I doubted she realized it, probably thinking they were just rheumy from the drugs. I reached for her hand and held it.

"You've had quite the adventure," she said. "Peter told me everything. Your encounter with the lion, the buffalo. Bringing you here. The doctors have gone back for now, but I've spoken with the nurse. Your care here has been remarkable for such a poor place. The people are just wonderful."

"I feel blessed," I said.

"What a stunning course of events. I simply couldn't have even imagined. I'm so glad you're going to be all right. I rushed here as soon as I heard."

"Even before getting hurt," I said to her, "it's been such an incredible experience. I've seen and learned so much. Nothing like I thought. The African culture here, the ingrained wisdom of the people. I couldn't help but learn some things about myself."

"What kind of things?" She sat carefully on the edge of the bed.

"I learned a Bantu credo. They sing it. I remember some of the first part. Something like *'Hatima ya mwanadamu si kutimia'* is how it starts. It has to do with a man fulfilling his destiny through courage, children, relationships. I know it sounds silly, but it penetrates right to the soul when you hear and understand it. There's a second part, another verse, too, but I don't recall it exactly just now. Honestly, it made me think of us."

"From what Peter explained, there was no shortage in the courage department," she said. "My God, it's hard to imagine what you must have felt. A huge lion coming at you and an awful buffalo goring you. You certainly came away with remarkable trophies."

"I did," I said. "Kuu Tuzo. A phrase the Africans taught me. The Greatest Prize."

"A wonderful lion and buffalo," Bitsie said. "You have every right to be proud."

"Not the animals," I said. "My name for you. Being with me here, now. Kuu Tuzo. The greatest prize I could imagine."

She looked at me quietly, and I could tell her eyes were filling with tears as well. Through the pain I pulled her to me and we kissed. It was the kind of warm, lingering, sensual kiss

36

that goes beyond simple attachment or affection or caring, the kind that defines relationships that are deep and meaningful and intimate and enduring. A renewed relationship that would fully and endlessly fulfill each of us, I knew.

Our lips moved against one another's for a very long time. When we finally parted I said, "I don't give a damn about anything we've argued over. None of it is important. I just want you to be happy."

"I feel exactly the same way," she said. "About you." A tear was trickling down her cheek.

"You were right about everything," I said. "Let's do it just as you want. That's what would make me happiest. Believe me, I'm just being selfish."

"No you're not," she said. "I don't care about things being my way."

"And we should talk about children again," I said. "There's still time. You're still young. Or we could adopt if you'd rather."

"Oh, God, I've wanted a child so much," Bitsie said. "You know that."

We embraced again. "I've remembered it now," I said.

"What?"

The last part of the credo. You know, the one I just told you about."

"What is it?"

"As nearly as I remember, '*Mtu lazima kupata na kutimiza hatima yake, Katika nchi ya mababu zetu.*' Something like that. I'm sure I've massacred it. But it means roughly a man will fulfill his destiny only in the land of our ancestors."

" 'In the land of *our* ancestors?' " she said, not comprehending the Bantu meaning—as I had not—upon first hearing it.

I kissed her again. "It means where I did. Here," I smiled.

"In Africa."

BEAR HUNT

The swells of Alaska's inside passage tossed our drenched little Zodiac inflatable boat as my guide, Nick, and I glassed the shoreline of the remote island bay through the area's infamous rain and mist. It was nearly impossible to keep our binoculars dry and clear. The rain would let up, then start again a few minutes later, and the thick mist was always with us. We constantly wiped the lenses and tried to shelter them with a hand, hat, or shirt, but the unpredictable wind always seemed to spread a coating of droplets just when we wanted to check something on the beach.

"There!" Nick hissed so urgently I jerked my head involuntarily in the direction he was looking through his field glasses. What seemed to be an animal shrouded in mist stood at the water's edge only two hundred yards away, and when I wiped the glass and put the binoculars to my eyes, I was staring into the face of the biggest bear I had ever seen. He was staring right back.

At that moment a big rogue roller lifted the Zodiac high and sent us surfing toward the shore in the direction of the bear. The boat bottomed out suddenly against the mud flat with a hard bump when we were carried to the trough. The force of the prop and drive shaft slamming into the sea bottom stalled the idling engine completely.

Nick swore as he turned to restart the outboard. The distance between the island and our boat had closed fast, and I saw the bear turn to square up directly at us. The guns were still cased to keep the salt water away from them. Nick revved the thirty-five horse Johnson engine to a full roar and turned the boat toward open sea, mud and gravel churning up behind in a dark swirl. The rain had picked up again and of course the visibility had dropped, and as I looked back toward the island, I could no longer see the bear or even the shoreline. I couldn't help but wonder if a thousand pounds of wet, brown malice would burst from the dense fog at any moment. The lump in my throat kept me from even swallowing. *This could be it*, I thought.

I glanced at Nick who had an odd look on his face. At first he seemed mad at me. Again. But then he mumbled, "Orneriest lookin' damn thing I ever seen," and it was clear he was scared, too.

I had first contacted Nick almost a year before about the possibility of a brown bear hunt with him just after returning from an Alaska vacation. It was a trip that affected me more profoundly than I could have possibly understood at the time. Alaska is legendary for the raw beauty of its endless and majestic expanses. But more striking were its stunning contrasts; nature at its fiercest and most unforgiving—a remorseless killer—and at the same time an unlikely bountiful provider for a stunning variety and quantity of life.

And, of course, there were its bears. I had seen my first brown while it was quietly fishing along a salmon stream near Skagway and was overwhelmed by a sense of its uncontained power. After returning home, I read everything I could get my hands on about the Alaskan brown bears, which I learned are the largest and deadliest land predators on Earth. Having hunted deer, birds, and small game all my life, I was riveted by the prospect, at the same time frightening yet curiously exhilarating, of hunting such an awesome beast. I couldn't help but wonder why, of all the people who travel to Alaska, I was affected in this way. But my dark fascination and emerging sense of destiny with the Alaskan brown bears grew into a compulsion, and I came to realize I must go back. To face my own bear, on his terms and in his territory.

I researched areas, regulations, and guides, talking to as many experienced Alaska hunting veterans as possible. Nick Kay had come to my attention as a professional who guided only a few lone hunters for several days each on isolated and rugged Chichagof Island, located in the waters of the inside passage in southeastern Alaska. Chichagof, I had learned, with its wooded mountains, alpine meadows, tidal grass flats, and most important of all, abundant wild salmon spawning streams, hosted the largest population of coastal brown bears in Alaska. Nick, I also learned, had a reputation for being direct sometimes to the point of rudeness, but always producing for his clients. The combination was fine in my book.

In our exchange of letters, he had written, "...and be sure to bring enough gun. I can't stand hunters who come up here with their favorite .30-06 deer popgun. Nothing short of a .338 magnum. Bigger the better, long as you can handle it. A worst nightmare is crawling through alders you can't see five feet after a crazy-in-pain brown that wasn't hit with enough power..."

It hadn't yet occurred to me that slugging through dense brush after a wounded bear might not be the worst nightmare at all.

After more research I bought a new .375 H&H magnum safari model for the trip. The three-seven-five is a reliable bolt-action rifle with a four-round magazine. With one more in the chamber, it carries five big shells. It is regularly used on dangerous game such as African lion or Cape buffalo, and is famous for its heavy, fast, bone-busting, and deep penetrating bullets. I selected the most deadly ammunition available, the cigar-sized, three-hundred-grain, high-power, expanding round with a jacketed, tough, bonded bullet. I topped it with a quality four-power scope.

A local gunsmith modified my new rifle's trigger to lighten the pull and reduce the travel, making it quick, crisp, and responsive. Despite the heavy recoil, my practice was constant, with two or three hundred rounds put through the gun at the local range over a period of months. Shooting at various distances—at first from fifty then up to two hundred yards—eventually 95 percent of my shots consistently landed inside a four-inch circle at any range. The sessions then moved to the woods, firing at an old fifty-five-gallon steel drum filled with sawdust and rigged to roll down a hill by pulling on a rope. After several months and hundreds more rounds of ammunition, it got so the tumbling, bouncing barrel took clean hits four out of five times from various distances and firing positions. I quit only after the metal became shredded into hunks of unusable pieces from all the bullet holes. I was just about ready for Alaska.

With preparations complete, in late September I drove to the airport, registered my gun, checked all my gear, and boarded the early morning nonstop to Anchorage. After a change there to a commuter flight then several stops along the way, the plane arrived to light rain and fog in Ketchikan just after five in the afternoon. Nick stood waiting inside the terminal and walked right up to me, although we had never actually met. As thin, tall, and tough looking as I had expected, his blond hair and hazel eyes did not match the image my mind had created.

"We'll grab your stuff and get over to the general aviation ramp," he said. "Gotta catch the local hop over to Hoonah before it's too dark."

We collected my gear as soon as it was off-loaded while I attempted an unsuccessful exchange of pleasantries. Nick picked up my cased rifle and daypack, and I grabbed my big duffle bag.

He nodded at my gun case. "What'd you bring?"

"Three-seven-five magnum," I said, smiling with pride. "It's real nice. Three hundred grains, holds four in the magazine and one in the chamber. Lots of firepower."

"Nothing in the chamber if you're hunting with me," he snapped. "Causes too many accidents. More likely you'd use that chambered round to kill yourself, or worse me, instead of a bear."

Nick led the way from the tiny terminal and toward the parking area for light planes, his angry scowl still on his face. "There'll be plenty of time to rack a round," he continued outside. "And if you're worried about needing more than four shots, it's why I'm behind you."

That was the most I'd hear Nick talk at one time, and with the most emotion, on the entire trip.

Nick had arranged a charter in a single engine Cessna to the Tlingit Indian village of Hoonah on the northeast corner of Chichagof. With a population of a few hundred, the small town spread along a harbor is home to almost all the native people inhabiting the island, which is about seventy-five by fifty miles in size. Irregular in shape, with hundreds of bays and streams dropping down from the thirty-five-hundred-foot low coastal mountains, Chichagof offered thousands of square miles of barely touched wildlife habitat. Perfect for our purposes.

We flew under the ragged, wet clouds and landed as the last of the twilight was fading at the local Hoonah airstrip, a leveled gravel bar by the harbor just on the edge of town. Our contact was waiting with his car, a short, barrel-chested Tlingit man to whom Nick referred only by his first name and didn't bother introducing me.

"Greg here'll put us up for the night," Nick said, "and take us out in his boat to where we'll make camp tomorrow morning."

I nodded to Greg and loaded my gear into his open trunk. We all piled into the old car.

"Can you drop us at the Snail Clan House?" Nick asked. "You can take our gear to your place, and we'll walk back when we're done."

Greg nodded.

"Ever been to a potlatch?" Nick asked me.

"Not that I know."

"Well, you're going to one tonight. Gotta meet up with a guy who's supplying our provisions for the trip. Only chance to see him tonight is at the potlatch."

I must have looked puzzled because before I could ask, Greg said, "A potlatch is a sort of party that's important to the Tlingit traditions. It's to celebrate some important event, or show appreciation, like to a sister clan. There's gifts passed around, traditional songs and dances, storytelling, that sort of thing."

"Sister clan?" I said, still puzzled.

"I guess Tlingit culture is fairly complicated to out-siders. All our people are divided into two broad tribes, Eagle and Raven. But within each, there're lots of sub-groups, or clans. Each one is bound together by kinship—blood or mar-riage. And by individual traditions and customs, too. Here in

Hoonah, the two main clans are the Brown Bear Clan of the Eagle tribe and the Snail Clan of the Ravens. Sister clans."

We turned onto the road bordering the harbor, with weathered, wood-frame buildings on the landside. Occasionally we passed an old totem pole, its paint worn and fading.

"Time was," Greg said, "clan members, the whole extended family, all lived together in one huge lodge house. Today, the Snail Clan House is more of a community center."

"So the native Alaskans have a tradition of getting along pretty well together," I said. "These potlatches to show appreciation, clan or lodge houses, sister clans and the like."

"I'm not sure I'd go that far," Greg said. "Among the Tlingits, yes. But between us and other tribes, like the Haida or Eyak, there's a history of rivalry, even warfare and taking slaves. But that's ancient stuff now. We're all Americans, just trying to make our way like everybody else."

We pulled up in front of a well-kept frame, two-story house. It was elaborately decorated with symbols of animals, birds, fish, and people above the small front door. The figures looked like those on some of the totem poles we had passed, but were painted rather than carved. Inside, the house was filled with native Alaskan people, with the exceptions of course of Nick and me.

"Wait here by the door while I check with our supplier," Nick said.

An older lady hushed the gathering and began a story. As nearly as I could tell, it was the tale of a Tlingit hero, Natsilane, who was a renowned hunter. According to the story, the lesser men of his clan were jealous of him and lured him to a small island under the pretext of hunting for sea lions there. The other men quickly left in the boat, stranding Natsilane to the fate of a slow death. But the heroic Natsilane dove into the water and began swimming through impossible hazards and across vast, stormy seas toward land. Close to drowning, he was happened upon by a canoe of Land Otter Clan men who offered to rescue him and take him to their lodge house. As the story went, after hesitating as to what to do, he refused and eventually swam back to his own camp, to retaliate against his tormentors and become chief of the clan.

"Great legend," said a tall, slender native Alaskan man who had walked into the clan house just as the story was wrapping up. He introduced himself as Matt Richardson.

"I had no idea of the interesting traditions among the Tlingits," I said. "The story is fascinating. But I wonder why the hero refused to be rescued by the Land Otter people."

Matt laughed and said, "You've got to understand the native history and cultures to know that. Land Otters are a clan of the Haida tribe, the traditional archenemies of Tlingits. They didn't trust each other. Land Otters, in Haida tradition, have a history of helping travelers or people who are sick, injured, or stranded."

The Land Otter Clan, I thought silently, mulling the odd-sounding name in my mind. "The Good Samaritans of early Alaska, then," I said at last.

"To some," Matt said, "but the Tlingits didn't see it that way. They would have attributed a sinister motive to the Land Otters' helpfulness. Tlingits believed an offer of help from a Land Otter was a setup to lure them to a fate of death. To Tlingits, Land Otters were sort of middlemen between the living and the afterlife."

"Like the Grim Reaper," I laughed.

"Sort of, I guess, to the Tlingits. But not to the Haidas. They saw them as more akin to Saint Peter, or maybe Saint Christopher. You know, the patron of the lost. But the story is designed in Tlingit tradition to show their hero, Natsilane, was nobody's fool."

"Well," I said, "maybe Natsilane's hunting prowess will inspire me. I'm off to get my brown bear tomorrow with my guide, Nick Kay."

"If you're after a good brown," Matt said, "I saw a monster boar over at Bronsett Bay a few days ago. And nobody's hunting over there."

I looked at him in surprise. "You a bear guide?"

Matt smiled and said, "I used to take people for bear over here. But now I just deer hunt for meat. That's why our camp is set up over there. Those grown over logging clear-cuts have some great browse and some of the best deer hunting on the island. But it's a little tougher to get to."

"Bronsett Bay," I said. "I'll keep it in mind, mention it to Nick."

"Good luck," said Matt. "Maybe I'll see you over there."

After I thanked Matt and said goodbye, Nick returned. Everyone was leaving, and Nick and I walked the few short blocks toward Greg's house. I told Nick what Matt had said about the big brownie he'd seen.

"Maybe we can go over there and take a look," I said. "Over at Bronsett Bay."

Nick walked for a long time looking at the ground before saying anything.

"You want to hunt with this Matt guy or whoever, hire him," he finally said. "You want to hunt with me, I'll put you on a nice bear, doing it my way."

I didn't bring up Matt or Bronsett Bay again. But Nick would.

Before dawn the next morning we made way and headed out of Hoonah Harbor in Greg's fishing tug, the *Sea Eider*. Our gear was stowed on deck with the eighteen foot Zodiac in tow. It was still dark as we passed Halibut Island in the harbor mouth, Pinta Rock with its harbor seals barely visible, and Scraggy Island before entering the Icy Straits headed north along the Chichagof coast. About an hour out, we heard three quick *whooshing* sounds off in the dark water, like steam under high pressure venting from a relief valve.

"Humpbacks blowing," Greg said. "These waters also have dolphin, orcas, and some sea lions, so keep your eyes open if you're interested."

After an hour, it was getting light and I could tell we were slowing and moving in closer to shore. Greg finally stopped the engines and dropped anchor.

"Let's load our stuff in the Zodiac," Nick said. "We'll camp on a gravel spit here by Eagle Point."

I could see by the tidal boundary the tide was in. Still, we dragged the Zodiac well up and away from the water as best we could and made our three-tent camp on a gravel ridge in front of an area of dense, dark green, and knee-high beach rye. There was a sleeping tent for me, another for Nick, and a big mess and supply wall tent for everything else. It was over a hundred yards across the grass flat to the tree line where the giant, impenetrable appearing rain forest spruces began.

"Less chance of a curious bear sneaking up on us out on this open gravel bar," Nick said. "Gallagher and Chicken Creeks come in south and north of here. There's a few smaller ones, too. All have decent salmon runs. It's mostly what the browns eat in the fall."

"Sounds good," I said, feeling excited.

With camp setup complete, we put our daypacks, rifles, and some lunch in the Zodiac and worked north toward Chicken Creek. The weather was cooperating for now, low, ragged clouds but no rain and visibility of a mile or so. We stayed roughly a quarter-mile off the beach and cut the engine about every fifteen minutes to glass the shore near the mouths of salmon-choked streams. Looking through our binoculars, fish splashed in the shallow, stony creek outlets as they struggled to work their way upstream to spawn. We continued scouting the area around our camp and searching the shoreline for the balance of the afternoon, seeing only a big sow with two half-grown cubs.

We had hunted our way back to camp just as the last light was fading. Nick made us a typical camp meal of stew and baked beans from cans heated over the propane cookstove, and fresh bread and butter. It was garnished with wild sea plantain greens he called "goose tongue" that grew on the top of the beach along the tree line. I washed my dinner down with water, and Nick with a beer from the supply he had brought.

"We'll turn in early and get a start before dawn tomorrow," Nick said. "My experience, you spot most of your bears first light or last. Specially the big ones.

"And one thing," he said. "If you have to get up during the night, look around and stay close to the tents. Bears are active at night and go up and down these beaches. Clams, dead fish, sedge grass, some berries, that kind of thing."

I felt the hair on my neck stand on end.

"Should be in good shape out on this gravel bar like this," he said, "but with a bear...well, you never do know."

It gets darker on Chichagof than I've ever seen. After dinner and cleanup, I closed my tent and climbed into my sleeping bag, my .375 magnum next to the cot, loaded with a round in the chamber. *To hell with Nick*, I thought. At least for tonight.

It was in the middle of the night when I heard it. Walking around the tent, brushing against it, turning over stones. It was pitch black, and my heart began to beat fast and hard. Then I heard it scratching at the canvas entranceway. Overcome with fear, I considered groping for my flashlight and rifle, but didn't want to anger or encourage it with any noise or movement. I felt if I kept absolutely silent and didn't move it might go away.

The flap tore open with an audible rip beneath what I knew was the bear's razor-like claw. I felt it breathing and understood its head must be inside. The whole shelter moved as the bear slid its neck, shoulders, and front feet into the tiny tent. He had to be only inches away and it was too late to go for my rifle in the total darkness. Any sound or movement, I was sure, would trigger an attack. I could smell its wet, matted, musky fur, and feel its breath on my face. It stunk of rotting salmon.

Panic swept through me like an electric shock. I was barely able to think and unable to act, facing certain mauling, even death. My thoughts raced. If I could just scream, Nick might get here before the bear could kill me. I opened my lips wide, took a deep breath, and tried to exhale in a scream with all my might. But nothing would come out, not a sound, no matter how hard I tried.

I bolted upright on my cot, squirming halfway out of my sleeping bag. I reached down and grabbed the flashlight on the floor, switching it on. The flap was tied securely shut, the tent empty except for me. My heart was still pounding. Usually the bear stayed longer, but did not get this close. This had been a relatively easy one.

I knew I was not going to be able to go back to sleep for a while, so I pulled on my pants and boots and stepped outside. There was still a flicker in the campfire Nick had made, even though a light rain had started. From the looks of the fire, I had been in bed just an hour or so.

The sound of movement in the gravel floated from deeper in the darkness. It seemed as though it were coming toward me.

"Couldn't sleep?" Nick asked as he stepped from the dark and into the dim light of the campfire. He had a beer in his hand and a cigarette in the corner of his mouth. "Bad dream, maybe."

"First night jitters, I guess."

"Bear'll do that to a man. They're unpredictable, like a beautiful woman." Nick laughed for the first time.

"You ever been in a tight situation with one?" I asked.

"Twenty years I been doing this, I've seen it all. Secret is, don't let 'em surprise you. Keep the upper hand. High ground. Good view. Work the wind in your favor. And be ready all the time."

"What would make them attack?" I asked, feeling uneasy with the nighttime as I so often did. "Anything special to be aware of out here?"

"Most encounters, they're set on getting away from you no matter what. But a sow with cubs, a dominant boar used to being top dog and getting its way, or an adolescent male feeling its first oats, any of those can spell trouble."

Nick took a long drink of his beer while I stared into what was left of the fire. "Course, there's always the wounded bear."

"What do you do if one comes at you?"

"Well, for starters, never take that first step back. You'll have an almost irresistible urge to run. Even drop your gun, panic sets in. You give up all your advantage and act submissive, like prey to the bear. Trigger his urge to chase and kill running prey.

"So whatever else, don't take a step back. Stand your ground. If you're not gonna take him, shout, wave your arms. Fire a warning shot over his head if you have to. Ninety-nine percent of the time, they won't attack in the first place, or if they do, you'll turn them. But for God-sake, don't take that first step back."

"Sounds hard to do with a thousand-pound brown barreling down on you," I said.

"It's what you have to do to keep him away most of the time. If he ever gets to you, chances of survival go down about 5 percent for every second he's on you. Ten seconds, 50 percent chance of coming out alive. Twenty seconds, zero. It's what the statistics say."

"Not good," I said. "I've heard they can tear a moose open with one swipe of a claw."

"On a man, a bear'll generally go for the head if he means to kill you. A lot of victims have their scalp or face bit clean off. Or tooth punctures through the skull."

"I'll remember," I said. "Don't take a step back. Keep the advantage. And don't let the bear get to the point where he could be on top of you. Ninety-nine percent seems like pretty good odds, I guess."

"Yeah," said Nick. "It's good." He took another long drink of beer. "Unless you're the one percent. Then all that don't mean shit."

The next day we ran down to Gallagher Creek in the Zodiac, seeing nothing on our way. We beached the boat about a mile south of the mouth and spent the morning and better part of the afternoon stalking up the slippery streambed and following game trails through heavy brush along the banks. There was snow on top of the higher mountains, but the hillsides, creek bottoms, and beaches were all clear. Several times we heard something in the tangle ahead, but never saw what it was. The going could be tough as we made our way at times through dense alders that limited visibility to twenty feet. I constantly worried about what might suddenly appear out of the thick foliage. *Stay ready, maintain advantage, stand your ground*, I thought.

The following several days were similar. Lots of glassing and working up the creeks and meadows. We saw the occasional small bear or sow with cubs, but nothing to shoot. Finally, we spent a day dawn to dark seeing no game at all.

That evening at dinner, Nick said, "Tomorrow we'll take a longer ride. New territory."

It was obvious he was getting discouraged, too. "What are you thinking?" I asked.

"We'll go to a different place, a bay around Idaho Inlet where we might try and find something. Place where they haven't been pushed much."

I was excited to try somewhere new and wanted to know more. "Does the bay have a name?" I wanted to locate it on my map.

Nick continued eating without saying anything and I thought he was going to ignore my question. I had my map out by then and had located Idaho Inlet.

Finally, in a low voice, he said, "Bronsett."

I recognized it immediately as the same place recommended by the Indian at the potlatch, the suggestion to which Nick had taken so much exception.

Now Nick motored the Zodiac well away from the shoreline of Bronsett Bay in the rain and mist, having just surprised the largest bear either of us had ever seen, and been surprised ourselves as well. *Stay ready, maintain advantage, stand your ground.* So much for that.

After we had collected our wits for a few minutes, Nick said, "He didn't seem spooked at all." *The world's greatest understatement*, I thought. To me, he looked about as spooked as a big, mean dog that had stumbled upon a small cat.

"Let's go south real quiet, beach the boat, and stalk back up here," he said. "We may still be able to jump him."

Nick had cut the motor again, and we paddled south for twenty or thirty minutes. After securing the boat on the beach, we uncased the guns and checked our ammunition. Four in the magazine, none in the chamber. Just like Nick said.

The rain had stopped and the visibility was up a bit. Occasionally a break would appear in the low overcast, revealing a patch of blue above thin clouds, until it quickly clouded over again. We worked cautiously north along the beach across sedge flats concealing jagged, melon-sized rocks. At times we crept along up by the tree line, using driftwood, big boulders, and fallen timber to hide our silhouettes and peer over at every bend or mound.

After about a half-hour, Nick crouched suddenly and whispered, "There he is!"

Some two hundred yards ahead was the huge Alaskan brown bear. It was splashing in the water where a fast-moving, broad creek, thick with thrashing fish, crossed the rocky beach and emptied into Bronsett Bay. As the bear moved around, its impressive size became all the more apparent. Its torso was round as a boiler, making its legs appear short even though it was really extremely tall at the shoulder. And then its massive head, improbably broad, the round ears seeming comically small in contrast.

"Biggest damn boar I seen." Nick spoke in a hushed voice. "Go way over a thousand pounds and the hide should square at least eleven feet."

At that moment, the bear looked directly at us, hesitated for a long moment, then turned and walked slowly in behind the trees, away from the beach.

"Crap," said Nick. "I don't think he saw us, but he might have whiffed us. Wind's onshore, but it's moving around when it gets to the trees here. Let's wait a minute then move up a little."

We crept forward foot by foot, constantly looking around. including into the trees to the side and behind us on the open beach. When we finally reached the spot where the bear had been, we could see its wet tracks on the rocks and in the gravel leading upstream along the creek side.

"Problem is," Nick said, "winds come off the water and rise up the hillside this time of day, when it's warmer up above than it is by the water. Our scent will go right up the creek. The bear'll know what we're doing. But we won't know nothin' about him."

I knew this was why I had come to Alaska, and I wasn't going to let this opportunity to face down my bear pass. "I'm going after him," I said to Nick. "What's the best way?"

Nick hesitated, and then said, "The water flow comes down through a gully cut in the folds of this mountainside. There are some fairly open old logging clear-cuts we can follow up, staying to the high side of the creek bed. Wind blowing up hill should keep our scent away from the lower stream bottom. It'll let us look down into the creek without spooking the bear.

If we stay off to the higher side, we may be able to spot him down there. Set up for a decent shot."

Maintain advantage, stay ready, work the wind, I thought. "Let's go, Nick," I said.

We stalked cautiously up the hill, holding close enough to the high creek bank that we could see down along the running water when the foliage permitted. We watched and listened for any telltale movement or sound. Nothing.

After an hour of moving uphill and upstream, the wet alders and low mixed forest along the ravine became so thick we could not see down into the creek bottom at all. We stalked, stopped, waited, listened, and looked. Hoping to detect the presence of the trophy-sized bear. Still nothing.

We moved farther uphill into some of the newer, more open clear-cuts. The water there ran down toward us through new second growth, logged-over meadows, and we could see along its upstream course for half a mile or more. Behind us the creek was choked with devil's club bushes, thick alders, and wet spruce deadfalls offering virtually no visibility. We swept the area in all directions with our binoculars.

"Bear's got to be in that heavy stuff behind us still," Nick said. "We'd see him easy if he were up ahead."

I nodded in agreement. As big as that bear was, we would have seen his tracks or sign of his passing if he had climbed up out of the creek on our side. And he surely was not anywhere in the clear ahead of us.

"Why don't I wait up here right where this really heavy stuff ends," I said. "I'll be able to see him if he climbs up out of the ravine, or moves into the open ahead. You can drop back to where the thick stuff begins, back downhill. The bear will probably be between you and me. Drop down to the creek bottom and work slowly back to me. Your scent drifting upstream might push him toward me."

"Worth a try," said Nick. "If you can get a clear shot, take it when he comes out. If not, try not to spook him and wait for me. We may still be able to get on him."

It sounded like a good plan.

"It'll only take me a few minutes to get down there and stalk down toward the stream," Nick said. "I should be back here in no more than twenty minutes, and I'll try to keep an eye on you, back you up, as I'm moving."

Nick started down the hill alongside the high edge well above the stream bank. I positioned myself on a small mound of dirt on the lip of a shallow natural gully about forty feet wide and four or five feet deep. Behind me to the south and uphill to my left was the logging clear-cut growing back in low brush. My view of the area was the best I could hope for. The gully where I waited was open, but the rim on the other side was the dense trees and undergrowth that covered the edge of the bank and descended into the creek bottom and back down-stream toward the sea.

I lost sight of Nick as he scrambled downhill, into the trees that bordered and filled the deep ravine. That's when I saw it move, just across the gully, in the thick, dark tangle of thorn bushes, alders, and cedars along the high embankment above the stream. Just inside the wet brush, very near the edge of the narrow depression, less than twenty-five yards in front of me. The outline of a small, round ear, barely moving. An eye, floating. A dark, massive, hovering shadow. I sensed it as much as saw it. Smelled the wet, musky fur, as I had that first night in my tent. As I had so many nights before. But now it was unmistakably real. Unmistakably huge and mov-ing, slowly. Directly toward me.

I heard a low woof, like a big dog just barely becoming alerted, and the sound of brush moving. Then came a distinct clack, the snapping of big teeth. The hulking shadow picked up speed and burst from the devil's club thorns on the edge of the gully in a quick lope. The thick, shaggy hide shook in rhythmic waves from front to back as it ran toward me, its mouth slightly open, head extended out and down, and its small eyes fixed on mine.

As soon as I saw the bear moving toward me, while it was still in the brush, I instinctively lifted the bolt handle of my rifle and cycled it back, forward, then down, chambering a huge three-hundred-grain round. I instantly flicked the safety off as I raised the gun to my shoulder, at the same time putting my eye behind the four-power scope. The bear, moving faster now over the far edge of the depression, completely filled the lens at this close range.

I had an overwhelming urge to turn and run. But with time running out and the crosshairs of the gun sight somewhere on his brown, moving chest, I planted my feet, steadied my legs, and pulled the trigger.

The heavy rifle lurched up as the round fired. No longer looking through the scope, I saw a puff of dirt and hair jump off the bear's chest, low just inside the front of his left shoulder, between the shoulder's inside edge and the center of his chest. The big animal stumbled to the ground on his left shoulder, his other three limbs still driving. He was back on all four in an instant and coming at me much faster than before. He hadn't lost a stride.

Even as the gun recoiled, I was cycling a fresh round into the chamber. With the bear up and moving forward, I threw the rifle to my shoulder. His speed had increased and he had quickly advanced much closer. I didn't even bother with the scope. I simply peered over the top of the barrel and fired toward the bear's head, now some fifteen to twenty feet away and still moving fast. The gun roared and bucked again. The bear lurched to his right, feet still churning, and began a frantic clockwise spin. As he moved around, I cycled the bolt once more and looked over the rifle. My shot had hit higher

60

than the first, near the side of his neck. I fired a third time. Sand and dirt flew up from the ground within an inch of the bear's head. A miss.

I worked the bolt a fourth time as he completed his full spin and lunged once more toward me, legs digging into the dirt. Again, I pointed directly at his head. The bear was past the bottom of the gully and coming up at me, only ten feet away, when I fired. His massive head jerked to the right and I could see a gaping wound in his jaw. Shooting down from my position slightly above him, I instantly realized the powerful bullet would go through his jaw and neck, and then penetrate deep down into his chest cavity.

The huge animal lay sprawled on his belly, front and rear legs fully extended but still moving in uncoordinated jerks. I cycled the bolt one more time. He raised his head, mouth open and eyes fixed on mine, and extended his face toward me, only a few feet away. He somehow managed to get his feet partially back under him and made a halting attempt to stand and move toward me once again. I put the muzzle of the rifle directly between his eyes, resting it on the fur of his forehead, and pulled the trigger. There was only a click on the empty chamber. All four rounds had been fired. *Four in the magazine, nothing in the chamber*, Nick had said. *Safer that way.*

The bear lurched forward then collapsed to the ground, his head hitting my legs, pushing me down into a sitting position. My rifle was still in my hands and my heels still firmly dug into the dirt where I had originally planted them. Pink, foamy blood coated the outside of his nose and lips. Darker red, wet splotches of blood stained his chest, neck, and patches of earth. Blood was smeared on me as well.

I watched as the last light of life seemed to drift from his eyes. The four rounds of ammo had finally done their job. Only six or seven seconds had elapsed since I first saw the bear

charge from the brush. And I had not taken a step backward.
It was over.

I pulled my legs from under the carcass, stood up,
and took a deep breath as the shakes set in. I looked downhill,
but Nick was nowhere to be seen. It was then I heard a muted
shout from up the hill and turned to see a man waving his
arms at me from a meadow in the distance above.

"How in the world did Nick get up there?" I asked myself aloud.

I began climbing up the hillside toward the waving figure.

"Congratulations," said the man as I drew closer. "I
watched the whole thing."

I could see finally it was Matt, the Indian man from the
potlatch who had suggested I try this spot. I walked up to him.
We were both smiling.

"You held your ground. Stood firm against a tough
one," said Matt.

"I didn't really think I'd see you here."

"Didn't you, now? Well, this is my favorite deer hunting
spot. I told you I might be over this way."

The clouds had ended halfway up the hill, and we stood
talking in warm sunshine. I looked down toward where the
bear lay and could see Nick working on him in the mist and
drizzle below. He'd be skinning, fleshing, and packing the hide
back to the Zodiac. Nick. Taking care of business.

"It's beautiful up here," I said to Matt. Looking over the
side of the mountain, the clouds were becoming scattered out
over the Icy Straits and I could see flashes of afternoon sunlight on the waves. A tiny puff of steam emerged far out on the
water, then another nearby. Whales spouting.

"It is," said Matt. "Beautiful. Local tradition has it each flash on the waves is the spirit of a departed ancestor signaling. One of the reasons I love this place."

I was still feeling a little shaky from the bear facedown as well as the hike up, and sat down on a log to rest. I stared out at the sparkling waters of Icy Straits and could then understand the native legend. As I watched the diamond-like flashes reflected from the waves, I was reminded of my own family—wife, children, parents, grandparents, brother and sister. I realized Alaska has a way of soaking to one's core, and this primal land provides context and meaning to our familiar, contemporary world. And makes it somehow easier to understand and attach meaning to one's own life. Strangely, I wondered if some future passerby would ever contemplate my soul from the reflections off the waves of the Icy Straits.

Matt said, "Why don't you come with me to our hunting camp just up the mountain here? There's some food, something to drink, a fire going. Nick can take care of things for a while."

I was exhausted and his invitation sounded good. I was sure Nick had seen me talking with Matt and knew where I was.

"I might just do that," I said, "if it wouldn't be any trouble."

"Our people would be glad to have you as a guest in our lodge," Matt said. "It's the kind of thing we do. It would be our honor."

"I guess I owe yet another debt of gratitude to the Snail Clan," I smiled. "After the potlatch and all."

Matt swung his daypack onto his back and picked up his lever-action deer rifle. "Oh," he said, smiling, "I'm not Snail Clan. I'm Haida, not Tlingit."

I was puzzled and said "But you were at the Snail Clan potlatch. I just figured..."

"Just there taking care of some business I had."

I recalled Matt had come in after and left before me, without talking to anyone else. I thought of asking about that, but then realized it didn't really matter anymore. I stood up and put my pack with all my things on my back, too. I looked down to wave to Nick just as a curtain of rain swept across the lower hillside. Nick and the bear disappeared into the mist.

"You ready?" asked Matt, as he started up the hill.

I turned to follow him up the mountain. I could see a plume of smoke curling up over the trees on the hillside well above. I knew there would be fresh salmon baking on the fire in the lodge, strips of venison in the smokehouse, and green spruce logs putting out richly scented smoke.

"I'm ready now," I said, and started up the hill, following Matt. Up to the camp of friendly, welcoming, helpful people. Where the sun shone bright and warm on the hillside, and where there was a warm, dry fire inside. Up to the lodge house.

Of the Land Otter Clan.

Author's Note

This is dedicated to the memory of Drake McLean. Born April 22, 1939, in Lansing, Michigan, he was by all conventional measures an ordinary husband, father, and attorney. To those who knew him well, he was a remarkable man of character and strength, and to me a loyal and valued friend. A man who faced his bear at times with hope or terror or determination, he always stood firm and never took a step back. After a long battle he succumbed, with a dignity born of courage, to multiple myeloma—his own personal bear—on November 23, 1997, in Rochester, Michigan. He is still missed, but even now as he resides in the lodge house of the Land Otters, his memory continues to provide strength to those he touched here. His battle was the inspiration for this story.

Epilogue

The following is an excerpt from the transcript of the Ten O'clock News, KUBL-TV Channel 6 Ketchikan on Friday evening, September 29:

> TV-6: On Chichagof Island this afternoon, a hunter was killed in an encounter with a brown bear. He was hunting with long-time Ketchikan resident and guide, Nicholas Kay. The body was airlifted by the Coast Guard to Juneau, where he was officially pronounced dead. In this exclusive TV-6 interview, Kay told us what happened.

> Kay: We were stalking a big brown we had jumped on the beach, and were separated for a few minutes when I heard some shooting. I ran back toward my hunter, but the bear was on him and I couldn't shoot without hitting them both. I was less than a hundred yards away, and ran up there to drive off the bear with my rifle butt or kill him. But when I got there, it was all over.

> TV-6: Was your client already dead, or was he able to say anything about what happened?

> Kay: I gave him CPR, tried to make a tourniquet from my belt, but there wasn't much I could do. I thought he was gone, then he opened his eyes and said, "I'm ready now." That was all. I'd like to say one thing. Hunters come up here for all kinds of their own reasons. This man wanted to kill his bear, but more than that, he wanted to face it, the right way. I think he did that.

TV-6: The hunter's name is being withheld pending the notification of his family. The Alaska Department of Fish & Game and local authorities are continuing to investigate.

UNDELIVERABLE: ERROR CODE 3276

From: "John Bascom" <john.bee@cheapnet.com>
To: "Eliot Tongas"
          <eliotstrophybearhunts@AlaskaiNet.com>
Date: August 16, 2014
Subject: Bear Hunt Final Arrangements

Hello, Eliot

I've dropped the check in the mail for the last payment on our fall black bear hunt with you at Que-eye-ow Island. My son-in-law, Curt, is sending his today, and this should complete the arrangements for our hunt to end all hunts the week after next.

Just something I wanted to mention to you about Curtis, although it probably isn't really necessary. He's eagerly looking forward to this, and I really want him to have a good time and a successful hunt. It's also important to his wife, my daughter, Beth, since she feels he needs to do this for his self-esteem. Unlike me (I've taken mulies and antelope in Montana, whitetails in the Texas brush country to name only a few), he's only shot a handful of small birds and local deer, and badly at that. I'm afraid he has something of a delicate constitution, being an English literature major in college and all. I think you get the picture. Anyway, he may be in over his head on this hunt. I'll help him as much as I can, but it would be great if you could be aware of his limitations and go the extra mile to nurse him through this. And, remember, this is just between the two of us.

I'm looking forward to stalking big bears up the wild rivers and over the Alaskan rain forest mountains of Que-eye-ow Island. I've been doing a little extra to get in top shape (not that it's needed) like running miles each night and serious weight training daily. I'm ready!

See you in two weeks.
John

From:	"Curt Kendall" <curtisken789@gmail.net>
To:	"Eliot Tongas" <eliotstrophybearhunts@AlaskaiNet.com>
Date:	August 17, 2014
Subject:	Last Payment

Greetings, Eliot

I just posted the balance of my bear hunt guide fee to you. I can hardly wait for the hunt to end all hunts to begin aboard your boat, Bruin Cruiser, on Kee-owe-ee Island in barely two short weeks. I've been reading up on bears and wanted you to know I'll be holding out for a real trophy, one that squares somewhere above 7 ½ feet. Boone & Crocket record book material. I'm accustomed to rigorous hunting for long periods and using my advanced skills honed over many hunts to take exceptional animals. Indeed I am ready, willing, and able to do whatever it takes.

I did want to make you aware on the Q-T of some issues with my hunting partner and father-in-law, John. He's elderly (up into his 70s, now), quite overweight, and getting a little "addled," if you catch my meaning. He tries hard enough by ambling a few blocks a night or two each week and attempts to exercise now and then with a pair of two-pound dumbbells. He puts up a good show by telling everyone he is "running" and doing "weight training," an innocent enough exaggeration if not a delusion! Ha ha. Anyway, my wife, Beth, and I want this to be a great hunt for him as it may be his last, given his age, physical condition, and flagging faculties. I'm sure you understand. I'll do what I can to prop him up and humor him along, but if you could be mindful of his "issues" also and make necessary allowances, it would be great.

Best,
Curt

From:	"Eliot Tongas" <eliotstrophybearhunts@AlaskaiNet.com>
To:	"John Bascom" <john.bee@cheapnet.com>; "Curt Kendall" <curtisken789@gmail.net>
Date:	August 24, 2014
Subject:	Kuiu Island Bear Hunt

John & Curt,

Received your recent e-mails and the checks you sent. Thanks. Everything is set for your arrival in Petersburg and my young assistant guide, Ben, will be here waiting for you, too. Be assured I am aware of the goals and special circumstances you each mentioned, and will do all within my power to accommodate your needs to make this a successful hunt in every way. Having guided bear hunters for over two decades, it is the thing I love most and eagerly anticipate as the end of summer arrives. I'm sure it will prove to be the hunt to end all hunts for both of you, as well as for me.

By the way, I thought you'd want to know the island is Kuiu (meaning in Tlingit "misty mountains") and it's pronounced like saying the letters "Q" and "U" together smoothly as one word, like "cue'-you"; just for your info.

Eliot
"Eliot's Trophy Bear Hunts"
www.eliotstrophybearhunts.com

From:	"Curt Kendall" <curtisken789@gmail.net>
To:	"Beth Kendall" <beffy.boo@hotmail.net>
Date:	September 1, 2014
Subject:	Arrived Magnificent Kee-owe-ee Island

Hey, Babes

Arrived at Bower Bay on Kee-owe-ee Island (an Indian name that translates "Island of the Great Bears" I think—Googled it but didn't get a hit) in southeast Alaska's inside passage. You wouldn't believe the beauty and isolation of this place. I'm amazed we can send e-mails over the sat-phone.

I reaffirmed to Ben, the guide I'll be hunting with (Eliot's assistant—I wanted the younger guide who can keep up with me), I'm after a nice boar bear, over 7 ½ feet in hide length. I've been doing my reading and know they sometimes get them that big up here.

We talked about hunting spots and I insisted on Halla-Luki Creek that empties into Chatham Strait behind some little islets just around from the mouth of Bower Bay where we're anchored aboard "Bruin Cruiser." I think the creek name means "Giant Bear" or something like that in Tlingit, the language of the local Indians. I'm not positive. Should be salmon running up it now. It's apparently harder to hunt than some other streams, but I learned online it has harbored a few monsters in the past. I think it's the one. Anyway, they tried to talk me into hunting one of the smaller and easier streams. Ha ha. Might be fine for your dad but they don't know me! I'm definitely up to it if that's what it takes to get the big one.

And speaking of your old man, he seems eager if clueless, and I mean that in a good way. I just hope he can handle the extreme hunting. Eliot's taking him up Raisin Creek tomorrow, one with few bears but an easy walk. Hopefully your dad will enjoy it if nothing else. I'll keep an eye on him for you.

I miss you but, honestly, am so excited about this hunt it's all I'm thinking of. I know the time apart doing "our own thing" will actually be good for us.

Expecting to get the big one soon if not tomorrow. I'll let you know when I do.

Curt

From:	"Curt Kendall" <curtisken789@gmail.net>
To:	"Beth Kendall" <beffy.boo@hotmail.net>
Date:	September 2, 2014
Subject:	Horrible Halla-Luki Creek Today

Dearest Beth,

Today was rugged. We hiked up "Big Bear Creek" all day. It was a tangle of deadfalls and thick brush. The underwater stones were like boulders. My feet kept catching between them. If there had been a bear, I couldn't have seen him at ten yards! But there was NOTHING. We heard something ahead a few times, but could never tell what it was. And my guide, Ben, kept getting so far in front of me he'd have spooked anything way before I could have been in a position to shoot. I only fell because I had to rush to keep up with him. I just can't believe they took me up there. Still, given the circumstances, I think I did extremely well.

I'm going to talk to the guides at dinner and suggest a different place tomorrow with more shooting lanes and a chance to see a nice seven-foot bear.

Your dad is still out hunting, but he and Eliot are expected back soon as it is beginning to get dark. I doubt he saw anything but just hope he's holding up.

Love and miss you,
Curt

From:	"John Bascom" <john.bee@cheapnet.com>
To:	"Nickie Bascom" <nickiegirl@cheapnet.com>
Date:	September 2, 2014
Subject:	End of First Full Hunting Day

Hello, Nickie-Dear, from Que-eye-ow Island

Well, I'm back from hunting up Raisin Creek all day and it was interesting. The going was hard but I did well. Only fell a couple times and then just because I was led into impossible areas. My waders never filled completely with water. It wasn't hard keeping up with my guide, Eliot, as he stopped to watch and glass for bears frequently. He actually slowed me down.

The creek was thick with salmon and we saw lots of bears. I had a shot at a nice boar Eliot said was nearly seven feet, but my sights were off. Through no fault of mine, I missed due to a defective scope, and my gun jammed when I tried a follow-up shot. Saw other bears over six and a half feet, but they were too small to take. Glad I took the time to get in shape and practice with my rifle. I'm going to re-sight it and check the function of the action tomorrow.

Your loving husband,
John

From:	"Eliot Tongas" <eliotstrophybearhunts@AlaskaiNet.com>
To:	"Sarah Tongas" <saratong@AlaskaiNet.com>
Date:	September 2, 2014
Subject:	From Eliot on Kuiu

Hello, Sarah

Well, we're off to an unusually shaky start. The one client, Curt, insisted against our advice that Ben take him up Halla-Luki, which as you know means Impassable Creek. Claims he read on the Internet about big bears there, but it's news to me. We've never taken one up that creek like I tried to tell him. He floundered and fell several times, and scared off a few doubtless smaller bears Ben heard splashing while they were chasing salmon in the shallows up ahead. The client couldn't keep up and came back beat-up and exhausted. Of course he blamed everything on Ben. He originally maintained he would take nothing unless it was over seven and a half feet, but this evening is talking about looking for one "near seven feet."

The other guy, John, is just as bad. He kept falling, and even when he didn't I constantly had to stop and wait for him, pretending to be searching the area for bears so as not to embarrass him. Then he wounded a seven-footer at eighty yards and blamed it on his gun. Like I haven't heard that excuse before! And neither can pronounce Kuiu for some reason. It's getting irritating.

Tomorrow Ben and I are going to take them up to the mouth of Little Fish Crick for John, and the headwaters of Raisin Creek for Curt. John and I will sit and watch (so he won't hurt himself—I told him there might be "wolves" there if we sit quietly, hah!), while Curt and Ben will wade slowly and carefully down the creek all day to the bay. It should be a lot easier going for both of them and hopefully will shut them up.

As usual, it's beautiful here and even with the first-day commotion, it's good to be out hunting I guess. Still, I've been thinking again about the opening at the fish cannery we talked about.

All my love from your husband—Eliot

From:	"Curt Kendall" <curtisken789@gmail.net>
To:	"Beth Kendall" <beffy.boo@hotmail.net>
Date:	September 3, 2014

Subject: Unbelievable Raisin Creek

My Darling Wife,

I didn't believe anything could be worse than yesterday, but today on Raisin Creek took the cake. The bottom was jagged, slick rubble and I lost my footing nearly every other step. The walking was so noisy the bears could have heard us coming a mile away. There were huge downed trees across the entire narrow creek at every bend. We saw a few tiny cub-like juveniles, but that was it. And Ben kept racing ahead of me again. It was dark by the time we got down to the bay where the skiff had been left for us. You wouldn't believe the water I drained from my waders back at the boat. I gave Ben and Eliot a piece of my mind at dinner this evening.

And your father is insufferable. I'm just being honest, not critical. He rants at dinner with his far-right political drivel and tries to bait me about my centrist political beliefs. Fortunately our guides see right through him and are sympathetic to my well-thought-out views as opposed to his psychotic diatribes. He keeps bragging about the size of the bear he missed yesterday, and the others he saw but "passed on." I'm sure! And he's blaming his poor shooting on his gun. Spare me! I'm embarrassed for him. I don't know how or why Nickie puts up with him.

We may take a break tomorrow and do a little fishing to let the bear-thing reset for a day. It was Eliot's idea, but I think it would be for the best.

I miss you desperately and can't wait to get home. I'm not sure this trip was such a good idea, but I felt it should happen only because it is probably your father's last chance. Pray for me. Still hoping to get that six-and-a-half-foot bear and get this over with.

Curt

From: "John Bascom" <john.bee@cheapnet.com>
To: "Nickie Bascom" <nickiegirl@cheapnet.com>
Date: September 3, 2014
Subject: Second Day

My Dearest Wife,

Well, I started this morning by shooting my rifle at a target Eliot set up on the beach. Amazingly it was back on "zero." And the action was working properly again. I must have bumped it a second time on my way in last night and knocked everything back as it's supposed to be. Like when I kick the lawn mower at home to get it running. Go figure.

No bears today, though. We sat on a hill above the mouth of a tiny creek that comes in from Bower Bay. I was looking for wolves Eliot said were often there, or bears fishing in the creek. It was filled with salmon, but no game. Eliot seems to think I may have winged that bear the first day up on Raisin Creek. By Alaska law, that would end my bear hunting. I'm sure I didn't hit it and told Eliot as much, but I hope he didn't bring me to Little Fish Crick just to keep me occupied and away from bears.

Curtis has been piece of work. Apparently he pretty much staggers down the rivers like a drunk and makes so much noise no respectable bear would hang around. That's what I put together listening to his guide, Ben, talking with Eliot out of Curt's earshot. They're going to give him a rest by taking us fishing tomorrow (which is fine by me) and leading him down easier streams after that.

And he is a pain in the backside at dinner, spewing his ultra-liberal crap. I had to call him out on it a few times to set him straight. The guides just rolled their eyes; no liberals in the Alaska outback. I think they respected me for speaking out.

I can't believe what poor Beth has to put up with. I had no idea. She is a saint!

Love you tons and can't wait to come home. Don't know why I did this except to help young Curt.

John

From:	"Curt Kendall" <curtisken789@gmail.net>
To:	"Beth Kendall" <beffy.boo@hotmail.net>
Date:	September 4, 2014
Subject:	Stream Fishing Today

My Darling Wonderful Wife Who I Miss So Desperately And Want To Be With,

Eliot repositioned the boat last night to the other side of Kuiu (your father simply can't learn to pronounce the name of this island; it's an embarrassment) where we set up crab pots then made an easy hike into the bush a few miles to a big pool below a waterfall on Slick Creek. Your father barely made it. I had to push his fat ass up the hills from behind while he clung to the back of Eliot's pack, who was in the lead. He got there flushed and breathless, but somehow alive. We fished in the pool below the falls, me doing it leisurely just to kill time and to let your dad catch a few, while he casted frantically as if his life depended on out-fishing me! Anyway, I purposely limited my catch to a couple small ones while your father got a half-dozen or so silver salmon and Dolly Varden trout. Then we repeated the disaster with your dad back to the boat. Emptied the pots we'd set out in Bower Bay in the morning and had a fine meal of steamed crab for dinner. Your lazy father was too pooped to help pull the pots up! What else is new? I had no idea of the struggles Nickie must have had in dealing with him all these years. I should drop her a note to buck her up.

This trip has made me realize how important you are to me, and how much I love and need you. Can't wait to get out of this place and back home to you.

Love,
Curt

From:	"John Bascom" <john.bee@cheapnet.com>
To:	"Nickie Bascom" <nickiegirl@cheapnet.com>
Date:	September 4, 2014
Subject:	Third Day—Fishing

My Dear Love, Nickie

We spent the day crabbing and spin-fishing on Slick Creek. The hike up there was a hoot. It was through the rainforest up and down the coastal mountains of Kuiu (which Curt insists on calling "Kee-owe-ee"—Jeeze!). Those guys are really out of shape, especially Curtis. To get up the hills, I had to simultaneously push on Eliot's (in the lead) back pack while dragging Curt as he clung to the back of mine. Ben just staggered along at the rear. They were all huffing and puffing when we got there while I just laughed.

Once at the falls, Curt fished like a house-afire attempting to outdo me, but I caught five big ones without trying for every little minnow he got. Maybe twenty all together. Then the hike back was more of the same, me pushing and pulling the others along. Curt tried to redeem himself by insisting on hauling the crab pots in by himself to prove something I guess, and nearly fell in a couple times. Ben finally had to do it for him. Poor Beth!

Tomorrow more hunting, Curt for bears on a wide, shallow stream more suited to him, and me for wolf on the shores of Bower Bay (we're heading back there tonight). Eliot still is insisting I've "tagged out" on bear. What a crock.

Love and miss you. Will try to see if we can get an earlier flight back if possible

John

From:	"John Bascom" <john.bee@cheapnet.com>
To:	"Beth Kendall" <beffy.boo@hotmail.net>
Date:	September 4, 2014
Subject:	From Kuiu Island

Dearest Daughter Beth,

Just a quick note to say Curt and I are well. No bear yet, although I nearly bagged a big one but for an equipment malfunction. Curt is struggling along as best he can and I think, in his own way, is trying.

Remember, Nickie and I will always be here for you. If you ever need some time to yourself, a place to stay, or simply someone to "talk to," just say the word. It must be very difficult. I hate to say "told you so," but...

Thinking of you. Stay strong.

Dad

From:	"Curt Kendall" <curtisken789@gmail.net>
To:	"Nickie Bascom" <nickiegirl@cheapnet.com>
Date:	September 4, 2014
Subject:	From your son-in-law

Nickie,

First, John is fine, through no doing of his own. I've been caring for him as best I can.

Spending this time with him has made the cross you bear all too apparent. You have my undying admiration and respect. And Beth feels exactly the same. If you ever are at the "end of your rope," need to talk, to get away, or simply be consoled, remember we will be there for you. We understand and love you all the more for your trials and tribulations. Hopefully you will find solace knowing Beth and I share your terrible secret and are ready to support you.

Your devoted son-in-law,
Curt

From: "Eliot Tongas"
               <eliotstrophybearhunts@AlaskaiNet.com>
To: "Sarah Tongas" <saratong@AlaskaiNet.com>
Date: September 4, 2014
Subject: HELP

My Beloved Wife, Sarah

Just when I thought it couldn't get worse...

John's rifle turned out to be fine after wounding his bear the first day, although he won't accept that fact. Keeps insisting he missed and he should still be allowed to take another. I took him up to Little Fish Crick yesterday, where, as you know, there are no bears. We wasted the day there looking for "wolves." Ha ha. Curt went with Ben on upper Raisin Creek and nearly killed himself again. He kept trying to get a shot at a few cubs they saw along the way.

Then I took them fishing on Slick Creek this afternoon just to give Ben and me a break. Both of them nearly died during the hike in, John hanging onto my pack and Curt onto John's while I pulled them both along. Then they went nuts trying to out fish one another, and later quarrelling over the stinking crab pots. And they both do nothing but harangue everyone about their lunatic political beliefs at dinner EVERY night! It's actually painful.

Tomorrow I'm taking John "wolf-hunting" (sure) again, and Ben will go down the easy Bower Creek with Curt. Only small, if any, bears in it, but at least he won't finish the job of killing himself there, which he seems so set on.

And see if you can get that cannery guy's phone number for me to talk to when I get home. Seriously.

Miss you—Eliot

From:	"Beth Kendall" <beffy.boo@hotmail.net>
To:	"John Bascom" <john.bee@cheapnet.com>
	"Curt Kendall" <curtisken789@gmail.net>
Date:	September 5, 2014
Subject:	Love from Beth

Good Morning, Guys!

Good to get your e-mails. You're both quite the jokers! All kidding aside, it sounds as though you are having an incredible adventure together. So glad for the two of you. Enjoy the country and each other's company.

Am eagerly anticipating your return with your trophies. Can't wait to see my two favorite fellows. Love to you both.

Beth

From:	"Nickie Bascom" <nickiegirl@cheapnet.com>
To:	"John Bascom" <john.bee@cheapnet.com>
	"Curt Kendall" <curtisken789@gmail.net>
Date:	September 5, 2014
Subject:	To my bear hunters

Picked up your latest e-mails early this a.m. and thought I'd answer right away. You two are such kidders! I'm so happy you have this time to bond together and are having such a lovely experience. But HURRY HOME. I'm looking forward to hearing all the wonderful details.

Love you boys,
Nickie

From: "John Bascom" <john.bee@cheapnet.com>
To: "Nickie Bascom" <nickiegirl@cheapnet.com>
Date: September 5, 2014
Subject: Your E-mail

Good Morning, Baby

Got your reply this morning. I'm not sure you fully understand what's going on here. For starters, Curt snores like a chain saw. We're in a bunkroom together and I can't get a moment of sleep. Then when I got up this morning, the young assistant guide, Ben, was GONE! I can only assume he couldn't stomach another day with Curt. Anyway, since Eliot claims I "got a bear" (which I clearly and cleanly simply missed only because of defective equipment), he's taking Curt down the park-like Bower Creek today while I sit on this rotten boat. Crap.

I'll try to e-mail you again tonight. Love you. And I WANT TO COME HOME!

John

From: "Curt Kendall" <curtisken789@gmail.net>
To: "Beth Kendall" <beffy.boo@hotmail.net>
Date: September 5, 2014
Subject: Replying to your e-mail

Morning, My Darling Wife

From your e-mail this morning, Beth, I'm not sure you appreciate all the nuances. I'll explain the details when I get home, but for starters, your idiot father insists on keeping a water bottle by his bed and sucking at it all night like an Oedipal pervert who can't relinquish his mother's teat. *Glug-glug-glug*, on and off all night. I didn't get a wink's sleep.

Then I learned my guide, the assistant, Ben, had left. Apparently he had pressing plans, but honestly I think he was intimidated that he couldn't keep up with me, mentally or physically. Anyway, Eliot will be guiding me down challenging and bear-laden Bower Creek today while your father gets some well-needed recuperation aboard Bruin Cruiser. Hopefully I'll see something near six feet out there and get this over with.

I did drop poor Nickie a brief note. She replied, trying to keep a brave face, but reading between the lines I could feel her pain.

I miss you terribly and only long for the comfort of your arms. I want to be home!

Your devoted husband,
Curt

From:	"Curt Kendall" <curtisken789@gmail.net>
To:	"Beth Kendall" <beffy.boo@hotmail.net>
Date:	September 5, 2014
Subject:	SUCCESS This Evening!!!

Hey, Beth. I DID IT!! Got a dandy bear late this afternoon with guide, Eliot, on Bower Creek. It was tough and challenging. I had to scale fallen timber across the creek and take a long shot at a monster bear, all while balancing on a slippery deadfall log. My first shot was spot-on, but I put a few more into him for insurance. Even so, that tough giant was able to keep going into the woods. Eliot followed and administered the *"coup de grâce"* from his .375 magnum with a shot or two, even though it wasn't really necessary. I set the timer on my camera on automatic and snapped a few pics of me with my trophy while Eliot went back to get his skinning equipment. It was awkward positioning the bear for the best effect and posing while the timer was winding down, but it worked sort of. I'll share with you when I'm home.

I watched while Eliot skinned out the bear. It's HUGE. While he was working on the carcass I asked, and he assured me it's the biggest he's ever seen, one for the record book. Of course, I told him to prepare it for a trophy and send it to us. It will memorialize a great trip and what I honestly feel was a major accomplishment for me. Can't wait to show it to you, our friends and family. And interestingly, he found it had a sizable tapeworm in its gut, which was an unusual but unimportant twist.

Your dad is jealous and I'm ecstatic. This has been the hunt to end all hunts. Honestly, Dear, I think the time apart enjoying our own interests separately has been good for us, as I've said all along.

Curt

From: "John Bascom" <john.bee@cheapnet.com>
To: "Nickie Bascom" <nickiegirl@cheapnet.com>
Date: September 5, 2014
Subject: Curt's Bear

Well, against all odds, Curt stumbled on what I now know was a small bear late this afternoon and barely wounded it before Eliot finished it off for him. I don't know all the details, but of course he's done nothing but boast. I wish I were dead.

But that's not the end or even the worst. I went through the shots on his digital camera after dinner and found this one:

For the love of God, could he be doing what I think he is to that little fellow? It's obviously a small, young bear. It would be the depraved union of bestiality and pedophilia! And he even took a photo of himself doing it while Eliot was gone! I'm sure he has no idea anyone has seen it. I can't get the terrible image from my mind. Poor, poor Beth.

Honest to God, this cannot get any worse. It's the hunt to end all hunts, and I mean that literally. Can't wait to be home!

John

From:	"Eliot Tongas"
	<eliotstrophybearhunts@AlaskaiNet.com>
To:	"Sarah Tongas" <saratong@AlaskaiNet.com>
Date:	September 5, 2014
Subject:	IT'S OVER!

My Darling Wife Sarah,

Well, first I got up this morning and Ben was GONE. He apparently took the skiff during the night over to the logging camp at the end of the bay and caught the morning Beaver supply flight back to Petersburg. I was furious at first, but when I calmed down I understood and only regretted I hadn't thought of it first. God bless poor Ben.

And my hell is finally over with these guys. The client, Curt, shot a small bear on Bower Creek this evening. He nearly fell off a wet log he insisted on climbing, then winged the poor bear in the leg and butt at unbelievably close range. I had to finish it off for him as it hobbled into the woods.

When I was skinning it out there was a really long tapeworm in the little thing's gut. I commented to Curt about the worm's unusual size. Oddly, he kept asking me if it was a "trophy" (whatever that means for a tapeworm), if I had ever seen one bigger, and if it would make the "record books." Of course the bear was too small to pay much attention to, just around six feet, but all he seemed to want to talk about was the worm. He said he wanted me to preserve and prepare it, and send it to him as some kind of bizarre trophy. It's no surprise he didn't care about that tiny bear, but a TAPEWORM? This one is a first. Now, I've had a bellyful with these morons, but if that's what he wants, by God...well, FINE!

And I'm calling the cannery guy as soon as I'm back. I know it's long hours starting on the gutting line, and minimum wage. But it's sounding pretty good right now. None of these clients to deal with.

Love you. Should be back tomorrow. Don't think less of me, but now the only thing I want is to hold you and have a good cry.

Eliot

From:	"Curt Kendall" <curtisken789@gmail.net>
To:	"Eliot Tongas"
	<eliotstrophybearhunts@AlaskaiNet.com>
Date:	October 15, 2014
Subject:	UNBELIEVABLE!!!

Well, I'm sure you think you're quite clever, don't you, Eliot? Of course, I got the shipping notice and tracking information on my "trophy" you said you'd mount and send. And you may not know I invited all our neighbors, friends, and family over to be here this afternoon when it arrived for an "unveiling party."

I'm completely confident, ELIOT, it comes as no surprise to you that when I opened it in front of a room full of excited, expectant people—the most important people in MY LIFE—out came the dried and salted TAPEWORM stapled to an old, warped scrap of plywood. It looked like a hideous, curled, six-foot length of shriveled old twine left out in the weather for several years, except of course, ELIOT, for the huge HEAD on the end of it. And then there was...the perfect touch...a delicate aroma of ROTTING WORM!

As you might imagine and most surely anticipated, the roomful of people stared, eyes watering from the acrid stink, in horrified, stunned silence. Silence but for the single exception of the jackass-like braying laughter of my idiot-moron-damned-rotten FATHER-IN-LAW, your obvious favorite—John—with whom I'm sure you planned this entire thing just to rob me of my legitimate spectacular trophy and, of course, to humiliate me, of which you did a fine job, ELIOT!

The only thing I have to say to you, ELIOT, is you are a despicable son of a...
****

>UNDELIVERABLE: ERROR CODE 3276<
>security server has truncated this message due to<
>   ****profanity****hate speech****threatening
          language****graphic violence**** <
>this message has been referred to the NSA for possible action as a terror threat<
****

From: Auto-Reply "Eliot Tongas"
To: "Curt Kendall" <curtisken789@gmail.net>
Date: October 15, 2014
Subject: E-mail Address No Longer Active

The e-mail address you attempted to reach for "Eliot Tongas" is no longer active.

"Eliot's Trophy Bear Hunts" is no longer in business
www.eliotstrophybearhunts.com PAGE NOT FOUND

"Eliot Tongas" may be reached at:

NordicBreeze Salmon Processing-Ketchikan Plant
Eliot Tongas—Apprentice Gutter
Offal Removal, Grinding & Steaming Line
Cat Food Division
info@nordicbreezepetfood.com
"NordicBreeze Choice Deluxe Alaskan Salmon—For Your Cat's Health & Happiness!"

From: "John Bascom" <john.bee@cheapnet.com>
To: "Curt Kendall" <curtisken789@gmail.net>
Date: December 20, 2014
Subject: MERRY CHRISTMAS

Holiday best wishes, Curtis, from Nickie and me to you and Beth.

It's hard to believe it's been over two months since we saw you at your "trophy unveiling." Ha ha, good one. I know you set up that gag yourself, but still, it was hilarious. It's great to see you have such a sense of humor, especially in view of that puny bear you (or should I say, Eliot) bagged.

Anyway, I got an e-mail from Atkins & Son, the hunting booking agent who set us up with Eliot, on a last-minute discounted cancellation hunt this spring in Zambia, south-central Africa. It's for Cape buffalo. The price is right and it should be a blast, but time is short. Given the great bear hunt we had with Eliot (what a guy!) on Kune-ee-whoah Island or whatever, I thought this would be something you may want to consider the two of us doing together.

I'm sure it would be the hunt to end all hunts. Let me know, and we both hope to see you two over the holidays.

Your loving father-in-law,
John

From:	"Curt Kendall" <curtisken789@gmail.net>
To:	"John Bascom" <john.bee@cheapnet.com>
Date:	December 20, 2014
Subject:	Africa Hunt

HELL YES! I'm up for it. It sounds perfect. Just the thought of going after dangerous game in Africa makes my blood hot. It should be the hunt to end all hunts. The cost is manageable, the timing is great, the experience sounds incredible... after all, with two seasoned hunters like us, what could go wrong?

Your hunting buddy,
Curt

MOLLY & ME

Me? What I love most about flying is the weather. Like a beautiful woman, she can thrill or soothe, cajole or flare with an unpredictable vengeance. I've flown deep troughs, fast-moving fronts, ice, zero-zero approaches, turbulence. And then those silky smooth days with brilliant sunshine when you can see forever and never want the flight to end. Like a woman, the weather's mysterious and unpredictable. Yet when you understand her, work with her rather than against her, overcome the risks and enjoy what she has to offer, weather can make flying all the more satisfying. What I love most about flying is the weather.

It was a Friday afternoon in the summer of 1987 when we—my fifteen-year-old daughter, Molly, and I—were getting ready to depart from the little country airport near Romeo for a father-daughter weekend getaway. The sky was a grim eight-hundred overcast with dark gray clouds spitting fine droplets.

"Why does the weather have to be so bad?" Molly asked, hunching her shoulders against the mist and bowing her head slightly. "Are we gunna be able to go?"

"They call it an 'occluded front,' " I explained more or less idly while preflighting the plane. I drained a few ounces of fuel from each of the wing sumps to flush any accumulations of moisture.

"Is that bad?"

"With an occluded front, all kinds of weather systems mix together, unpredictably. No telling what you'll get. I checked with Flight Service, and for now it should be flyable up to Beaver Island. Just these clouds and light rain. Hopefully this will all drift to the northeast like it's supposed to and won't wreck our weekend."

By the time we were ready to take off it was late in the warm afternoon. We accelerated down runway 18, lifted the nose, climbed about seven hundred fifty feet, then leveled and turned north under the soggy, ragged cloud bases. I gave Selfridge approach a call on 126.9 to pick up our instrument clearance. The controller assigned an altitude of six thousand feet, and I advanced the prop and throttle to begin our ascent into the thick clouds.

I've read trout and salmon are found only in the most beautiful places, and in the case of Beaver Island, also the most remote. We were on our way to an island smack in the middle of northern Lake Michigan. We had bought the cottage there a few years before as a perfect retreat from the traffic, crime, and pollution of the city—perfect if you like fishing, hunting, big water, and doing pretty much nothing else. Having the single engine Cessna to run back and forth was the only thing that made it all work.

Beaver Island is known for its unique 1940s look and feel, and its surrounding waters had at one time been sought out for the quality of the king salmon fishing. But with commercial gillnetting picking up, the salmon had become harder and harder to find. I knew getting them would be chancy. Still, I thought it would be nice give it a try. Catching even one, after all, was considered by fishermen to be quite the achievement anymore.

"This is going to be soooo much fun," Molly's voice scratched through her built-in headset microphone over the onboard intercom, stretching out the word *so*. "I told my friend, Carrie, I was going fishing with you. Her parents are divorced, too, and she doesn't get to hang out much with her dad, either."

Molly's mom and I had divorced years ago while Molly was still a toddler. I doubt she had much of a recollection of me in her home. I had made it a point to see her and her older sisters regularly while they were growing up. But as she entered her teen years, she became less and less interested in spending time with her father, and more and more drawn to socializing with high school friends. When I'd call to set up a weekend visit, it would be, "Dad, I'll call you back. Scott's here now and we're just leaving." Of course, no call would come. Or, "I can't this weekend, Dad. I have drama club rehearsal. Can we do it next weekend?" Naturally, there would be something just as pressing the following weekend. I called less and less frequently. It got so we only saw each other near holidays or for special events. And I was occupied with my job, my new wife and home. There wasn't anyone to blame, really, except me. It just happened that way.

We hadn't seen each other for quite a while when the handwritten letter arrived a few weeks before our trip. "Dear Dad," it began. "I miss you," Molly wrote. "I want to get to know you better...we hardly see each other..." It wasn't accusing or hurtful or angry. Just reaching out in a young girl's heartfelt way. "I love you so much..." she ended. I called as soon as I finished her letter and set up the weekend adventure. Just the two of us.

We had broken out of the overcast at fifty-two hundred feet and climbed in clear air to our assigned altitude. Molly looked at the thick, ivory cloud tops below, then at the sun and blue sky between the thin snow-white cirrus wisps above us. "I can't believe how awful the weather was at the airport and how great everything looks up here," she said.

"When you get far enough from the ugly stuff, it can actually look pretty nice," I said.

She stared out the window for another minute. "Carrie was excited for me, but she was like, so jealous, too," she finally said. "She goes, 'I wish my dad would take me some-place,' and I'm like, 'well...write him a letter like I did.' " Her laugh was almost a giggle. After another, longer pause she said quietly, "Thanks for setting this up, Dad."

"I'm glad you wrote," I said. "It's fun for me, too."

As we passed Saginaw the tops were getting higher, and I requested eight thousand feet to stay in the clear.

"I've missed you, too," I said.

Crossing the Traverse City VOR navigation beacon, we turned northerly toward Beaver Island. We were in and out of the tops by then, and I could see they were only getting higher ahead. I requested and was cleared to descend to four thou-sand feet, into the murk. No chance of remaining in clear air, anyway. In the descent I couldn't even see the wingtips. About ten miles south of the airport, we were cleared for the NDB 27 approach. When the ADF needle swung around over the runway, I turned east, then did the procedure turn back inbound, still in solid clouds and rain over what I knew from experience was Sand Bay. The Cessna descended slowly to five hundred feet above the ground. I could see the trees below us on and off as we clipped through the cloud bottoms. Nearer the airport, we continued in and out of the irregular bases, and I wasn't sure we would see the runway. When we finally saw it through the thin, ragged fragments hanging down from the overcast, we were still too high and fast to land. It was raining harder, and there were low, fractured cloud pieces right down in the big trees on either side of the airfield.

"Are we going to be able to land?" Molly asked. She looked a little frightened.

"Sure," I said.

Beaver Island is famous for eating small planes and their occupants. Last year in exactly the same conditions, a charter had gone down trying to duck under the scud. It hit trees near the top of Angeline's Bluff while trying to land to the east, killing the flight crew and leaving an injured mother and two kids in the wreckage all night before they were found and rescued the next day. Thinking of that, I overflew the runway, dropping down to three hundred feet above the trees at the far end, turned onto a tight left downwind, retarded the throttle to 15" manifold pressure, and rolled in some flaps.

We flew the pattern just above the scud in the treetops, careful to maintain every inch of our precarious altitude, and banked probably too steeply onto a very short, low final in the clear for runway 27. I did a final gear-down check, pulled the throttle back to idle, and extended the remaining flaps. Touchdown was picture perfect.

We took the beat-up Jeep I keep at the airport and dumped our gear at the cottage, which sat on an oak-and-birch-covered old dune just at the edge of the east-side Lake Michigan beach. It was getting dark early with the rainy overcast, and we headed into the tiny village of St. James on the northeast end of the island for something to eat at the Shamrock, a small town bar and grill everyone who has ever been to Beaver Island has visited.

We didn't need to spend much time looking at the menus. Molly ordered a hamburger and fries and I got my usual fish and chips.

"What's the plan for tomorrow?" she asked.

"I thought we'd try for salmon out on the big lake. They're not catching them like they were before the gillnetting started. But August is the time when the really good ones used to come in, fattening up before the spawn. If there're any the nets have missed, we should have a shot at a nice one. I've seen a few up to eighteen, even twenty pounds or more at this time in years past."

"Oh my God, I'm not going to have to clean them I hope. That's so gross," she said. "And I won't put a worm on the hook!"

"It's not like that," I laughed. "And I'll do all the 'gross' stuff."

Molly seemed satisfied and attacked the hamburger that had arrived.

We finished dinner and drove back to the cottage under dark, drizzling skies. Molly went to bed early, taking a book with her. I watched the late news on the old rabbit-eared TV, picking up the Canadian channel from the Soo before turning in. I usually drop right off and sleep like a log at the cottage, but for some reason the sounds of the confused surf breaking just below our deck kept me awake. After a while the soft rumble of distant thunder began, and I watched as the cloud bottoms flashed with electricity through the rain and haze out over the lake. Finally I drifted off.

The next morning we had a quick, cold breakfast at the cottage and drove to the marina in town. The sky was still overcast, but the bases were higher and smooth. The rain had stopped sometime during the night and the visibility was up a bit, all good signs.

We parked the car at the marina and walked out on the fuel dock. I used the marina's dingy to row out to my boat—a twenty-foot aluminum Starcraft I/O with a cuddy cabin— moored in the harbor just off the dock. I ran the blower and bilge pump, then started the engine and wiped the rainwater from the windscreen and the seats. I climbed out on the bow, unshackled the mooring line, got back in the cockpit, and motored the boat—the dingy dragging behind by a line fastened to a cleat—over to the dock where Molly was waiting.

After loading our personal gear, Molly jumped aboard and we took four sturdy boat rods with Penn level-wind reels from the cuddy cabin. They were each wound with four-hundred-fifty yards of clear twenty-pound test mono. We cut the first fifty yards of old line off each reel and tied on new brass snaps with barrel swivels. I showed Molly how to do it using an improved fisherman's knot. After a little initial trouble, she got the hang of it quickly. We secured the snaps to an eye on each rod, tightened the lines, set the drags, and put the rods in holders.

We stowed our personal gear and got under way, headed for the harbor mouth. There was a light, mixed chop on the dull, blue-gray waters of the harbor under the overcast skies. I opened the throttle when we cleared the Beaver Harbor Lighthouse, moving up on plane, then headed south along the shoreline about four miles into Sand Bay where we throttled down. Medium swells advanced from the south with the occasional line of foam along the higher crests. The boat rode them well.

"All this water," Molly said. "How do you decide where to stop?"

"Sand Bay here is a big, deep, sandy bowl," I said as I unlocked the downrigger stanchions and rotated their booms out over the water. "It's easier to set up here in deeper water where there's not much for our gear to hang up on." I repositioned the four seven-foot boat rods to the holders attached to the riggers. "And to tell the truth, Sand Bay is where we've gotten the occasional really big one."

"Like the twenty-pounders you told me about last night?"

"At least," I laughed.

The plotter showed a smooth bottom at one hundred sixty feet give or take. I took two J-plugs out of my tackle box in backs with green and rose respectively, both over silver bellies. Then two Northport Nailer spoons in pink and white, and green and silver. I put two of the J-plugs on the snaps of a pair of the seven-foot rods, attached the lines about three feet behind the lures to clips on the back of the heavy lead downrigger balls, cranked them down into the water a few feet and locked them. I lowered a temperature gauge, getting a reading every twenty feet. The surface temperature was 64 degrees, then it was 61 all the way down through eighty feet, 54 at one hundred feet, and 49 degrees at one hundred twenty and below.

"What's the temperature all about?" Molly asked.

"Salmon are most active and like to feed at about 54 degrees," I said. "When we know the depth of that temperature, we can place our best lures right at, just above and just below there. Today it's at a hundred feet. And there's a sharp drop in temperature beneath, and a rise above. They call it a 'thermocline.' When the break is at 54 degrees—like today—it's usually pretty good fishing right around there."

I lowered the two downrigger balls with their attached J-plug rods a bit deeper. After locking them in place again, I clipped stacker lines from the two other rods, a Northport Nailer spoon on each, to the two cables ten feet above one ball, and twenty feet above the other, adjusting the ball depths as I worked. The port ball was then lowered to its final running depth of a hundred five feet, and the starboard to one hundred. I tightened the drags on the reels and set the line tension on the rods, causing the tips to bow down toward the water as we ran.

"It seems more complicated than I thought," Molly said.

"It's mostly just experience."

We trolled a lazy zigzag pattern heading generally south for about an hour. We got a few false releases on the stacker lines, which we reset, and bumped bottom a few times causing a ripple of unfounded excitement each time the rod tips bounced. We had to raise the riggers several times to clear seaweed from the balls and lowest lures before resetting them again. The overcast began to break up, and the few shafts of bright morning sunshine on the water seemed like more good news. The wind freshened a bit as it swung southwesterly, and the waves picked up to two and a half feet or so with the occasional well-developed whitecap beginning to form. Good salmon fishing weather.

Molly and I talked about the island, fishing, the flight up, school, her friends, and probably a dozen other things. Then she was quiet, looked out at the water, and finally said, "I hate the divorce, Dad."

"I know. Me, too."

"It's so unfair. And I never understood why. I always thought it had something to do with me. Maybe if I had behaved differently..."

"You kids have always been great," I said emphatically. "The divorce was about me and your mom, no one else. I couldn't have asked for better..."

The rod on the starboard downrigger—the one running directly behind the ball at a hundred feet—jerked straight up, then bent down almost double and finally began thrashing up and down. I bolted to the back of the boat and snatched it from the holder. Molly stood stunned, her mouth open, but no words coming. With no one at the wheel, the wind caught the bow and began swinging the boat sharply about. I knew from experience that would cross and tangle all the lines and cables, causing us to lose the fish and maybe our gear as well. I handed the rod to Molly and ran to the wheel, turning the bow back to hold a heading of south.

"Reel," I said. "Reel!"

The rod pulled down parallel to the water, and the drag of the big level-wind reel screeched as line peeled off. "Keep the rod handle pointed straight up," I told Molly.

"Why?" She looked panic-stricken. "It's too hard!"

"Use both hands and haul back on the rod. It makes the fish pull against the flex in the rod, like bending a leaf spring or a shock absorber. Tires him out, and keeps him from snapping the line by jerking straight against you and the reel."

The fish initially broke toward the beach but then turned for deep water, threatening to take the line across the downrigger cables and the other lines still trailing behind them. I knew we had to raise both downriggers and haul in the other rods, but only after turning the boat ever so carefully to the north to stabilize our course in the brisk south-south-westerly wind. There was so much to say to Molly, but at that moment we had to land the fish.

I throttled down as low as the engine would go, and slowly, gently, carefully nosed the boat around, keeping the rigger cables with the other lines well clear of the line with the fish. We kept coming about easily, the gear running cleanly behind us, until we were headed north with the wind on our stern. I was at last able to leave the wheel without the boat spinning about in the wind. I quickly released and retrieved the remaining lines and cranked in the downrigger balls. One of the rigger cables tangled and bound on its spool, freezing everything. I shook it loose with my free hand, leaving a bright ruby abrasion across my palm from the thin, braided, stain-less-steel line held taut by the heavy ball still attached in the water beneath. With the gear finally up and out of the way, I put the boat in neutral and let her drift as we fought the fish.

"Keep the line tight," I said. "Otherwise the fish will be able to shake the lure out, or jerk the line from slack to taut. That'd break it."

"I'm trying. But sometimes it just goes loose, then gets real tight again no matter what I do."

"That's because the fish swims toward the boat sometimes. When he does it, reel as fast as you can to keep the line tight. When he turns to run, reel slowly or just hang on. The drag and flex in the rod will do the work by making him fight for the line he's taking out. It'll wear him down, then we'll be able to bring him to the boat."

"My arms are getting weak. It's getting real hard to hold the rod up."

I put a hand on the rod to take some of the weight from Molly. The fish was still pulling hard and occasionally breaking into fast runs of forty or fifty yards at a time. Finally he seemed to tire and lay like a brick on the end of the line.

"Whenever he stops running or thrashing, let's lift the rod back and reel in as we lower it again," I said. "We'll be able to capture some line back and work the fish in close to the boat until he's played out."

We took turns handling the rod. When the line finally got twenty feet or so from the back of the boat, the fish dove straight for the bottom, peeling line against the drag as it went. Then it stopped. I looked at the plotter. It showed two hundred feet of water and marked the fish hanging on the bottom.

"We'll just keep pressure on him until he gets exhausted and starts to come up." I tightened the drag and pulled straight up. I gave the rod to Molly and told her to do the same thing.

After a while, the rod tip began to rise. We would reel in line until the rod doubled over again, and then pull up until the tip began to lift once more. We repeated the process for fifteen minutes or so, Molly and I taking turns.

"Look." I peered over the stern as I spoke. "I can see the silver flashes of the scales about fifteen feet down and only five or six feet back. That fish is huge!"

Molly was holding the rod and looking into the water off the back of the boat. The rod suddenly jerked hard and line began to buzz off the reel faster than it had at any time before. I quickly loosened the drag to keep the line from snapping. Molly struggled to hold the rod up. The fish continued its hard run out toward deep water. "I think it's going to visit its cousins in Petoskey," I said. She smiled as she hauled back on the rod with both hands, not even bothering to reel against the intense pressure of the run.

The fish took out several hundred yards of line before stopping. I thought it was going to strip all four hundred yards from the reel and be lost. We began taking turns pumping back the rod and taking up line as we lowered it again. After what seemed like hours, the fish was off our stern once more.

Most of the time a spent salmon will turn on its side as it's dragged to the boat. This fish stayed upright and swam back and forth as we slowly edged it closer. I grabbed the big net from the cuddy cabin while Molly played the fish.

"You'll have to lead it to the net," I said. "If we try to scoop at him, it'll feel the net and lunge away. If one of the free hooks on the J-plug snags the netting, it'll rip the plug out of its mouth and we'll lose it for sure."

I lowered the net gently into the water without splashing while Molly patiently pressured the fish toward the opening. When he was just in front of the mouth, I eased the net around him. The fish bolted, but right into the net. I lifted the mouth of the net clear of the water, with the net bag and the fish still in it just below the surface. It was too heavy to pull in by myself. Molly put the rod in a holder and grabbed the net handle. We both hauled with all our strength and swung the net and fish up out of the water and into the boat. We were both breathless.

"Oh my God, look at it!" Molly said. "Do you think it's a twenty-five pounder?" She was beaming.

"Would you look at that fish," I said. "It's freaking huge."

We were both breathing heavily and grinning. The fish nearly spanned the width of the boat. It lay quietly in the net, no struggle left in it. A single barb from the two gangs of treble-hooks on the J-plug was through less than a half inch of its bottom lip.

"You're some fisherman," I said, hugging her and laughing. I felt like a kid myself.

"I can't believe we caught it," she said, laughing too. She hugged me back.

"I could never have landed this alone," I said to her.

"No one could have," she said.

We were both too excited and tired to fish any-more. We secured the rods, downriggers, net, and other gear, then cleaned up the boat with buckets of lake water. I put her in gear, and headed north toward the harbor. The sun was shining on us, but I could see a squall line passing across the island, the broad silver sheets of rain extending from cloud to ground and sweeping the entire island like a broom. When it finally reached us, the drops fell in big, cool splashes that felt good. The rain became intense at one point, but still I could see all the way through to the sunlight on the other side. It drenched our boat and washed the deck clean of the remaining iridescent fish scales the salmon had shed. After it passed, the sun came through again and the wind freshened out of the west-northwest. The air felt cooler and drier, and the remaining haze had cleared completely.

I advanced the throttle and put the boat on plane once more, the hull pounding occasionally as we crested the larger waves and slammed down into the troughs. That threw a gusher of spray up to either side and into the cockpit where we both were clinging to handholds. The wild ride and the chilled spray felt invigorating. The offshore water had become a magnificent royal blue under the clear, sunlit sky, going to lovely aqua-green above the sand flats nearer shore. With the bow riding high, I turned on the pump to purge the rain and lake water from below. Bilge water poured overboard from the outlet on the aft hull, leaving a streak of foam with tiny reflective scales like Christmas lights sparkling in our wake. We rounded the harbor-mouth buoy, passed Whiskey Point and the old Coast Guard rescue station, then throttled down in the harbor as we headed back to the marina fuel dock.

I tied up at the dock and both of us began unloading our gear. The attendant, an old fellow with a weathered face and baggy jeans, walked over to us with the fuel line in his hand, looked at me as if he was going to say something, then looked in the bottom of the boat.

"Well, I'll be...." he said, staring wide-eyed at the fish. "I don't believe I've ever seen one that big."

"Yeah, it's a dandy, Phil. My daughter and I just got him a few miles south of the harbor. No fuel right now," I said, "I'll take care of it next time I'm up."

It was an effort to lift the salmon and haul him out onto the dock.

"We don't see these much no more," he said. "Never seen one this big."

"Me and Dad got him in Sand Bay," Molly said.

A skinny boy about ten wearing shorts and a dirty T-shirt had been riding down the road on his bike and had apparently noticed us. He jumped off, letting the bike drop on the rain-dampened ground near the fuel dock, and ran over to us. He stopped about three feet from the fish, bent forward at the waist, not daring to approach closer but wanting to get a good look. He held his arms stiffly out to his sides and angled behind him as if to maintain a precarious balance as he both strained to see the fish but remain safely clear of it. "Jeezo-Pete!" he said. "What is it? Where'd you catch *that?*"

A couple from one of the moored yachts was looking at us from the long wooden dock that separated them from the concrete pier where Molly and I stood. "It's a shark," I kidded the boy. "Got him with a worm off the end of a broomstick here on the fuel dock."

"I'm getting my dad," he said loudly, but only stepped back a few feet and continued staring.

"I'll get my scale from the shop," Phil said.

The couple from the yacht had walked around and out onto the fuel dock. "What a beauty," the man said. The woman retrieved a small camera from her purse and snapped a picture.

"He bit a J-plug at a hundred feet," Molly said to them. "A pink and silver one. We both had to land him."

Somehow the boy's father had arrived and was standing next to him with his hand around the ten-year-old's shoulder. "Good one," the father said, looking down at the fish.

Phil returned with the portable fish scale and placed the hook attached to the bottom through its lower lip. We both had to lift the scale with the fish dangling below. Phil stared intently at the numbers etched on the side.

"Sumpin' wrong. This cain't be right." He jerked the scale and the fish up and down roughly. "Must be rusty." He bounced it again. "Guess it's right," he finally said. "A hair over thirty pounds! Ain't never seen one this big 'round here."

Molly was beaming. "We caught it together. Neither of us could have done it alone. Everything happened so fast."

A car had stopped on the road shoulder by the marina office. Three young men who looked to be in their early twenties got out and walked over to us.

"Whoa," the man in the lead said as he got close.

"Boy!" another of them said.

Several other people from the yacht dock had appeared and were making their way toward us.

"Why don't you start loading our gear in the Jeep," I said to Molly. "I'll find something to wrap this fish in."

I located some old newspaper in the marina office and took it out to the fuel dock where the knot of people was still standing around the salmon. I thoroughly wrapped the fish, carried it by myself to the Jeep, and hefted it into the back end. Then I went back, took the boat with dingy in tow out to its mooring buoy off the dock, secured everything, and rowed in again. The people had drifted off the fuel dock. A few were standing at the rear of the Jeep looking in the tailgate window.

We headed out of town, down Kings Highway to where the pavement ended. The still-damp dirt two-track dipped through the jumbled cedar swamp where a horse-faced old doe and two big fawns—spots fading but still visible—ran across in front of us. We made a left where the track climbed up out of the swamp again and ended at Hannigan's Road. We drove east in bright sunshine past the abandoned Mormon-era farms, the road becoming sun-dried to the finest, billowing sand and dust as it humped like a hog's back where it crested an old pasture before starting down again.

The fallow fields were choked with juniper bushes, the open areas alive with orange hawkweed, Indian paintbrush, and coreopsis. Orange and rust-splotched Michigan lilies grew in clumps along the trailside. A gray goshawk with a massive wingspread flushed at our approach from a wild apple grove along the dirt road, soaring away over the brushy meadow and into the woods. Down where the cedars started again a big snowshoe hare still in its mottled-brown summer coat dashed from the roadside into the forest. Then driving through the moist dark of the thick cedars, the old swamp-soggy fallen logs on the side of the trail lay blanketed with thick, green, wet moss. And over gravel-bottomed Jordan Creek where it wound across the swamp, beneath the road through a culvert, in the springtime flowing heavy and full of suckers up to spawn from the big lake and stacked against the shoulder of the track, but now, late in the summer, barely a trickle a man could jump across if he wanted.

Back at the cottage, Molly unloaded the Jeep while I filleted the big salmon at a makeshift fish-cleaning table fashioned about seventy feet behind the cottage. We whiled away the afternoon, Molly going for a swim, then showering and curling into the big easy chair with her book. It was mid-afternoon by the time we ate the sandwiches I had made for the boat but had been too excited to have earlier. With our late lunch, neither of us felt hungry until well into the evening. About eight-thirty, the sun still hanging low in the midsummer southwest sky, I started preparing dinner.

Molly had wandered into the kitchen where I was working. "I'm not sure I like fish," she said.

"You'll like this, Beans," I smiled, using the nickname I had given her when she was little. "You caught it. And anyway, there's nothing better than fresh-caught salmon."

"I guess I'll try it. And...*we* caught it." She was making fun of me.

I'm not much of a chef, but I've prepared salmon at the cottage since we began fishing for them when we first got the place. I cut the fillet sections into roughly twelve-ounce servings, basted them in melted margarine, seasoning like always and baking until they were just cooked through. Then I applied a light honey-glaze and finished them briefly under the broiler on both sides until there was a golden-brown, slightly crisp patina. We sat down to dinner with the fish still hot from the oven, served with brown rice, applesauce, peas, fruit juice, bread and butter.

Molly took a first cautious bite. She smiled before digging into the rest of it. "This is great! Maybe we should have had it mounted, though."

"It always tastes this way when it's fresh and you've caught it yourself. And besides, if we took it to the taxidermist, we'd have nothing for dinner tonight but hotdogs. You can't have your cake—or in this case your fish—and eat it, too," I kidded her.

"I can," she laughed. "I get to eat it, but I'll always have this weekend. This fish will go on forever."

"We'll always have Beaver Island and our thirty-pound salmon," I said to her.

Molly and I talked about the day, our fish, Beaver Island, and about the divorce. There were no interruptions this time. By the time we finished the final bites of our meal, when our conversation began to naturally and comfortably settle, the sun had set. A huge, full, cream-colored moon was just rising in the dusk across the lake over the forested bluffs north of Harbor Springs.

"It looks like a harvest moon," Molly said.

"That's what they'd call it if this were October. In November it would be a 'hunter's moon.' But the Indians up here call these big midsummer moons a 'truthful moon.' They claim the bright moon rays melt away lies. It's said a person can only speak the truth under a moon like this."

In my room that evening I opened the double French doors to the deck and let the mild night air in before turning out the lights. The treetops were absolutely still. The rhythmic, soft gurgle of the low surf breaking against the shoreline was soothing again. I knew I'd have no trouble drifting into a sound, all-night sleep. I heard the faint, distant yapping of a lone coyote deep in the hardwoods, but it was receding, and after a few more moments I couldn't hear it at all. Then there was only the surf. The full moon had risen higher into the sky and become an elegant silver disk bathing the dark waters of Lake Michigan in the most comforting, soft light reflecting subtly from the ripples on the lake.

As I drifted into a drowsy haze my mind wandered to the morning. Even though I hadn't called for a briefing, I understood from the sky, moon, wind and waves the weather for our flight would be through fair skies. Oh, there might be the lingering, isolated post-frontal puffy cumulous here or there, perhaps with even a brief summer shower beneath. But overall the flying would be smooth for our trip. For the two of us. Molly and me. What I love most about flying is the weather.

CHEWORE SAFARI JOURNAL
a novella of eleven stories

Visiting Africa, much less hunting there, had always seemed an unattainable dream. Yet in the fall of 2013 that dream was made real when my wife, Nickie, and I took a ten-day hunting safari in the Chewore area of the Zambezi River Valley in northern Zimbabwe. These stories—only slightly fictionalized—chronicle our experience. The events are real but the characters, other than Nickie and I, are inventions.

One — Renewal by the Waters of the Chenje

Our pilot, Ahmad, had turned his head away, but still I could see his lips moving from the side as he said something to Nickie in the seat just behind him. I couldn't make out his words through the noise-suppressing headset I wore to help mute the loud wind-stream sounds and the roar of the old Cessna Centurion's lone engine. He was pointing through his side window to something on the ground.

"Elephants in the dry river." Nickie leaned across the back seats and forward, shouting at my ear loudly enough to be heard through the cuff and over the drone of the engine as I sat in the front co-pilot seat.

I looked back across her, peering down through the window on her side, and saw the group of a half-dozen elephants in the sandy riverbed. They seemed big, even at our altitude of several thousand feet above the dry middle Zambezi Valley of northern Zimbabwe. I felt a ripple of excitement.

They were the first game animals we had seen in Africa although there would be many more over the next eleven days. We had left the commercial airport in Harare only an hour earlier on our charter to the remote Chewore safari area nestled twenty miles south of the Zambezi River and equally near the borders with Zambia and Mozambique. Traveling from Detroit the day before, the marathon flight included a grueling sixteen-hour leg from Atlanta to Johannesburg, where we spent the night before catching this morning's connection to Zimbabwe.

The plane continued its descent beyond the elephants, seemingly skimming just above the taller mopane and acacia trees as we banked right in an easy turn to the east. The dirt runway appeared ahead through the heat haze that limited forward visibility to a mile or two, the landing strip worn to red dust bordered by dry yellow hard-grass then endless scattered small trees and low scrub. The whine and clunk of the gear descending was followed by the *thump-thump* of our touchdown and the rumble of the wheels on uneven ground as we rolled out. The plane bounced to a halt and pivoted about in a cloud of reddish-brown powder raised by the prop. Then I could see the white bush-lorry parked off to the side at midfield and the people waiting for us. *We really are on safari now,* I thought and could feel my heart beating.

We piled out of the Centurion and Ahmad began unloading our gear. Our professional hunter walked casually over and introduced himself with the detached nonchalance marking Englishmen everywhere.

"Wil Fredericks," he said, extending his hand. "And this is Levitt, our tracker." He nodded toward the middle-aged, thickly built black African. "Marusi here is our all-around man, and Favor, our number-two tracker." Wil motioned to-

116

ward the two younger Africans standing behind and off to one side of Levitt. They all smiled and nodded without speaking. We shook hands.

"Three groups of elephant in the Maura," Ahmad said to Wil with a friendly smile.

Wil looked toward Ahmad but didn't respond. I thought I saw him nod, though barely perceptibly.

"The guys will load your gear and we'll be off to camp," Wil said. "Would you like to ride up top?" He directed his eyes to the padded bench seat built for the trackers in the truck bed high behind the cab.

I glanced toward Nickie. She had been nervous about coming with me to hunt the African wilderness. "I'll ride in the cab with Wil," I said. I wanted to start getting to know him and talk a little about the hunt. "Would you like to join us, or enjoy the view up above?"

"I'll ride up there," she smiled and scrambled up the iron rungs welded on the steel framework fashioned to make the big diesel Toyota Land Cruiser 4X4 into a safari vehicle.

We set off, bouncing along the dirt two-track, the cab windows rolled down. "It's been bloody hot," Wil said. "No rain for five months now and these late-season temps have really begun to rise."

"How's the hunting been?"

"Good. We shot a nice lion last week. He charged as we were checking the bait in daylight. Very odd. Seems as though he was quite possessive about it and felt we were stealing his meal." He smiled slightly. "Had to stop him at twenty yards."

"What about buffalo? That's why I'm here." I was hoping he'd say the place was lousy with huge bulls.

"They're around. We put the resident herds at some three hundred fifty animals or so, and others drift in and out from surrounding areas. There can be as many as six hundred at any one time by most estimates."

"Great!" I could feel the anticipation building.

"The concession is large, and they can take some work to locate. Chewore-south is some three hundred thousand acres, hundreds of square kilometers. All kinds of terrain. Thick jesse stands, mixed scrub. Areas of tall, dense woods. Then there's the grassy savannahs, dry rivers, floodplains, gullies. Lots of places for them to disappear."

"How do we hunt them?"

"We'll scout the area in the truck. Or walk the ridges above the rivers, or the beds themselves. If we see promising sign, fresh tracks or scat, we'll set out and follow. Sometimes the trackers will actually spot them, but then they're usually off and on the alert. Always looking back at that point. Very difficult to move up on them. It's best if we find new spoor and follow up. We can catch them unawares, although they're awfully cautious animals. Constantly being harassed by lions, you know, so they're always looking for danger. Part of the challenge."

My heart was racing again. "It sounds exciting."

"That's why hunters love Chewore. There are other concessions that are easier, more animals. More accessible and less expensive. But few have the romance and challenge. The terrain can be punishing, but it all adds to the satisfaction when you're successful."

"Can't wait."

"What other game are you interested in?"

"I'm here to get a Cape buffalo and it should be our main focus. If we get that done or the opportunity presents, a nice kudu bull would be great, maybe an impala ram if it's good."

"There should be plenty of impala around. A good kudu is a bit of the toss of the dice, though. Anything else?"

"For something different I'd take a nice old warthog boar with long, heavy tusks or a big, dominant male baboon like I've seen on TV shows with those fierce-looking canines. Make for interesting mounts, something different as a conversation piece."

"Game can be fickle. Only one hunter this season failed to get his buff, though, and that was a bit odd. He missed on several clean opportunities. And it was early, just after the rains stopped. Everything was still thick green, which ruined the visibility. Something of the jitters, too, I suspect."

"Actually, just being here is a dream come true. The buffalo would simply be a bonus."

"This time of year it's quite dry, and they're oriented near water, the odd springs or seeps in the dry rivers. They really can't stray far from those for any length. We'll have a go and get you a shot on a nice nyati."

"Sounds good."

"I'll be honest with you. This is mostly a dangerous game concession. Lion, leopard, elephant, buffalo. Hippos and crocs up north in the Zambezi. The plains game are chancier. But we'll give it all a try."

We passed the graveyard for the bones and discarded remains of hunters' trophies cooking in the late season heat a few hundred yards before we pulled into the Chenje Camp compound. As we turned into the tight cluster of a few permanent and tented structures, a group of about ten Africans, the camp staff, greeted us while beating tribal drums, gyrating elegantly in an animated dance, and singing loudly and enthusiastically in their African dialect. I jumped from the cab as soon as the truck came to a halt and grinned at our reception committee as Nickie scrambled down from the trackers' seat above the open bed. She was smiling, too. I couldn't help but feel warmed and welcomed by the authentic and traditional African greeting, and I could tell Nickie felt exactly the same.

We walked over to the staff and introduced ourselves, shaking hands and asking the names of each man. Few knew enough English to respond to our own welcoming words. "Thank you...what an elegant way to be greeted...and what is your name, young man...those drums are wonderful, what drum skin and wood is used?"

Smiles and a few single-word responses, "...yes...okay...Godfrey..." Eyes cast to the ground, not presuming, not daring to look into the faces of these new, odd American hunter-guests.

A white couple walked from a small thatched structure and greeted us. "I'm Sharon," the pretty, middle-aged woman said, smiling warmly, "and this is my husband, Jerry." A slender and tall white-haired gentleman with a distinguished appearance. "We're your camp managers. Welcome to Chenje," she extended her hand.

"Would you like something to drink?" Jerry asked in an unmistakably British but uniquely accented English I would come to recognize as distinctly Zimbabwean. "The staff will get your gear to your tent."

Jerry and Sharon led the way to the thatch-covered, open-sided dining area with its bar and adjacent roofless patio up on the edge of the Chenje River. Wil walked next to me.

"We'll need to sight your rifle after you've relaxed and settled in," Wil said. "Make sure it survived all the baggage handlers. What did you bring?"

"A .375 in H&H," I said.

"What kind of ammunition?"

"Three-hundred-grain expandables and a box of the same weight in solids."

"And the brand?"

"Safari Grade Premium trophy bonded. It's what I've used in all my hunting for twenty years."

"Perfect. That's what I use. They hold together well on large game. Some other manufacturers produce ammunition with too high a velocity for these large bullets. Tend to break up on the bigger-boned and thicker-skinned animals like buffalo and elephant. They'll fishtail a bit at the higher speeds as well. Accuracy goes all to hell. The trophy bonded are a bit slower but stable, penetrate well, and the rounds stay intact."

"Will we use the expanding or solids?"

"We'll shoot expandables unless we come upon a really big loner dagga-boy. When they're grouped up the solids can pass right through and strike another animal. Those big bonded soft-points you have will do the job on just about anything we're likely to encounter and will most always stay completely within a properly hit buff."

Wil walked to the bar while the rest of us found comfortable chairs around the fire pit that contained only sand and the burnt-out remains of mopane wood during the heat of the afternoon. "What would you like?" he asked.

"Just something soft," I said. "Nickie and I don't drink alcohol anymore, although I hope that doesn't discourage you from enjoying your cocktails," I motioned to the seated group with a hand. "It's not that we disapprove. Most of our family and friends enjoy something to relax. We simply lost interest and gave it up a few years ago."

"We don't drink much and never during the day," Sharon said. "But a little wine with dinner is nice or a relaxing sundowner with a few hors d'oeuvres beforehand. We have just about anything you'd like, and you can help yourself to the bar anytime."

"I believe I'll have a plain tonic on the rocks with a dash of lime juice if you have it. Maybe the quinine will keep the malaria at bay," I smiled. "Nickie?"

"Fruit juice of any kind with a few ice cubes, if you would, Wil. To take the edge off this heat."

After finishing our beverages and sharing a few minutes of pleasantries, we made our way to our quarters. The camp spread along the bank of the Chenje River with its pools still holding water below us. The grounds were manicured with a green lawn clearly watered day and night, and dirt walking paths between the structures. Carefully positioned logs created a neat edge along the paths.   A groundskeeper worked methodically picking up leaves and sticks, then sweeping the earth smooth with a leafy branch he carried. Towering mopane, mahogany, and acacia trees provided broken shade. A few vervet monkeys scampered among the branches.

Our tent was substantial, roomy, and well appointed. All our gear had already been placed inside. The ridgepole height within was a least seven feet, and the interior dimensions had to be around eight by twelve. The pitched roof dropped down to sidewalls of about five feet in height. Each end had a zip-down entrance through sturdy netting with a heavy canvas flap that could be closed if the occupants wished. The sides were lined with window flaps with a canvas cover on each that dropped away to expose netting. There were similarly fashioned ceiling vents. The forward entrance opened to a grassy area not ten feet back from the bank above the Chenje, then some twenty feet down and forty or fifty feet farther to the water's edge. Two camp chairs sat outside on either side of the entrance.

The rear access opened to an adjoining mortar-walled bath area with running water, toilet stool, shower, a masonry bench, and movable shelving made of metal tubing. Fresh bath linens awaited us on the shelves. A second, very large canvas tarp atop long poles sunk into the ground covered both the main tent and the bath, although the tops of the five-foot walls that made up the plumbed area at the rear were completely open to the outside. A woven thatch laundry hamper sat partially hidden, pushed back just beneath the sink. Sharon had explained our laundry would be picked up shortly after our departure into the bush each morning, and we would find it ironed and folded upon our return each evening. Everything we had seen was immaculate.

Twin beds were pushed together to create a makeshift double. There were nightstands with a battery-powered reading lamp on each side. An overhead light in the main tent and another in the bath worked only when the camp generator was running, which we soon found would be a few hours in the morning and evening.

Once we had unpacked and settled in, I walked over to the riverbank. The Chenje was really just a stream, the pool only forty feet or so in width but extending out of sight up and down stream. There was no visible current.

"Hey...take a look at this," I said to Nickie. A big Nile croc swam slowly up the pool, its nose and eyes just above water while the tail was visible inches below the surface gently swaying from side to side. It wasn't but sixty feet from where we stood.

"Oh my God," Nickie said. She had walked to the edge and was standing next to me. "I hope it stays down there."

"Get a picture," I said.

"I'm going to be sure our tent is closed tight tonight."

I grabbed my rifle case and day-bag, and we walked over to the parking area to meet Wil. The range was farther down the road we had taken from the airfield, about a half mile from camp. It dipped down across a shallow ford through the Chenje. A family of waterbuck, a female with two young, watched us from the far bank as we splashed across before dashing off. Climbing out on the other side, a big wart-hog displaying huge tusks trotted stiff-legged and tail raised into the bush in its hurried gait. A sharp turn, then down a little drive took us to the sighting area.

"Game already," I said to Wil, motioning back to where we had seen the animals, as we climbed from the truck.

"They're awfully bold around camp," he said. "No hunting allowed by law within a kilometer. They seem to learn quickly."

Wil placed a piece of cardboard on a tree downrange, a circle inked in the center as a homemade target. I uncased my rifle and settled in at a surprisingly nice and sturdy wooden bench. I adjusted the scope slightly and chambered a soft-point, the round I'd be using to hunt. My hand holding the forestock rested on a sandbag put there to steady the rifle.

"What's the range?"

"I'd say ninety meters."

I took my time until the crosshairs were completely steady on the bulls'-eye and smoothly squeezed the trigger. Everything felt just right as the rifle recoiled sharply. I knew I had fired with a perfectly centered hold.

We approached the target. The hole was absolutely dead-on left to right and no more than three-quarters of an inch high.

"That one will do," Wil said. "It would be exactly centered at a hundred meters or so."

I was satisfied and ready for the morning.

It had become quite dark by early evening as we made our way to the patio to enjoy a cool drink and a few snacks before the appointed mealtime. Camp managers Sharon and Jerry soon joined us around the new fire. Our PH, Wil, drifted in a short time later. He was joined by a young man, an apprentice professional hunter who introduced himself as Matt. Our waiter, Pihwa, offered a tray of little meatballs on crackers.

"What are these hors d'oeuvres?" I asked after sampling one. "They're delicious."

"Ground buffalo loin with spices and other seasoning blended in," Sharon said. "From our hunter last week. We'll have game for most meals if it's all right with you."

Nickie largely has an aversion to wild game, but seemed to genuinely enjoy these.

"If it's like this, the more the better," I said.

"Are there any diet restrictions or health issues we should be aware of in serving you?" Sharon asked.

"We eat about anything," I said. "The only real health issues I discussed with your booking agent stateside. I just turned seventy and have had four abdominal surgeries in the past two years. Cancer of the prostate and bladder. Both were removed, and I have a urinary diversion, a collection bag worn externally beneath my clothing on my belly."

"Sounds like a bloody bother," Jerry said. "I've had a bout with cancer myself a few years back, but it's all good now. No fun at all, though."

"Other than requiring some extra time and care mornings and evenings, I'm not expecting it to be a physical limitation for the hunt. I do require a lot of extra water—I'll probably drink twice what your other hunters do and pee three times as often. It's more of a nuisance. Doesn't slow me a bit, really. The only issue in the field may be my stamina. My last surgery was barely a year ago, and I'm just now feeling my old self. Having turned seventy and been on the mend, I'm not sure I have the same spring in my step as in the past. We'll see."

126

"Your cancer has been under control?" Sharon asked, sounding both concerned and hopeful.

"They claim they can find no sign now. It was an unusual and aggressive cancer I'm told, and quite advanced by the time they figured it out. So one never knows. But so far, so good."

"I'm so glad," she said. "It's been seven years since Jerry's."

"For now, I'm feeling great and ready to go. One thing about cancer, it focuses one on the present. Every day is a gift from God, and I wake up each morning thankful and ready to enjoy it."

"God is truly great," Jerry said.

"Amen. There was a time not long ago when I felt I'd never be able to have this opportunity to experience Africa. And it seems an impossible miracle I'm here. I felt if I were ever to do this, the time was now. Who knows what next year holds? I'm truly the luckiest man alive."

That evening in our tent—the generator off, lights out, and complete, moonless darkness outside—I drifted slowly toward sleep. My thoughts were still on the day, on being here, and on the hunt for my buffalo that would begin in the morning. At some point during my in-and-out journey to slumber, an elephant trumpeted close and loud, no doubt just on the far edge of the Chenje pool by which we slept. It was accompanied by the frantic and piercing *whooo-WHOOOP* of hyenas. At times I could hear something unmistakably large moving just outside the tent and casually munching. I would later learn it was hippos enjoying the manicured grass at night. I couldn't help but marvel that I was actually in wild Africa, cancer receding in the rear-view mirror, a second chance, renewed and reinvigorated beside the waters of the Chenje

River. And then, thinking only of what the morning might bring, I finally slipped into a deep and dreamless sleep.

Two — Tsoma and the Mbada

The native African people of Zimbabwe belong to a host of age-old tribes including Shona, Tonga, Batoka, Ndebele, and Venda. Each has its own spiritual and cultural traditions, and its own language.

The safari district where we hunted was named for and defined on its western edge by the Chewore River. Bounded on the north by the Zambezi River, to the east by the M'Kunga, and on the south by the Zambezi Valley Great Escarpment wall, it was completely uninhabited. But the surrounding tribal areas were dotted with tiny subsistence villages of a few thatch-roofed, mud-walled huts each. There were no paved roads, motorized vehicles, electricity, or pure water other than what could be wrung from the seeps and elephant digs in the dry rivers. Each village might have a band of a few goats and a small garden. The area is unsuitable for large-scale farming or cattle. Hunting by the native people is generally not allowed and subject to stiff legal penalties, although the meat from hunters' trophies is often donated to the villagers. Unemployment in Zimbabwe as a whole exceeds 80 percent, much higher in these rural areas. The life expectancy of a black Zimbabwean man is thirty-six years; longer-lived women can expect to survive to an advanced age of thirty-nine. Mortality comes in the form of malaria mosquitoes, tsetse-borne sleeping sickness, AIDS, poisonous snakes, Nile crocs, ubiquitous lions, and assorted predators, all augmented by malnutrition and an almost complete lack of health care.

Yet despite all hardships and odds, these tribes and their villages have survived for countless thousands of years.

Africa is the undisputed birthplace of humanity. Modern Homo sapiens first graced the Earth there more than a hundred thousand years ago. The predecessors of modern man—"Lucy" and her kind who spent equal time in trees and on solid ground—stalked the African bush more than two million years ago. It is safe to say every human alive today, whether their roots be European, Asian, Native American, or otherwise, descends directly from the African forerunners of these Zimbabwean villagers.

Our field and camp staffs came largely from the Shona villages of the adjacent Dande South tribal area. The strength and resilience of these people are inspiring. Their practical wisdom and fascinating customs were fortifying. While reading, writing, and mastery of English are rare among these villagers, still they have rich oral traditions that serve to teach moral and life lessons more than to simply entertain. Our number-two tracker, Favor, was a young, fit, and cheerful man from such a Dande South Shona village. His father having been imprisoned for choosing the losing side in one of Zimbabwe's many civil conflicts, Favor was taken in as a child and educated by Christian missionaries. At their hand he learned passable English. One evening after we had made a kill and were waiting for the bush-lorry to be brought in, he used that skill to share with us a Shona tale about a leopard, called "mbada," and a bushbuck known in the local language as "tsoma." Given all of mankind's ancestral link to these people, the legend is as much everyone's as it is that of the Shonas. This is the story.

The leopard had to work long and hard to catch his food. He constantly chased, and occasionally caught, impala, warthog piglets, or even the odd young baboon. He was quite good at it and his kills of this game kept him full and fit. But these animals were not his favorite.

No, his favorite meal was the tender, delicately flavored meat of the bushbuck. But the bushbuck was quick, clever, and elusive. And when cornered, the small, elegant tsoma, unlike other antelope of the Chewore, would not hesitate to stand his ground and defend himself with his graceful, sharp horns. To hunt the bushbuck was often difficult, fruitless, and dangerous. And it distracted from his success on the easier prey. Yet he constantly tried. Finally, tired, discouraged, and losing weight, the mbada decided to make a deal with the bushbuck.

"Little Tsoma," the leopard called out. "Why should I waste my time and energy chasing you, and you waste yours eluding me? Can we not call a truce and be friends?"

"If I agreed to such a truce," said the bushbuck, "how could I know you would not attack me when my guard was relaxed?"

"We will strike a sacred oath before God," the leopard said. "Whoever shall break the truce, all their sons shall die. God will see that it is so. Neither of us could accept such a terrible thing. Our truce will therefore endure."

The bushbuck agreed. He spent his days leisurely eating grass and leaves. He had no need to be constantly alert nor to flee the mbada. The leopard for his part hunted the easier prey and lounged in the trees for much of the day and night. After a while, both became lazy and fat from lack of exertion.

One day the leopard was napping on a limb of a baobab tree just above the bushbuck sleeping below at the base of the trunk. The leopard began to think about how tasty bushbuck meat was. "I have no sons," the leopard thought to himself, "only daughters. And I am too old to have more children. There would be no consequence in breaking the oath between us." He decided to pounce upon and eat the resting bushbuck.

But the leopard had grown weak and sluggish from little activity. He stood up and sprang at the bushbuck too slowly. The tsoma caught the motion from the corner of his eye in time to swiftly lift his head. The leopard fell directly onto the raised long, sharp horns, completely impaling himself.

"Mbada," the bushbuck said, "why did you break our bond? Will not your sons now die?"

"I have no sons, Tsoma," said the dying leopard, "and would have no more. So the prophecy would never have been fulfilled. But now you have killed me."

"No," said the bushbuck. "It is your father who killed you. You see, he made a similar bond with my father. And your father broke it by killing mine. Now the prophecy is completed with your death. My role was never to kill you, but only to assist you in fulfilling the destiny put upon you by your father. It has long been the duty of all bushbucks to help others fulfill their destinies."

With that the leopard died, and the bushbuck lived to a ripe old age, siring many sons and daughters.

Three — Trial by Fire

My internal clock must have still been on stateside time because I lay wide awake in bed well before the generator kicked in at 5:30 a.m. on the first hunting morning. We had agreed on the day's schedule at dinner the prior night, which would become the ritual each evening. After dressing and morning preparations in the tent, we walked cautiously in total darkness along the dirt paths to the breakfast area. I hadn't forgotten the trumpeting elephant, howling hyenas, and munching hippos from the night before. A quick shot of fresh coffee with toast and juice, then into the bush-lorry just as the eastern sky was beginning to lighten.

Wil drove the Toyota from the right side, English style, with Nickie in the center of the bench seat and me squeezed against the opposite door. Our trackers, Levitt and Favor, rode in the truck bed along with backup driver and all-around man Marusi. The required government game ranger assigned to our party joined them in the back, a tall, thin, good-looking young African named Gibson. My daypack was thrown in the back bed and our guns—mine and Wil's—were stowed, soft-cased against the dust but otherwise unsecured, on an open metal gun rack fashioned outside on the back of the cab. Gibson carried his AK47 with him in the exposed truck bed. We would learn he was never without it.

As the darkness gave way to dawn I was surprised at the rugged and varied terrain of the Chewore. The narrow two-tracks over which we drove were barely visible in places. Low branches scraped the truck sides and the men in back frequently had to drop down to keep from being slapped by overhanging limbs. The trail climbed steep hills and bypassed empty pans with only baked, cracked mud in the bottom. We plunged over embankments through deep gullies cut by waterless dry-season streambeds consisting of only rocks, sand, and gravel. At times it seemed it would be impossible for the truck to climb up the bank of a nearly vertical gully face, but the 4X4, its engine roaring in low gear and big tires digging in, always made the grade. We drove up and down bedrock shelves and banged over basketball-sized boulders with bone-jarring violence. It was hard to understand how these trucks survived the assaults.

Elephant sign was everywhere, with dry, melon-sized droppings scattered about and broad, well-worn game trails crisscrossing the bush. Some of the hilltops looked as if they were war zones, trees pushed over or big branches cracked off. Huge rub marks appeared on larger tree trunks, the bark worn completely away in spots. Limbs that had been pulled down but were still barely attached by shards of splintered wood were stripped of leaves, twigs, and bark. Big, round pachyderm footprints marked the dusty trails. Brown grass was trampled into mats over broad areas of elephant activity.

Wil stopped the truck to examine baseball-sized, lumpy, dark-brown clumps of dung along the narrow road. "Buffalo scat," he said. "But it's old." He broke a pile open with the toe of his boot. "When it's fresh, the skin that forms from drying is lighter and thinner. The inside is moist, and sometimes even warm. This is at least a day old. They're far from here by now."

He studied the dusty trail carefully. "And lions walked along here," he said. "A pride of at least three. Probably trailing these buffalo. Bad news for us. It keeps the buffs nervous and constantly moving. Harder to pin them down or stalk up on them. But at least we're seeing some sign."

We continued driving throughout the morning without locating game of any kind. At times we would hike far back into the bush to a tiny wet spot or barely damp seep in an otherwise empty creek course, hoping to surprise something. Wil and the Africans were fit and adept at covering ground quickly over the tough terrain. I often struggled to stay with them or catch my breath on the steep, long grades. The trails could be thin and brush-choked, most harmless enough. But occasionally an unnoticed thorn bush would grab my flesh, or I might stumble slightly but noisily on some obstacle while straining to keep up and with my eyes diverted to the trail ahead or the brush alongside. This usually resulted in raised eyebrows or an irritated shake of the head from Wil, although he never actually said anything. It was clear enough he was a man who didn't suffer fools gladly. I had hunted all my adult life but was beginning to feel like an unschooled rookie in the punishing, strange African bush.

Down in the soft, shifting riverbeds we dismounted to walk the banks or hike the foot-sucking sand to a moist elephant dig or a still-wet pool at the base of a cut bank. The dry rivers showed recent signs of erosion from raging summer torrents, but this late in the season they looked more like images of the Sahara Desert. Elephant and buffalo tracks and dung were everywhere, along with the footprints of all manner of antelope. Still, we saw no game.

We searched, drove, and hiked all morning without result. The sun had risen high in the sky, and the relatively cool morning had given way to stifling heat. Buzzing tsetse flies swarmed us at every stop, biting the soft areas on the inside of elbows and behind ears. My skin was spotted with tiny, bloody fly bites and thorn gouges. I was happy whenever the truck was moving, the hot, dry air sucked through the cab windows, pulling most of the tsetses with it.

Wil looked at his watch. "It's just past noon," he said, "and this heat will only get worse over the next few hours. We usually take a midday lunch break and give the air a chance to cool a bit before setting out again later in the afternoon."

"Sounds good to me. Nickie, you up for a break?"

"Sure."

"Game doesn't move when it's hot like this, anyway. The buffalo will bed down in the thick jesse during the worst heat, and it's impossible to sneak up on them then. The forward visibility is no good in there. And it's too quiet—they're on the alert. It's about half an hour to our spike camp on the Angwa," Wil said. "We'll drive over there and see if we can jump anything on the way."

The truck banged along the trails, over hilltops, through swales, and across dry creek beds. I had been happy with my rifle's performance at the range last evening, but couldn't help wonder how the scope was holding up under the pounding.

We had just climbed a hill and were moving along the trail through the low, heavy scrub when there was a soft slap on the roof above Wil's head, like a branch brushing the top of the cab. The truck stopped abruptly. A group of about eight or nine impala drifted from the tall trees on the left of the track and crossed about seventy yards ahead. They paused just past the trail's right edge where the mopanes began again. It was the first game I had seen since leaving camp.

"Impala." I had never seen a live one but knew exactly what they were. "And would you look at that ram in the lead!" I said. He was larger than the others and had long, thick, gracefully curved horns setting him distinctively apart.

"I think we should shoot that one," Wil said, and opened the truck door.

I hopped out and Levitt handed my gun down. Wil moved to the front and set up the three-legged shooting sticks used as a steady rifle rest. I chambered a round and moved up by Wil just as the impala all trotted off into the thicker scrub. We could see them drifting through the brush, hesitating to look back occasionally, but not offering a shot through the dense undergrowth. They turned directly away from us before disappearing from sight.

Wil looked after the impala then casually glanced all around the surrounding bush. Without saying a word, he set off downhill to our left, the direction from which the impala had originally come. I followed, rifle in hand. Levitt moved up behind Wil, then there was me, Favor, and then Nickie. Ranger Gibson with his AK47 took up the rear. Marusi stayed with the truck.

After walking about two hundred fifty yards down the hill, I suddenly spotted an impala ahead moving across the hillside from our right to left. "There!" I whispered toward Wil and Levitt. The group of impala had clearly circled around at a safe distance and were headed back to what would have been our rear had we stayed in the truck. Everyone stopped and crouched. There were thin mopani bushes and low thornbush scrub between us and the impala.

The animals moved from the denser brush and across our path in a long string. "Wait for the ram," Wil said.

After seven or eight females paraded across, the big, impressive ram emerged at the rear. He was only forty yards from us. Wil had put up the sticks again and motioned me impatiently forward. I ignored the sticks and instead rested the rifle stock in the crook of a sturdy sapling, slipped the safety off, and picked up the ram's front shoulder in my scope, set on two-power. I felt rock-steady and ready to fire.

"Wait until he stops," Wil ordered. The ram was walking slowly across our front, completely unconcerned. There was no longer brush between the animal and us. I felt I had a clear, easy shot, but held up.

The wind was light and shifting. It was impossible to pin down its prevailing direction. The impala kept moving until they disappeared behind an isolated dense clump of scrub to our left, still only forty yards out. They froze. I could see tiny brown and white patches shifting nervously through the clusters of branches. Just like deer hunting in brush country back in Michigan. They remained motionless for what seemed an impossibly long time. Without warning, they bolted down-hill and directly away from us, never emerging from behind the obscuring bush. No one had moved or spoken. Busted by the wind!

Everyone continued down the hill, following Wil through several dry creeks and along a small, brushy flood-plain before working back uphill to the truck. He never said a word.

We had gotten back into the truck and were making way once more to the Angwa River spike camp when we crossed another dry creek, roared up the loose sand bank on the far side, and stopped at the soft slap of a tracker's hand on the metal roof. Wil hung his head out his window and glanced back at the trackers. Then he looked left across us, opened his door, and got out.

"Come!" he said.

I jumped from my side and took my rifle from a tracker, quickly and quietly working the bolt to advance a round from magazine to chamber. Wil set the sticks up as I moved to the left front of the vehicle. At least a hundred twenty yards down the riverbank an impala group stood in the shade of a glade by towering, still green-leafed mahogany trees. There were at least six animals.

142

"The ram is on the right," Wil said.

I picked up the animal in my scope right away and slipped the safety forward in the *ready-to-shoot* position. I had never fired from shooting sticks before. The rifle stock sat well forward, back near the floor plate of the magazine, pivoting about in the crook formed by the top of the three sticks above where they crossed. I had to lift up, almost on tiptoes, to lower the muzzle and crosshairs to the body of the ram. Still, the stock butt rode high on my shoulder, its heel barely touching me. The butt's toe extended into the air, well above the top of my shoulder. My adrenaline pumping, the sight picture wandered unsteadily about, the crosshairs moving erratically over the impala's chest. It was staring intently at me. Ready to bolt. Still, I couldn't stabilize the animal's image through the scope.

Remembering the missed opportunity on the earlier impala, I focused solely on this ram and getting a shot off before he, too, ran. He had turned slightly, quartering toward me and presenting just the front half of his chest as the only available shot. With the point of aim still drifting, I fired quickly—as soon as the center of the crosshairs swept across his chest—anxious to shoot before the gun's sight once again strayed from the target.

The rifle recoiled, lifting upward to an angle that must have been nearly forty-five degrees from horizontal. All I could see in that instant was the top of the receiver and the scope. When it came down again, the impala were all running. There was no carcass on the ground.

"What happened?" I said to Wil.

"I think you missed," he said. "It didn't act hit, and I didn't hear the bullet impact." A puff of dust was still drifting away behind where the ram had stood.

We moved up. Wil, the trackers, and Gibson searched the area methodically. They moved into the bush, through the riverbed, and farther down along the bank.

"No hair or blood anywhere," Wil said after twenty minutes or more of searching. "The trackers said it didn't look or sound hit, either. Looks to be a clean miss."

I was glad at least I hadn't wounded it.

Every serious hunter I have known—every devotee of the sport, each practitioner and regular participant, whether he hunts ducks or birds or other upland game, or deer or North American big game or exotic animals—everyone defines himself in large part by his shooting. Defines himself not just as a hunter, but as a man. Good shooting is as important to hunters as being a good lover is to all men. Shooting is very much a part of who a man is, of his self-image and the way he imagines others view him. And I suppose, but do not know, this may be true of women hunters as well. But it is most certainly true of men.

Of course, it is the depth of bad form to brag outright about one's shooting. Those who do so are patently admitting to feeling inferior about it. No, it is mostly said in the manner of "that buck was running full out at a hundred fifty yards when I fired, and to my great surprise, he crumbled into a heap. Always said I'd rather be lucky than good..." The implication being, the hunter is actually quite the remarkable shot while amazingly also possessing the qualities of modesty and understatement.

And when the shooting goes bad, it is quite a humbling thing. My late friend, Cliff Higgins, and I were mulie and pronghorn antelope hunting in Montana years ago. Cliff, only forty-nine at the time, had recently received a devastating diagnosis of metastasized bowel cancer but still chose to complete our long-scheduled trip. He was an avid hunter, an expert with firearms, owning and shooting a vast collection of sophisticated weapons. A former Army ranger who had operated behind enemy lines with the Montagnard tribesmen of Cambodia during the Vietnam epic, he had distinguished himself in armed combat. Later a police officer, he went on to lead a successful group of small but important manufacturing companies in Michigan. A father, husband, and admired leader in his community, he possessed wealth and respect. Yet foremost in his mind in that Montana autumn was his shooting. Having missed a mule deer buck, then wounded and finally brought down his antelope, he obsessed only on his shooting.

"I think my scope was banged in the back of the pickup," Cliff said to me in our tent after missing his buck. "I was dead-on. It's the only explanation. Our guide should have been more careful stowing our rifles." And he was probably right, too. But the point is, it was so important to him.

After wounding his antelope, he talked only about the follow-up shot. "It was hit well enough," he said, "but was still able somehow to run off at full tilt. He made the mistake of going in a semicircle around me. I took my time, held just in front of his chest, and without stopping my swing, dropped him at a hundred yards with one more shot. Just like we do on running deer all the time back in Michigan." Cliff, dying of cancer, an impeccable résumé of achievements, but wanting to talk only about his shooting. He died a year later. I still remember him fondly with the deepest respect and admiration, and miss him dearly.

Just as intense were my feelings of disappointment and self-loathing after missing a standing impala ram at one hundred twenty yards on the bank of a dry river in the Chewore safari area of the Zambezi River Valley in northern Zimbabwe at noon on a broiling hot African day. I knew exactly what I had done. I had never become comfortable on the sticks, never said anything or made any adjustments. I had snapped off a shot on a wing and a prayer without a stable sight picture because I was afraid the animal would bolt. I had wanted so badly to avoid another messed-up opportunity on a quite fine impala ram, I chose to take a very low-percentage shot. I was not about to do it again.

Later in the truck after a respectable period of pouting, I said to Wil, "I couldn't get settled on the sticks."

He said nothing.

"I've never used them before. I'd like to learn more about them. When we get to the spike camp, I'd like to do some shooting at the range with them. Have you show me a few things."

"We can stop right here and shoot," he said.

I knew all the camps had sighting ranges and I wanted to shoot at a measured distance both from the sticks and from the bench to compare the results. "I'd rather do it at lunch," I said.

The Angwa camp had been shut down for the season, but there was a local African caretaker present to prevent looting by the locals. The guys—Levitt, Favor, and Marusi—set up a nice field lunch under the thatch-covered portion of the patio. There was a wonderful, miles-long view of the huge, sandy, dry Angwa River from our position on the high bank. While we ate, a large group of impala, including a good ram, browsed and rested under the shade of broadly crowned acacias on the floodplain across the river. *No shooting within a kilometer of camps* was the rule, and our ranger, Gibson, was there to enforce just that type of thing.

After lunch Wil set up the sticks in the yard and called me over. "Let's dry-fire a few to get you comfortable," he said.

"It's just as effective." It was obvious he didn't want me shooting near the mothballed camp for some reason.

I had pocketed the spent casing from my missed impala and loaded it into the chamber. I rested the center of the stock in the cradle formed by the tripod of sticks where they came together and crossed near the top. Wil had set them up as he had for my impala.

I had to tiptoe to level my rifle. "It's way too high," I said. Just as it had been with the missed ram.

Wil demonstrated how to raise or lower the pocket by moving only the left tripod leg in or out. "Get it to where it's comfortable for you."

I lowered everything until I felt stable and comfortably bent slightly, leaning forward. That part felt perfect. I put the crosshairs on the small knot on a tree trunk about fifty yards away. "It's still not too steady."

"Your stock is too far forward," he said. "The center of gravity should be well behind the resting point on the sticks for stability. Otherwise the whole rifle will tend to teeter about. Put just the front of the stock in the *V*. Then steady everything by gripping the underneath—from below where the shafts cross together—with your palm. Wrap your fingers up and over the sticks, stock, and barrel to hold the rifle firmly in the crook." He demonstrated quickly. "Don't pull down, though. Just stabilize the forestock and barrel on the sticks by squeezing slightly. If you have to move them—say your game moves—simply lift everything straight up with your gripping hand and set it down again in the new location. The height and orientation of the sticks and rifle will remain the same."

I practiced his instructions several times, then dry-fired my spent cartridge again and again, aiming at the tree knot, taking care to squeeze rather than jerk the trigger, and doing so only when I was rock-solid on the target. I got to where the crosshairs never moved from the target—before, during, or after the shot. I felt much better. *I wish we had gone over this at the range yesterday,* I thought.

After lunch cleanup and a short nap, we piled back into the Toyota around 2:30 p.m. and headed into the hills along the Angwa River. More driving the narrow trails, brushy ridgelines and fairly open, flat savannah stretches between the hills. An hour or more into our drive I heard the familiar slap of a tracker's hand on the roof. Wil stopped, leaned from his window, and said a few short words in African to the trackers. He jumped out and took his rifle from one of the men. I got out and Favor handed mine down.

Wil took off down the road and then veered left into the bush along a game trail. Levitt had moved up behind him, carrying the sticks. As usual, I followed Levitt with tracker Favor behind me and ranger Gibson taking up the rear. Nickie stayed at the truck with Marusi.

They were moving fast and it was an effort to keep up. We followed the trail for thirty minutes until it played out into a web of barely visible diverging paths in the grass among the trees and scrub. Levitt and Favor moved to the front and picked their way among the faint trails. It was a mystery how they could tell which one a certain animal had used recently, but we pressed on. Finally, we came to a high ledge marking the side of the hill. It looked down into a deep, wide valley choked with low brush and scattered large trees. Wil stood at the edge and carefully scanned the lowland below. It was the first I had caught up to him, and I was more than a little breathless.

"What are we after?" I said.

"Levitt spotted a nice eland bull crossing the track ahead and around the bend. Only ninety meters beyond us. I couldn't see it from the cab."

149

When I told Wil on the first day which animals I was interested in, eland was not among them. I was aware they were large and rather homely antelope. From the pictures I had seen, they looked every bit like the big Brahma bulls the cowboys ride in rodeos. Each animal taken in Zimbabwe requires payment of a trophy fee, and I vaguely recalled it was high on eland and definitely not in our budget. I was exhausted, my feet sore and calves aching from keeping up with Wil. We had yet to see a buffalo or kudu.

"They're fairly rare here," Wil said of the eland. "This is the first one I've seen this season."

I knew from my research hunting begins in April in the Chewore after the summer rainy season and peters out in the hottest, driest months of September and early October. It was now late September, and we were the only hunters left in the entire Chewore.

"Quite the accomplishment if we can bag one. Problem is, once they spot you and start moving, these eland usually won't stop. Hard to get a shot." He turned and began the return trek up the hill.

Back at the truck we took a break to have some water from the cooler and relieve ourselves off in the brush. When I had finished, Nickie walked over to me. We were alone.

"What was it?" she asked.

"Eland."

"Eland? What are those? That isn't something we're after."

"According to Wil it is."

"Can we afford that? It wasn't in our budget."

"I'm actually not interested in eland. But Wil is. I guess it's his safari, not ours."

"We need to say something to him."

"I didn't know what was going on," I said. "I'll talk to him. Leave it to me, I'll handle it." I wanted to straighten things out without Nickie getting in the act. Without pissing Wil off. We would, after all, be constantly together for more than a week. But still...

Back in the truck again I waited a few minutes before bringing up the eland. "That was quite the hike back in there," I said to Wil.

He was silent.

"Honestly, eland is not something high on our list. It would be a budget buster."

"I don't think the trophy fee is much higher than for most game," he said.

"I recall it's about fifteen hundred dollars." I thought I remembered something like that but was really just guessing. "That's a deal breaker for us. I'd rather skip the eland and devote our time, money, and energy to our top priorities. Buffalo is still number one and I don't want anything to distract from that. Afterwards, or if a chance opportunity presents beforehand, a kudu and impala would be good. But eland isn't on the list."

Nickie turned and smiled at me. She was happy.

We continued winding our way through the back-trails of the Chewore. After a time we turned onto a wider dirt road that appeared to be regularly traveled. We continued on for about ten miles. At one point four elephants moved across our front, two large, tusked cows with a half-grown adolescent and a calf following in tow. They moved off into the bush, then paused and stood about a hundred yards in. We had pulled forward and stopped to snap a few pictures. It was the first elephants we had seen on the ground since landing at the airstrip the day before, but we were to see them every day for the rest of the safari.

We had turned off the dirt road and onto the primitive interior trails again when Wil stopped the truck. Once again we collected rifles, and the trackers jumped down. We took our time getting organized with no particular sense of purpose or urgency.

"Where to?" I asked.

"There's a damp pan back in here with some water still in it and lots of green vegetation growing in the bottom. I thought we might surprise a nice bushbuck."

"Bushbuck?" I said. I wasn't familiar with them but remembered seeing them on the Chewore trophy list. I recalled the fee had been quite reasonable, a few hundred dollars.

"A small antelope," Wil said. "They're quite beautiful and make a wonderful trophy. Very unique. Our hunters love them, and the meat is excellent."

After complaining about the eland, I was embarrassed to be interested in the bushbuck, but I was. "Let's go," I said.

We hiked back a mile or two to the spring, Nickie coming along. It was a pretty walk, and the little sunken pan was lush and moist. Just looking at it seemed to take the edge from the afternoon heat. The thick canopy of leafy treetops helped with that, too. There was no game other than a lone baboon that barked angrily, but the leisurely stroll in and back was refreshing. Everyone seemed happier and more relaxed.

Back in the truck, the trail led us to the bank of a large dry river. "What's the name of this one?" I asked.

"Maura, where you saw the elephants from the plane," Wil said.

We drove down the bank, turning and following the bed for a mile or more. I could tell the sand was loose and deep from the way the truck swayed and plowed through it, nearly becoming stuck several times. Off in the distance on the adjoining low floodplain thick with brown grass, we spotted large herds of impala and waterbuck. They were too far off and in the open for a shot or stalk. Wil drove up a worn spot in the sandy bank and into low riverine bush. We followed the river from up on the bank for another several miles, passing the skeleton of a large elephant and beautiful spreading acacias with thick garlands of red flowered vines in their crowns. Finally we drove back down into the river and followed its course for a few hundred yards before stopping on a raised gravel bar.

Once again we all jumped from the truck. "There're some seeps farther down," Wil said. "We'll walk up on them and see if we can't surprise something."

Everyone set off down the river, Nickie and then Gibson at the rear. Marusi joined us this time. The loose sand gave way under our feet, making the walking difficult. Once more I struggled to keep pace with Wil and Levitt.

Rounding a bend in the river, Wil suddenly looked back and said, "Lion!"

A big lioness was drinking at a tiny, wet seep scooped in the river bottom. We saw each other at about the same instant, and it took only a fraction of a second for her to stand, turn, and spring up the bank into the brush. I thought she was long gone, but when we walked the hundred or so yards up to the waterhole, she was crouched on the edge of the bank just barely in the brush and staring confidently at us. We were only some forty yards from her. She watched us for a full minute before slowly turning and melting into the bush.

We continued on, slugging through the loose sand. After another mile, we rounded a sharp bend in the river, Wil as always in the lead, followed by Levitt then me. Wil stopped abruptly and stooped down, motioning us to a halt with his palm. He took the sticks from Levitt and positioned them, calling me forward with a waggle of his fingers. I moved up.

"Get on the sticks," he said urgently.

I did as he said. "What?" I asked.

"Bushbuck in that elephant dig."

I looked down the river. It was wide, with undulating sand ridges and spotted with little depressions of every description. The riverbed was visible ahead for at least a half mile. The bushbuck could have been anywhere, and I wasn't seeing him.

"Where?"

"Right THERE!" Wil hissed impatiently, but didn't point with a finger or otherwise indicate the location. "Shoot."

I had no idea where he was talking about, but scanned the area until I spotted the tiny-looking bushbuck standing in a shallow, damp depression on the very edge of the riverbed next to the embankment. With his legs below the front rim of the seep, he was visible only from the shoulders up and perfectly camouflaged against the backdrop of sand and riverbank. He was quartering toward me, alerted with eyes fixed on mine. I adjusted the sticks, lowering the pocket, and steadied my rifle in the cradle they formed, left palm gripping the sticks and fingers wrapped up around the forestock and barrel. The bushbuck offered only a quartering frontal shot. I carefully moved the crosshairs to just above and inside his right shoulder—to my left—and held my breath with my aim absolutely solid. The trigger squeeze was prompt but smooth. The big .375 magnum buffalo gun roared and bucked. When it settled down again, I looked over the top. Nothing.

"Did I hit it?" I said to Wil.

"Good shot. He's down."

We all hurried forward. The bushbuck lay stone dead on his side in the bottom of the depression. My shot had

154

struck precisely where I had intended, if anything an inch or two high, above his shoulder angling down and across his chest, exiting on the other side at the back of the ribs. It had been over before he hit the sand.

Levitt was at my side. He pumped my hand excitedly. "Naka tsoma," he grinned. "Kupfura raka naka, Boss."

I shook Levitt's hand and grinned back.

"He says it's a beautiful bushbuck," Gibson explained in his clipped and precise accented English. "He says it was an excellent shot." He grabbed my hand and shook it as well.

"What was the distance?" I asked Wil.

"At least a hundred meters. More."

Favor was smiling and shaking my hand. Nickie had made her way up.

"It's magnificent," she said. "I couldn't see the animal all the way around the bend from where we stopped, but I saw you shoot."

I stooped down to examine the bushbuck. I doubt I've ever seen a more elegant animal. About the size of a typical Michigan whitetail doe, its rich tan coat had a reddish cast that made it seem to glow. It was embellished with rows of lovely white spots like those of a fawn deer, but combining to form an effect of subtle, widely spaced stripes. The face was small with a distinctly noble appearance and slightly darker than the body. The high horns had a unique triangle-shaped cross section, thick at the bases but tapering and gracefully twisting to tall, sharp tips. The overall impression was of a rare and regal treasure. I felt awed by my trophy, grateful to the animal for granting me this moment, for providing such a memorable and inspiring experience.

"It's a nice bushbuck," Wil said. "A very old male. Past his breeding prime. These are the animals we want to harvest. He's fulfilled his purpose and has been removed near the end of his natural life to make way for others. He'll look splendid in your study."

"And the little bushbuck has fulfilled its duty to you," Gibson said.

I was puzzled, as I had not yet heard Favor's story of the tsoma and the mbada.

"In Shona legend, the role of the bushbuck is to help others find their destinies. Then their life is complete. Your destiny was to come to Africa, to secure your position as an able hunter. But you struggled with the impala, and your success was in question, questioned more by you than by others. This bushbuck sacrificed his life to settle the matter. His final act was to redeem you from your doubts and deliver to you your rightful destiny."

"I'll have the guys cut a stout branch from the river bank and lash your bushbuck to it," Wil said. "They can carry him back to the truck. It's too soft to drive all the way in here."

We began making our way back to the truck. I couldn't stop thinking about Gibson's words. It had been a day of highs and lows, seeing little game in the morning, blowing an easy opportunity on a walking ram, and then completely missing a standing impala. A trial by gunfire. And now, redeemed by the sacrifice of my magnificent bushbuck, I felt elated by the culmination of my first day and could only wonder what the rest of the safari would bring.

Four — Joy and Mourning Among the Mopanes

O n our way back to camp after our first day, we stopped briefly at dusk to scout yet another lovely spring, this one with still, green water in a chain of deep pools carved from solid white bedrock. Then, with night pushing out the last gray light, we headed back.

It was completely dark when we finally came to a halt at the Chenje camp. Stepping from the truck, I was greeted by our waiter, Pihwa, holding a tray of iced drinks.

"Would you and Madam care for a sundowner?"

Tired and dusty, we were not about to pass up the offer and enjoyed the virgin fruit juice concoction over ice by a fresh fire before going to our tent to shower and change.

Everyone was gathered around the fire pit as Nickie and I arrived back at the patio on the edge of the bank above the Chenje. It was too dark to see down into the pool in the river and the afternoon heat had only barely begun to yield. Matt, our young assistant professional-hunter-in-training, fixed a plain tonic and lime over ice for me and another juice cocktail for Nickie.

"How was your day?" Sharon asked.

"Missed an easy shot at an impala before lunch, then lucked out on a nice bushbuck this afternoon." I said it with intentional understatement and a deliberate hint of self-deprecation, embarrassed by my initial despair in missing the impala and the childlike excitement, the sense of redemption, I had actually felt in then cleanly taking the little tsoma. "Came across some other animals as well. We saw plenty of remarkable African country. All in all, quite a day."

"I saw your bushbuck," she said. "It's beautiful. I had the cook remove some loin chops. We'll enjoy them for dinner this evening as a celebration."

"What a nice touch," I said.

"And there's a bit of another surprise. A truck bringing in supplies from Harare this afternoon experienced something of a mechanical problem. The driver will have to wait for a part to be sent in tomorrow morning. He'll be joining us for dinner."

"Sounds great," I said. "I'm looking forward to it."

We had sampled a few appetizers and put a dent in our sundowners when everyone turned to look at our headwaiter, Pihwa, who had marched in and was standing ceremoniously at parade rest between the fire pit and formally set table a few feet away. He wore stiff khaki shorts, freshly creased from pressing, and a starched white shirt with buttons up the front, epaulets on the shoulders, and cuffs at the end of the short sleeves. The handsome young black man appeared very official.

Pihwa's English was clipped and precise as he spoke, accented in the fashion of a person of some education whose native tongue is an African tribal language.

"Good evening. First let me congratulate our guests on their wonderful bushbuck. For your enjoyment this evening, we will be serving you bushbuck loin chops with a lovely raisin sauce. We have steamed fresh broccoli and cauliflower as our vegetables. We will start with a salad of chilled asparagus spears, slivered baby carrots, and green onions complemented by a light vinaigrette dressing. There is fresh baked bread and butter for your pleasure. As dessert, we are proud to offer our carameled custard. Enjoy your meal."

We were to receive such a formal, impressive introduction to our dinner each evening.

The table was beautifully set with linen napkins, fine stemware, and china plates. Our food was served with as much ceremony as had accompanied its announcement. The perfectly cooked filets and accouterments would have seemed at home in a five-star New York or Paris restaurant.

We were joined for dinner by Sharon and Jerry; of course, our PH, Wil; the apprentice, Matt; and the stranded driver, a nice white chap who introduced himself as Rollie. No blacks ever joined us for meals, at the Chenje base camp or in the field.

This was our second evening in camp, and it had become apparent the European-descended Zimbabweans were a pleasant if reserved lot. It was up to Nickie and me to keep the conversations moving.

"In doing our research back home, I learned your operation has quite the fine reputation with clients," I said to Sharon. "They say you and Jerry run a tight ship and everything is first-rate. I'm learning how true that is. How long have you two been doing this?"

"Oh, thank you. We try. We've been here at Chenje about seven years now."

"And before...?"

"I worked as a bookkeeper for a small business in Harare for a few years. Before that Jerry and I had a very fine business dealing in agricultural products. Fertilizer, insecticides, other farm chemicals and supplies."

"Before 2000, Zimbabwe had a huge agricultural economy," the truck driver, Rollie, added. He seemed the most outgoing of the bunch. "It provided for all the country's domestic food needs and exports of things like cotton, tobacco, and millet to the rest of the world. We were known as the 'bread basket of southern Africa.' Agriculture was a major source of employment, foreign exchange, and tax revenue."

"So your business must have been quite successful," I said to Sharon. "Did you finally sell it then?"

"I'm afraid not," she said.

"Our president's land 'reforms' changed all that," Rollie went on. He said *reforms* with obvious heavy sarcasm. "He's held power since 1980, sometimes with brutal tactics."

"He's actually a dictator, then?" Nickie asked.

"Oh, we have a constitution and elections," Rollie said. "It's just that any serious competition is promptly eliminated by whatever means. The president has complete control of the military and police."

"Then it's about the same thing," I said. "A dictatorship."

"In the nineties, thousands of minority Ndebele rural people who supported his opponent were tortured and murdered. It's simply not the proper thing to discuss in detail at dinner. But in 2000 he instituted land confiscation, *redistribution* of farms and businesses owned by whites to blacks—mostly to his military and political cronies. The white-owned farms were seized without compensation and given to his powerful political allies."

"My God," I said. "That must have been awful for the farmers."

"They were ordered from their land with twenty-four hours notice," Rollie continued. "Often their homes were burned and white families killed in the process."

"Couldn't anything be done about it?" Nickie asked.

"No chance, I'm afraid. And these were people who had built their farms from nothing over generations. The farm workers, black Zimbabweans, were driven away, too. And the new owners had no idea how to run modern farms. They lacked the capital and technical knowledge of chemicals, seed hybrids, pest control, crop rotation, agricultural machinery, and the like. Farming collapsed as an industry. Less than half the farms were still producing a few years later, and that's mostly still true today. And it dragged all sectors of the economy into complete ruin. Unemployment reached over 90 percent nationally and the currency disintegrated." Rollie seemed on a roll.

"In the States, the housing market tanked a few years back," I said. "That pulled everything else with it, too. When unemployment hit 10 percent everyone was in a panic. It's simply impossible to imagine 90 percent, though."

"That was over ten years ago. Unemployment is still around 80 percent here today. And now most business is transacted in the South African rand or the U.S. dollar. There isn't a national currency anymore. It's really never come back."

"So with no customers, your business was *kaput*." I had turned to Sharon and Jerry.

"We lost everything," Jerry said matter-of-factly, as if describing a long-ago event recounted so many times over so many years the emotion had been leached away.

"I worked with my father on our family farm," Wil said. "He was third generation. We produced tobacco for export and raised some livestock. I always assumed that would be my life." He said it without a trace of self-pity.

"The white population dropped in half afterwards," Rollie said. "We're only 2 percent now. Those who could get out, did. But a lot of us had nowhere to go, or simply didn't know anything else. Europeans immigrated here in the late 1800s and built the modern economy with capital and know-how. But over a period of more than a hundred years, the later generations here had no ties left to family or friends in other countries. Everyone simply has to make do now."

"Then you got into hunting after your family farm was taken?" I said to Wil.

"I'd always loved hunting with my father on our farm, so it was a natural direction to take when we lost it. As a teen-ager my father and I worked closely together. I was essentially the number-two man for all practical purposes, supervising the scores of workers. Many had lived on our farm with their families for generations. Marusi and Levitt were actually born there. When I wanted to sneak some beer but was too young to buy it, I'd order one of the older men to go into town and get it for me," he laughed. "What could they do? I was the boss, next in line to be the owner. It was a good life. But this is exciting work, too."

After dinner Nickie and I moved to the fire pit area again to relax before retiring to our tent. We were joined by Wil and Sharon.

"Did you hear the elephant trumpeting last night?" I said, trying to make conversation. "And that piercing howling. Was it hyenas?"

"I think the hyena was giving the elephant a hard time," Sharon laughed.

"I've always found hyenas fascinating," I said. "You know, on the TV shows. Are there a lot here?"

"Oh, yes," she said. "We hunt them here regularly."

"That would be something—to bag a big hyena."

"We're done with our quota here," Sharon said. "But I believe I heard our Zambezi River camp has one permit left. I could check if you're interested."

"How do the quotas or permits or whatever work?" I asked.

"The government oversees the lease of these safari concessions like Chewore to an operator such as ours. It's done as either an auction or competitive negotiation between operators and the wildlife department. The money is theoretically used for local infrastructure such as roads and bridges. It's put back into the community, they say, but who really knows?"

"The land title may be owned ultimately by the politicos, the same group that got the farms and businesses," Wil said. "A lot of the cash ends up with them, I'm sure."

"Based on the government's assessment of game levels, a limited number of permits are authorized for each animal deemed eligible to be hunted in the concession," Sharon said. "The safari operator must commit to purchasing all of them. For the use of our clients. When they're gone, then we're done hunting that animal. If clients don't take them all, then we— the safari operator—absorb the cost and they go completely unused. Of course, we're hopeful all the permits are used by our clients each season."

"Alright then, when I pay a trophy fee, it basically represents the money paid to the government for the permits?" I said. "Is that right?"

"Yes," Wil said. "The safari operator may mark it up slightly, anywhere from zero to as much as 20 percent, depending. To defray some of their other costs. But the majority of the fee simply represents what must be paid to the government. We only collect the fee if the game is actually shot, not simply for trying."

"And the licenses, the permits to take game, are tightly limited?" I said.

"Oh yes. We estimate, for instance, there are some one thousand elephants in this concession. Only eighteen permits were allowed this year, six tusked bulls and twelve tuskless cows. For balanced management purposes."

"That's a small enough percent," I said.

"And we only take old animals past their prime, in the case of cows, those without a calf. It's all to make sure the herd stays large and healthy. As you saw today, John, there is no shortage of elephants here, including plenty of calves and adolescents."

"A hyena would be wonderful," I said, glancing at Nickie to gauge her reaction.

"We still have a leopard tag," Wil said. "And I noticed some big tracks when we were scouting the river banks today. I'm sure several were males. They're the only ones that can be taken. If you'd like to try, we can hang some baits in those areas and see what shows up."

I was stunned at the prospect of taking a legendary Zambezi Valley leopard on my first and probably only safari. Leopard hunts, I knew, were traditionally fourteen-day affairs dedicated exclusively to that single animal. Even then it could be hit or miss. Serious safari hunters considered it the trophy of a career, often the triumphant culmination of a lifetime hunting the African bush. To think I, a novice on a ten-day buffalo and plains game hunt, might bag a leopard was mind-boggling.

"It must be expensive," I said. I knew from my reading some operators charged separate, additional fees for establishing bait sites.

"Actually, the trophy fee is slightly less than for your buffalo. That would be the sole cost, and then only if you take

166

a big tom. We can use the carcasses of your kills over the next few days, and there's still some good meat left in the bone-yard from our hunters last week to get things started. We could hang some while hunting your buffalo in the days coming, and Matt can scout a few areas and put up baits separately while we're out."

"Let me talk it over this evening with Nickie," I said. "I'll let you know in the morning."

In our tent later, I was selling my heart out to Nickie. Thoughts of our budget had flown from my mind.

"This is once in a lifetime," I argued. "We'll never have this opportunity again. I hadn't thought it possible we would have a chance at leopard. My God! Just think. A rare, magnificent Zimbabwe leopard."

"But the money..." she insisted.

"I've just checked the trophy sheet. A hyena is inexpensive. The leopard is a few thousand, but so is the buffalo we came for. Honestly, I doubt we'll get both, with the law of averages and all."

"I just hope you know what you're doing." She pulled the covers to her face just as the lights dimmed, turning away from me on her side of the bed.

In the lorry just two miles from camp the next morning we came upon a pack of wild African dogs with their black and brown blotched coats, long legs, and lean, round, solid-looking bodies. We slowed as they milled fearlessly and carefree about the truck, panting with open mouths in the fashion of dogs everywhere. As we continued along the track, a collection of small puppies, only weeks old, bounced along in the headlights ahead. Finally they veered into the bush and we sped up. I took it as a good omen.

"They're protected, you know," Wil said. "They're mercilessly efficient hunters."

"Why do they need protection, then?"

"The locals hate them. Kill them at every opportunity. The dogs wipe out their livestock."

We rode on in silence as the sun slowly lit the eastern horizon.

"Let's go ahead on the baits," I said a half hour later. I had told Wil I'd let him know about the leopard and hyena this morning.

"The ribs and hindquarters of your bushbuck are already in the bed," he said. "Along with a nice elephant hind leg from the bone-yard. We'll add to the baits as we collect game."

The prospect of hunting carnivores sent a ripple of tingling excitement along my spine. I did not understand, could not have understood at the time, that the decision to hunt them—that a big male leopard hitting one of our hanging baits—would eventually lead me to the only shooter bull Cape buffalo I would face on the entire trip.

The next several days were similar to the first. Each was sunny, dry, and stifling hot during the afternoon with chilly overnight temperatures. We drove the trails and walked the bush as we had on that first day.

And we saw plenty of game. Still, there were endless hours of scouting, long periods when we saw nothing, convinced the Chewore had gone barren. Then our complacency would be broken by the dash of impala across the road or the burst of acceleration from a little red duiker we had not seen grazing in the brown grass. I was always surprised by the first desperate leaps of a tiny grysbok antelope, bounding along looking very much like a fat Texas jackrabbit on steroids, with their miniature bodies and overdeveloped hindquarters. Unlike the impala, the duikers—German shepherd-sized—and the housecat-sized grysbok with their inch-long horns never stopped once they began their escape. They simply disappeared forever into the long grass.

One afternoon, I don't recall if it was the second day or later, Wil stopped the truck to investigate an area of buffalo sign. We walked parallel to the road for a half mile or more, looking at tracks and dung piles, when Wil suddenly signaled to Levitt to bring up the sticks. A group of impala stood in the open at the edge of a long clearing just where it turned to thick mopani scrub. Wil motioned me up to the sticks.

"The ram is on the right."

I set up my rifle and looked through the scope, dialing it to its full four-power. The impala were clearly more than a hundred yards away. After a moment I picked up the large, well-horned ram standing broadside and looking back at me.

"Shoot when you're ready."

Even having taken the bushbuck cleanly, I was still a little nervous from my initial miss on the first impala ram. I took my time, aiming for the center of the chest, well behind the shoulder, rather than a tighter heart-shoulder shot. The animals began to move forward, and I suppose I rushed my shot a bit when I fired. When the recoil subsided, everything was running.

"They all began to move just as you fired," Wil said. "Nothing you could do. You hit him a little back and down, but still a kill shot. We'll catch up with him easy enough."

Wil took off in the direction of the impala carrying his rifle in one hand and the sticks in the other. We zigged and zagged through the brush at a run for several hundred yards. Finally, Wil said breathlessly, "There!"

The ram, visibly hit back and low in the lungs, stood motionless. A careful shot through the front shoulders this time dropped him for good.

"Very nice," Wil said of the impala, bending over him. "A big old ram." The horns were thick and long. They curved gracefully from the top of its head well out to the sides before sweeping in then out slightly again, ending in sharp points. The animal had lived only a few minutes after my first shot.

Everyone moved up to us. The field staff shook my hand, and Wil snapped a few pictures of Nickie and me with the impala. I had him include a few with the men as well.

Marusi had brought the truck forward, and the Africans began loading the impala. "Another leopard bait," Wil said. I thought I saw a faint smile, but maybe not.

Not long after killing the impala—it might have been the afternoon of the same day, or maybe the next—we again jumped a duiker while driving along an open area of brown grass and thornbush scrub. This time, unlike before, the duiker dashed off a few hundred yards and stopped. We could see the top of his body barely above the grass.

We had stopped, and Wil jumped out. I followed from my side, taking my rifle from Levitt still up in the truck bed.

We moved down the trail toward the duiker. When we had closed to under a hundred yards, the little animal started moving again. We could see just the top of his head bouncing above the grass as he trotted along. At one point he turned and crossed the trail ahead, moving off to our other side. It happened too quickly to shoot. We followed. Then he turned again, angling just a bit back toward us.

"This chap has a death wish," Wil said, nodding in the direction of the little antelope. "There's a small opening in the brush in the direction he's headed. If he crosses it, take him then."

I set up on the sticks Wil had positioned. The duiker trotted into the clearing, only about forty yards out. He was still moving, and I put the crosshairs toward the front of his shoulder to compensate. I fired, the duiker still going broadside across us.

He flopped over on his side like a dropped sack of flour, exactly as the bushbuck had. We all moved forward. My shot had cleanly penetrated through the forward side of both shoulders. He lay motionless with no sign of life in his eyes, but with one hind leg barely twitching. Levitt took a big folding pocketknife from his jumpsuit and opened the long blade. Bending down, he carefully felt for the depression between two ribs just behind the duiker's shoulder and inserted the blade all the way. The duiker never reacted but his leg didn't twitch again.

"Another old guy," Wil said. "This would be barely a snack for a leopard, but he'll provide a nice meal back at camp."

I was impressed by the elegant, diminutive beauty of the antelope. He was solid reddish tan on top and lighter sand color on the belly. A small animal, no larger than a Michigan whitetail fawn, he was nonetheless a beautiful old male. The horns were black, straight, and only six inches long. I was thrilled with the trophy.

We saw game throughout each day but more frequently in the afternoons. We might surprise them or spot something in the distance while driving, or just as likely see animals at a spring or on the floodplain along a dry river.

One afternoon we were walking the bed of the Angwa River when a group of animals crossed well ahead. I couldn't tell what they were, but Wil moved us quickly forward. We crept across the sand, tight against a bank where the brush growing there and the natural curves of the river course provided concealment. Finally I could see about five impala making their way from one bank to the other.

"Bait for our leopard and hyena," Wil said. "Take one of the females."

I got on the sticks, but by the time I had set up, the impala had moved quickly off and up the bank into the bush. Farther down the riverbed, more animals were moving across. I couldn't get a good look.

"Come," Wil said, as he scaled the low bank, moving forward and parallel to the river at a fast trot. As we neared the spot where the animals had been crossing, he ran in a low crouch. I got down, too, and followed. After a while, he slowed and stalked carefully forward. Finally he paused where the riverine bush ended and opened to floodplain. We could see all along the area above and down into the river.

Wil shook his head. "Gone," he said. "There was a nice eland bull. I felt sure we'd get on him." He turned and strode back toward where we had left the truck.

I waited in disbelief before slowly following him. This time it was I who rolled my eyes and shook my head. *I thought we had settled the eland business,* I mouthed silently.

I was glad Nickie had not come along on this stalk. And it would not be the last time we were to deal with eland.

I had told Wil early on of my interest in a big, alpha baboon or a nice warthog tusker-boar if the opportunities presented. And by this time in the hunt, I had decided I'd also take a good waterbuck if possible. I had seen the big, imposing bulls in the distance on several occasions and had been impressed with their size and overall handsome appearance. We needed leopard and hyena bait. Our budget was yesterday's news, and the excitement of hunting Africa had driven out more mundane thoughts about frugality. Actually, we could easily afford a few additional trophies. Still, with a high-price-tag leopard unexpectedly a possibility, the robust trophy fee on a gangly eland I didn't really care about would be the unacceptable last straw. It had become a matter of principle.

We had seen occasional troops of baboons in the hills, but either a clean shot had not been possible, or we had been after other game at the time and didn't want to spoil it by shooting something we felt we could easily get later. Baboons, I soon learned, were very alert and cautious animals. One glance and they would dash away into the thickest stuff, barking to alert the others, not to be seen again. At one point I took a shot at a big one Wil had put me on, but it was running at a distance through dense brush, resulting in an unsurprising clean miss. An unwise shot in any event.

The truck crested a hill of mixed tall trees and a low understory of scrub when we all spotted a lone baboon sitting in a tree across a valley about seventy yards out.

"Take this one," Wil said.

I jumped from the cab and grabbed my rifle from Levitt, chambering a round. Everyone else stayed put. Moving around the front, I steadied the rifle in the crook of a good sized mopani bush alongside the two-track. The baboon was alone, which I found unusual. It sat on a limb, leaning forward slightly, about twenty feet off the ground. Looking at it from the side, the animal presented a surprisingly narrow profile. I took careful aim and fired just below its forward-hunched shoulder at a point that would cause the big magnum round to penetrate its upper arm and pass through its barrel chest from side to side. My aim was solid, my trigger pull good.

The baboon fell from the tree at the shot, disappearing into an overgrown old streambed at the base of the tree. Nickie and Marusi remained with the truck, but everyone else moved forward. There was blood and hair in the little gully where the animal had fallen, but no baboon.

The trackers moved methodically but swiftly through the depression, up into the bush, and down into the gully once more. Now and again I could see little patches of barely visible blood. Otherwise, it was impossible to understand how Levitt and Favor could unravel the trail. They lost the track once, and it was the ranger, Gibson, who was there to pick it up again. I was glad he was with us. Finally there was the sound of thumping and dry foliage crashing in the brush-choked ditch very close ahead. The baboon burst up the bank directly between Wil and me, only thirty feet from us. Neither of us could safely shoot without endangering the other. It took off again in a direction away from the gully and stopped about forty yards out this time. I had run up the bank, and Wil was positioned squarely between me and the baboon. It would have been simple enough for me to end it, but again I had no safe shot, although Wil did. Not wanting the wounded animal to escape, I shouted, "Take him, Wil!" He fired once and it was over.

My original shot had been high on the side of the shoulder, about where I had aimed left to right, but considerably above my intended point of impact. The bullet had penetrated the hunched shoulders near their tops, where the chest narrows back as it joins the neck. Both shoulders were sadly broken without any penetration of the vital areas in the chest or neck. Later, at the range on our last day, I would learn the pounding my rifle had taken in the back of the truck caused it to shoot four inches high at eighty yards, compared to dead-on at a hundred meters as we had determined on the first day. Exactly consistent with the high shot on the baboon.

The animal was not what I had expected, either. It was obviously quite old, its teeth completely missing on its left side. The body hair was thinning. I had seen photos of the big, dominant males with their imposing frames, large heads, prominent brow ridges, dense fur, and impressive canines. This was not one of them.

"You shot the oldest baboon in the Chewore," Wil joked.

It's true it was old and on its final leg, undoubtedly an outcast from its troop. It would have faced a lonely death in the bush or the jaws of some leopard. This animal, if any did, needed to be harvested. Still, it was the first and only time on the safari I felt truly sad after shooting something. I learned long ago the folly of blaming others for my disappointments. I knew it was on me, but I resented Wil's selection of this animal anyway. *Take this one,* he had said—just to put something in the bag, to check one off the list, to get on with other things. And I, without any experience or basis for selection, without hesitating or questioning or declining, did.

Five — "Whack 'em, Stack 'em and Pack 'em."

Ted Nugent, musician and hunter, on taking game

Things would soon become even more interesting when it was time to take my waterbuck. We had regularly seen the young cow with calves hanging around camp, or we would come suddenly upon another such family group out in the bush. And while walking the dry rivers there might be a herd of waterbuck up on the floodplain even with the odd bull among them.

In the evenings we would drive down to the savannahs bordering the Angwa or Maura or some other riverbed and there would invariably be waterbuck, impala, or a warthog sow scurrying along with quick little steps and tail carried erect, her piglets stutter-stepping in trail. Then again we would occasionally surprise a family of these warthogs, a female with young, when topping a hill deep in the thickest Chewore bush. It was neither common nor unusual. But we saw a big, old heavy-tusked boar hog like that which I desired as a trophy but once.

We were scouting kudu on a narrow sand back-trail when a tracker tapped the roof of the Toyota. One of them leaned around toward the window and said something in African to Wil. He jumped out of the truck, taking the sticks from a tracker's hand, and moved well to the front where the roadside brush was shorter, providing some view into the bush. He moved a few yards in from the road's edge bent low for concealment, then put his field glasses to his eyes and studied the gray, leafless area of thick mopani scrub. From my position behind him, I couldn't see past the heavy foliage along the trailside next to the truck.

"Come," he finally said in a low, barely audible voice, his face still turned away from me.

We had done this enough that I knew we were on game, but I had no idea what or exactly where. I could see the general direction in which he was looking, but I couldn't tell if the object of his interest was a few or hundreds of yards from us, somewhat to the right or left, concealed in brush or in an open spot. Did it offer an immediate shot, or was it something we would need to follow? Was it a dagga-boy or a grysbok, or perhaps a kudu? Standing, bedded, running, or just poking along? There simply was no way of knowing.

As I moved up next to Wil, he set the sticks and signaled me urgently onto them. Everything was happening fast. I rested the rifle in the crook, a round loaded and safety off. Looking into the endless jumble of bare gray branches ahead, I saw nothing else.

"Shoot," he said.

"What is it?"

"Warthog."

"Where?"

"There!" Not pointing. Simply *there*.

At that moment a big-tusked warthog broke his statue-like pose about seventy yards in. He hurried stiff-legged and tail-high into the mopani in but an instant, disappearing from view. The boar was obvious enough when he first began moving, but his coloring was indistinguishable from the dense, gray branches, rendering him invisible when motionless. And I had no idea exactly where to look to begin with. I knew if there had been even a little communication—*warthog sixty-five meters out, John, standing in that thick brush just to the left of the fallen tree*—a hint of coordination, I would have had a good chance to get off a reasonable shot. As it was, that would be the last—the only—shootable warthog boar we saw on the entire safari.

But better news was not far off. We had been driving only another twenty or thirty minutes when Wil stopped the truck, looking out the windshield and to his left. A big water-buck bull was meandering along a ridgeline parallel to the road and only eighty or so yards in. We all quickly jumped from the truck. Again, Wil moved forward and set up the sticks. I followed, loading a cartridge into the chamber of the rifle Levitt had handed down. I set up fast and picked up the bull in my scope right away.

Wil had been looking him over. "He's a good one. Shoot him."

The waterbuck had stopped on the ridge top, standing mostly broadside but quartering slightly away. He had turned his head in our direction and was looking at us. I held on the side of his chest, a little behind the shoulder, and fired. As always with the big magnum, the rifle recoiled back and up so that I momentarily lost sight of the animal. When I saw him again, he was running along the ridgeline, then he disappeared down into a draw choked with trees and brush.

It had been a good hold, and I knew he was well-hit. We moved up to where he had been standing when I fired. The trackers picked up the trail right away. We worked down into the gully. Levitt and Favor were in front followed by Wil. Gibson hung back with me. Suddenly he grinned and pointed at the grass and leaves on the gully floor. They were splashed with bright, red blood.

We moved forward at the same deliberate pace, tracking up the far wall of the gully. Everyone's eyes were glued to the trail we were following, looking for sign. Gibson stopped, bent forward, and pointed ahead. There, beyond the far rim, past where the trees and bushes ended, the dead, gray waterbuck lay in a heap on his side in the open grass. He had run only about two hundred yards.

We rushed up. It was clear the waterbuck was stone dead. My heart was racing.

Gibson grinned and pumped my hand. "Dhumukwa!"

"What?" I said.

"The word for 'waterbuck' in Shona. It is the emblem, the ensign of the wildlife service. My employer of sixteen years. A very special animal to us."

The others were smiling and congratulating me as well.

Nickie had trailed near the end of the group, but Marusi had remained with the truck. She walked up close to the waterbuck, grinning.

"It's *huge*," Nickie said.

The animal's sheer size was striking. We had only seen bulls at a distance, but this one seemed monstrous. Examining him carefully, it was clear he was shot through-and-through both lungs. He'd never had a chance.

"How much will this weigh?" I asked Wil, still marveling at the mass of the animal.

"It should go five hundred pounds I'd think."

"Is he a big one?" I had no personal basis of comparison.

"They don't come bigger than this, eh?" Wil said. "Another old boy."

The substantial horns were thicker and lacked the pronounced curve of the impala's, sweeping just slightly back then forward again as they tapered gently at the ends to dulled points. The shafts had stacked, protruding growth rings formed sequentially along their length giving way to smooth, shining dark horn a few inches from the tips. The animal's hair was long and dense and rough and mottled gray, unlike the short, fine tan coats of the bushbuck, duiker, and impala. This bull's bulk, color, and coarse texture of his hide added to his rugged appearance. He was beautiful.

Wil used his handheld radio to call in Marusi with the truck. Nickie and I stood admiring our trophy. We snapped photos in the fading light.

After a few minutes we could hear the lorry in low gear straining through the bush. The men had to hack away brush and small trees with their machetes and hand axes to form a path. Once the Toyota was in position, they attached a steel cable from an electric winch on the frame to haul the water-buck aboard. Still, six of us had to push and strain to urge the carcass into the truck bed.

"You've had quite the few days," Wil said back in the truck and on our way to camp once again. It was completely dark. "Let's see. A very good Chobe bushbuck, an impala ram..." he paused.

"Don't forget the duiker," I said. "It's one of my favorites."

"Yes, of course. Then there was the baboon, and now this fine waterbuck."

"And I thought this wasn't a plains game concession," I kidded.

"They only migrate here in these numbers late in the dry season—when their water is gone elsewhere." He said it *wahhh-TUH*, drawing out the first part, not pronouncing the "r" and emphasizing the last syllable. "All these little springs and seeps in the hills and streambeds of the Chewore are what they're after. It's seldom like this in our high season when it's wet most everywhere."

"Again, I'm luckier than smart. I booked this time only because there was an opening."

"Our hunting is usually over by mid-September. Few clients can tolerate this heat. You're the last one of the year."

"I had no idea it would be this hot. It's not so bad, though. With the low humidity and cool nights it's bearable. And all the game makes it worth it."

"You've accumulated quite the collection. I hope you have a large study at home."

"Whack 'em, stack 'em and pack 'em," I laughed. I admit I was feeling euphoric.

"What?" Wil grinned. He was relaxed and quite jovial, enjoying our success. I hadn't seen him like this before.

"A saying of Ted Nugent's, one of our celebrities back home. A rock-and-roll star. He's quite the hunter, has a cable TV show he does on hunting. Nugent's the eccentric one, though. It's what he says about bagging game—'*whack 'em, stack 'em and pack 'em.*' It's funny."

Of course, it wasn't about numbers. Having hunted most of my life beginning at age twelve when my older half-brother gave me his beat-up, hand-me-down .22 rifle, I had pegged rabbits in the brush and squirrels in the hardwoods for the sheer joy of it during our occasional family summer vacations to the Missouri Ozarks.

As a boy I was strangely drawn to hunting like a moth to a flame, even though no one in my immediate family shared my passion for game. My father had been an infantryman in Italy during World War II fighting the Nazis, wounded twice in battle, but had no interest in sport firearms ever. I never saw him fire, much less own or even hold a gun. Nor did my grandfathers and uncles. My half brother, Walt, had inherited our old single-shot .22 from his father but rarely fired it. It's a certainty he did not hunt. My cousin, three years older than me, was the only friend or family member who hunted. As a young teenager, I was fascinated and looked up to him for it. My parents must have interceded on my behalf with his, because cousin Shel suffered to invite me along on one occasion when he and his friends hunted in the Missouri hills for rabbits and crows. I got one of each, and my zeal for hunting was secured. I can only imagine what an irritating nuisance I was to those older boys. I hunted with him just once, but from that day forward I worshipped Shel.

In my youth, *Outdoor Life* was a fixture at my bedside. Then there was the subscription to the *American Rifleman* magazine and my Junior NRA membership. I used the old .22 regularly to blast tin cans to scrap and puncture paper competition targets purchased for a penny apiece. I kept detailed track of my scores, planning to enter a formal shooting competition one day. It never happened. Finally on my fourteenth birthday, my parents—reluctantly acknowledging my love of shooting—presented me with a basic 20-gauge Remington 870 pump shotgun. Later as an older teen, I used it to shoot rabbits and quail along the many brush-choked creek bottoms that ran beside the weedy, fallow forty-acre farm plots in the Missouri hills beyond the outskirts of Saint Louis. Today I own many fine shotguns, rifles, and pistols, but I still—some fifty-five years later—grab that beloved, scarred old Remington 870 to try for a few grouse during autumn in the Michigan woods near home.

As a youngster, I took for granted my fascination with hunting, but later wondered how I, without a family tradition for the sport, became so drawn to it. Author Robert Ruark called it answering the *Horn of the Hunter*, a primitive, perhaps genetic stirring felt by many but certainly not all. I knew from studying introductory archaeology in college the earliest human and humanoid fossils, dating back millions of years to our small-brained, long-armed forebears, included indisputable evidence of handcrafted stone hunting weapons, deliberately butchered carcasses, and the bones of now-extinct animals with man-made spear points embedded in their remains.

There are those who have told me hunting in humans evolved to provide food and not sport, that sport hunting in the age of agriculture is somehow cruel and wrong. But I know it not to be true. The typical ethical hunter, as distinguished from the exploitive poacher, is in it for the experience, not to simply cause death and never intentional suffering. Having visited commercial slaughterhouses in Detroit's Eastern Market as part of my job in the early years, the fate of an animal before the hunter's gun is a much kinder one. And there is clear evidence of hunting for sport throughout all recorded human history and across every civilization. After spending fifty years in Michigan deer camps, it is clear hunters cross all economic and social lines. The man who you help drag his deer from the woods is as likely to be a corporate CEO as a cab driver.

It's been argued animals hunt only when they need food, or primitive cultures, such as the early American Indians did likewise. This fails the test of history as well. Primitive societies hunted to obtain religious symbols, personal decoration, to prove one's worth, or as a rite of passage—exactly as modern people do. And zoologists confirm animals hunt not only for food, but for the inborn joy of it. One needs only to consider the well-fed tabby cat that brings back a bird or chipmunk from the backyard, or the pampered lap dog that enthusiastically chases and occasionally even catches a squirrel. And it's been shown wild predators behave exactly the same. It has struck me that the instinctive need to hunt, such

184

as I first experienced as a young boy, is God-given in the very fiber of our being for many of us—even if it is not the calling of everyone—and it would be the greater blasphemy to deny it than to act on it.

And for me, it has never been about numbers. Particularly in later years, I have many times passed on an only average buck, or stopped kicking up grouse, even when the cutover aspen stands and brushy clover field edges were thick with them, after just a bird or two had been taken, happier with the experience than the amount of game.

But now, in the wild Chewore of the Zambezi River Valley, my larder was filling with exotic game. *Whack 'em, stack 'em and pack 'em.* And, more than halfway through our ten-day safari, I couldn't have imagined the best was still to come.

Six — Bere and Mbada

On another morning several days into our safari, after we had taken the waterbuck, we made a particularly refreshing trek back to a lovely spring. It was one of those in a small ravine with a chain of little fresh, clear pools supporting thick, green-leafed foliage along its banks. It was quite pleasant.

There were many hunting rules in the Chewore. In addition to those requiring the presence of a government ranger, prohibiting shooting near camp or from a vehicle, before light or after dark, another regulation forbade hunting at major water sources. Essentially if the pool was named on the published maps—a recognized landmark—it could be scouted for sign, for tracks or scat or spotting something to follow, but not actually hunted. On the other hand, if it was simply a puddle or elephant dig in a river bottom that held a little moisture, shooting there was permitted. This one was not mapped, and we took our guns along as we looked it over. There were old tracks and scat, but nothing promising. After a refreshing break at the spring, we headed back to the truck.

Hunting the Chewore could mean hours of dreary boredom, of driving back-trails or walking dry streams. Yet occasionally the boredom would be interrupted at the least likely of times, and in the most unexpected of places, by the sudden and usually brief appearance of game. We had begun devoting our mornings to baiting for leopard and hyena. Sharon had learned there was one last hyena tag still available from the

Zambezi River camp to our north. That camp was used only by fishermen for the rest of the season. I claimed the tag immediately.

We set up a hyena bait along a dry streambed that cut through the hills not too far from camp. The site had a barely visible track running along the top of a very high bank. It was a drop of at least eighty feet, maybe considerably more, to the sandy, bone-dry stream course below. The face of the dirt bank was nearly vertical, almost a cliff, but with just enough grade to allow the field staff to work their way up and down, clinging to the odd hand or foothold. They dragged the ribs of my waterbuck with neck and backbone still attached down into the gully and across the sand to a little clearing on the opposite side. The carcass was then chained to a big tree trunk to prevent predators from dragging it off. Our shot would be from up above, on the edge of the bank, down and across into the baited area. It was about seventy yards.

"We've taken some nice ones here in past seasons," Wil explained. "The guys have spotted some fresh tracks up along the road and down below by the streambed."

"Will we build a blind?"

"We'll stalk in early in the morning. First thing. We'll leave the truck about a mile back and walk in on this trail. They make an exception for hyena hunting—we can shoot an hour before dawn. They're almost totally nocturnal, you know. We'll need to leave camp by shortly after five. And we must be very quiet coming in. These hyena have remarkable senses, especially their hearing. We walk in barefoot. Can you do that?"

I thought I had prepared well for this safari while still back home, losing a few pounds and walking three to four miles every day. But by the second day my feet were blistered and bloody, and I had lost a toenail. I had taped everything well enough, but each step over rough ground or on a steep

188

grade delivered a blast of pain. And the two-track trail in was littered with sharp stones and jagged sticks, some with thorns. I wasn't about to let injuries ruin my safari, but I recall thinking *there isn't a hyena in the world worth walking barefoot with open, bleeding blisters on this miserable rubble for a full mile.*

"I've got some soft-soled tennis shoes for relaxing back at camp. I'll use those." I'd thought it would be nice to get a hyena, but it wasn't a priority.

Wil looked down in silence. Finally he said, "Can you pull some thick socks over them at least?"

"Sure." It was a minor concession.

"We won't need a blind," Wil said. "We'll come in and have our look over the edge. If hyenas are still there, we shoot. It may be quick. Are you okay with an offhand shot?"

"If I have to. I'd rather have something to brace on."

"I'll have the guys set up some homemade shooting sticks using small branches and strips of old truck-tube rubber. We'll put them in position and leave them here. We'll know within a few minutes of arriving in the morning if there's something to shoot. If not, we'll pull back and head to camp for a late breakfast. Then set out to find you that buff you've been craving."

It was just before four thirty the next morning when I heard the camp staff lighting the wood fires under the outdoor boiler that supplied our hot water. Then the generator came alive with its rumble. A few minutes later I heard the familiar voice of our waiter outside the tent.

"Good morning, Boss and Madam." He left two cups of hot coffee outside our tent as he did every day.

"Morning, Pihwa."

Nickie stayed in bed. I cleaned up and went over to the mess hut for a quick cup of coffee and a dry scone from the jar on the counter before meeting Wil at the truck at five fifteen sharp. We made the twenty-minute drive and parked a mile shy of the bait as planned. It was still black out, and we used flashlights at first but shut them off a quarter mile from our destination. We had picked our way along the trail for a half hour. Occasionally I, like everyone else, would kick a stone or crack a twig. In the dark I was spared from watching Wil roll his eyes or shake his head.

The trackers finally dropped behind as we approached within a few hundred feet of our shooting position on the high bank. Wil and I worked forward, giving the edge a wide berth until we were absolutely abreast of the chosen spot. Then we cut quietly toward the bank where the sticks had been prepositioned in a gap in some brush. The sun was nowhere near up, but it had become barely light enough to see for a hundred yards, no more. We crept forward and peered down toward the streambed and the bait. Nothing.

We waited and scanned the area for only a few minutes. Then Wil sent Levitt and Favor down to check the bait. They quickly returned and spoke softly to Wil in African.

" Bere aiva pano," Levitt said. Wil nodded.

"What'd he see?" I asked.

"Bere. Hyena in Shona. He says the bait's been fed on. There are plenty of fresh tracks down there and up here on the road. We were just a bit too late."

We were to repeat this ritual every morning for the balance of the safari. I never shot at or even saw a hyena the entire trip. Still, it was exciting and fun. I found myself looking forward to and enjoying these early morning outings each day, right up to the last.

Baiting leopard was almost as interesting. Wil had commented in an uncharacteristic burst of communication each time we spotted leopard tracks while scouting the rivers. They were usually in brushy or wooded areas along the upper banks or on the game trails etched in the bush beside the rivers.

"These are big ones," he might say. Only males could be hunted, and the size of the tracks indicated the likelihood of the age and gender.

We began selecting sites to hang leopard bait, using meat left over from the bone-yard at first, and later the carcasses of our impala, waterbuck, and bushbuck. We would drive the lorry to the site, the bait in the back, and select a particular tree and branch suitable to the wind and terrain. Favor, our number-two tracker, was lean, young, fit, and eager. He was selected to climb the trees. A rope would be thrown over the chosen branch, one end lashed to a carcass and the other hoisted by Levitt, Marusi, Gibson, and Wil on the ground. Young Favor would then secure it in place on the limb and hide it with brush and small branches. I, as the client, was forbidden as a matter of proper safari protocol from helping. It was fine with me. Usually the meat had begun to ripen, and it was good planning to remain well upwind.

Once the bait was secured high enough that lions and hyenas couldn't reach it, but was still convenient to the tree-loving leopards, a scent bag would be dragged. This consisted of the guts of our trophies lashed into a ball or sometimes in a net sack. The trackers would drag it from as much as a half mile away to the bait tree, successively from several different directions. It took some time and was most unpleasant.

"It's to lure the leopard in," Wil said. "Give him the smell of something dead to follow. Probably doesn't do much good, but it makes us feel better," he smiled.

He set up motion-activated game cameras at each site like we used for scouting deer areas back in Michigan.

"If we catch a male on a bait, only then will we build a blind and hunt in early morning and last light," Wil explained. "Leopard are nocturnal and quite shy. The cameras are capable of recording the exact time of each photograph. If we see him visiting near morning or evening, we're in luck. If it's only in the middle of the night, it's bad news, but we'll still have a go first and last thing. No shooting at night allowed, though. And it's absolutely critical we positively identify it as a male regardless of its size. Huge fines if we make a mistake. You can only be sure by waiting long enough to have a look at his jewels," he smiled.

We would check the baits and cameras regularly in the ensuing days. There would be photos of leopards feeding on a few of them, all at night. Several females including one with her half-grown cub. And one very big, beautiful, thick-necked male that was to impact the outcome of our buffalo hunt.

Seven — The Gray Ghost

O ne cannot help but be struck by the comedy of the tiny, ill-shaped grysbok bouncing frantically through the yellow grass. And the warthog seems as if he were assembled from a discarded collection of unwanted parts, a Frankensteinian experiment on the animal world gone terribly wrong. The bushbuck, on the other hand, exudes harmonious elegance, while the duiker is a study in diminutive beauty, an artistically rendered miniature of an idealized antelope. Baboons are the blue-collar, scruffy, rudely barking rabble of the bush while impala are the common proletariat, the working class of the Chewore with their long, homely faces, roughly featured and oddly angled. But one can never forget, cannot help but be awed at the first glimpse of the majestic wild bull kudu.

If the lion is king of the jungle—I have no doubt it is true—the kudu bull is the crown prince. Strikingly tall and magnificently proportioned, his soaring, spiraling horns are the perfect adornment, a princely coronet upon a regal body. It is said when George Washington, general of the Continental Army and first president of the United States, entered a room, a hush fell. All others paled in comparison even though he behaved humbly. He was always silently and spontaneously acclaimed by those in his presence a man above men, not so much for his achievements as simply his bearing. So it is with the kudu bull amongst lesser, amongst all other animals. It is true enough the elephant is more massive, the giraffe wondrous, the zebra unique, and the leopard deadly and beautiful and stealthy. But nothing compares with the kudu.

Perhaps it is his coat, appearing lush, tailored and smooth in satiny-rich, understated silver-gray. The immediate urge is to reach out and stroke it. Or the very light gray, almost white, thin, faint and widely spaced stripes running vertically up its flanks and horizontally along the backbone. The same contrasting light gray forms a distinct chevron, a coat-of-arms of a knight of the court, on the face below the eyes. The kudu's head is prominent and noble and pleasingly proportioned. A mane runs both above and below the long, strong neck, dark and stiffly bristled on top and feathery light gray beneath.

The bull kudu's legs are long, his body is athletic and sculpted with muscle honed through the rigors of survival in the African bush. While the Cape buffalo is muscle-bound and massive and brutish and unafraid, the kudu is built as an animal of action. His movements are confident and unhurried even though he is capable of remarkable speed and power. The impala flees in frantic, terrified, escaping leaps, while the kudu runs as does the American working quarter horse, with chest forward and legs driving beneath, taking the thick bush in a purposeful attack, an NFL running back cutting and powering through the opposition to reach his chosen objective. Like the human athlete or the quarter horse, the kudu runs without fear. One can never forget that first glimpse of the majestic wild bull kudu.

Kudus are trophies of opportunity, residents of the brushy forests where the advantages are all theirs, unlike on the more open savannahs. The first time I saw a kudu bull while hunting, it was three or four days into our safari. Our party was hiking to a spring a mile or so back in the bush to look for buffalo tracks. We had crested a small rise in the mopane-covered hills when we jumped a bull and cow standing in a wide depression some fifty yards ahead. They glanced at us only momentarily before taking off at a leisurely trot up the next hill, the two of them stopping at the top among the scrub to look back at us. They were still within a hundred yards.

We had actually gotten on kudu the very first day when I was stumbling noisily along behind Wil, catching the skin on my forearms on the *wait-a-minute* thorns, the little fishhooks that caught and held you until you backed them out, that ripped your skin open in a bloody, jagged line if you tried to simply press past them. When Wil had rolled his eyes and shaken his head at my oafishness. I had spoiled our stalk on a nice bull spotted by our trackers, one I never did see. The stalk had been abandoned. I had been clumsy and loud and clueless on those first days, but was finally doing better even if Wil continued his occasional silent, pantomime castigations of my bush transgressions. Experience is an effective if harsh teacher.

Now, days later, I was looking upon one of the most impressive animals I had ever seen. The bull's dark, massive horns rose up and diverged out in lovely curling ringlets. The sun filtering through the trees reflected from their shiny surface. The gray coat perfectly matched the bare mopani brush, the lighter stripes mimicking the sunlit, mottled hues of gray among the branches. The bull stood much larger than the cow, bigger by an order of magnitude than the duiker, impala, or bushbuck. Their camouflage was perfect. I would never have seen them had they not run to that spot before my eyes.

"What a magnificent kudu," I stammered, still starstruck at the sight. I wondered why Wil hadn't called for the sticks and motioned me to his side. He said nothing.

"Should we shoot him?" I finally asked. We had stood looking for nearly a full minute. The animals seemed unconcerned but I was certain they would bolt at any instant.

"A bit too young. He has a few breeding years ahead of him. We want something older."

I was stunned. I never challenged Wil's calls, never had a desire to, but it was as if we had stumbled upon a tall-tined, wide, rutting-necked ten-point buck in Michigan and someone called it off because he was too small. "Let's wait for a fourteen-point."

"Their coloring is perfect," I said. "I wouldn't know they were there had we not seen them moving."

"The gray ghost of the Chewore."

"Ghost?"

"It's what the locals, the hunting community says. Their coloring. The way they move. Blend in. One minute they're there, the next they're not. As much as anything, it's a comment on their mystique, I suppose. A compliment. There's something quite different about them."

During an afternoon a few days later we were driving the hillside trails through the mopanes when we rounded a sharp bend. A group of three beautiful kudu bulls burst from behind a fallen tree a few dozen yards off the track and charged deeper into the forest.

Wil stopped the truck abruptly and we all jumped out. Levitt quickly handed my gun down.

"The big one was quite good," Wil said. "Let's give them a try."

We set off into the woods in the direction the kudus had run. Levitt and Favor tracked in the lead and I followed Wil. Nickie and Marusi remained with the truck this time. We worked methodically forward, the trackers seeming to hesitate occasionally as they lost the trail, casting wide until they picked it up again. The bush was crisscrossed with game trails, and I was confounded at their ability to follow specific animals among the many that had obviously passed through.

At one point everyone stopped suddenly, and after a few seconds Wil pivoted ninety degrees and led us off in a new direction. Minutes into our detour I glanced back through the bush in the direction we had originally been heading. A huge gray elephant was moving through the dense stand of trees and low scrub, paralleling our path. He was only a hundred yards away. We picked up the pace and soon lost sight of the elephant. After a few more minutes we heard him trumpet loudly and what seemed to me angrily from the general direction we last saw him.

We continued on our detour until we reached a very high riverbank, as sheer as a cliff. Down below was a sand riverbed bordered by thick trees, with heavy mixed scrub and forest along the opposite bank extending on as far as we could see. A large herd of elephants was drifting through the bush alongside the river. They were in and out of heavy brush and I couldn't count them all, but was positive I had seen at least a dozen separate animals.

Wil only glanced down at the elephants briefly before turning another ninety degrees and heading back in the general direction of the truck. He had never said a word since we left the roadside. After another fifteen minutes he turned again, doubling back in the direction where we had spotted the lone elephant in the nearby bush. After a few more minutes everyone froze again and looked to the left. A huge tusked elephant was moving deliberately through the trees and brush directly toward us, ears flared to each side and eyes fixed intently on us. He was but forty yards away and steadily closing. It was obvious he was intentionally coming for us.

Wil carried a Winchester 70 bolt rifle with iron sights and chambered in .416 Rigby. He quickly squared up toward the elephant and noisily worked the action. It was not so much that act that commanded my attention, but the look on his face. His eyes were as wide as silver dollars.

"Back up!" he said.

My rifle had been slung over my shoulder, but I lowered it to port-arms, at the ready with a finger on the trigger and thumb on the safety. I was behind Wil and staring over his shoulder at the closing elephant.

Wil backed up, too. He looked briefly behind him.

"Don't look! GO!"

We all turned and hurried down a game trail away from the elephant. Wil was the only one still backing up. After a few minutes I looked back again and could no longer see it.

Once again we did a wide flanking maneuver and continued through the woodland in the general direction the kudu bulls had taken. I wasn't sure if we were still on a track or were just searching. Wil was characteristically silent. We finally came to another high riverbank and scaled down into the bottom. It was hard going. We walked the bed then climbed out on the other side, pausing on top. Wil used his radio to call Marusi and the truck with Nickie. How they got to us with the river ravines as obstacles, I'll never know, but they soon came bouncing up the two-track that followed the bank where we stood. We never saw those kudus again, and Wil never mentioned the episode.

We continued our daily drives and walks through the Chewore searching for buffalo. It was several days after the encounter with the elephant that a tracker tapped the cab roof late one afternoon as we drove a trail deep in the hilly forest. Wil stopped and we climbed out. My rifle was again handed down.

Wil moved cautiously forward along the roadside and studied the bush to our left. He motioned me forward and we all set off into the trees. After a few hundred yards he set up the sticks and finger-waggled me up. I rested my rifle in the crook as always and looked forward. Two big kudu bulls were standing in the scrub looking back at us. They were nearly invisible.

Before I could pick them up in the scope, they took off again at an unhurried trot. Wil collected the sticks and we continued to follow, this time deviating off to the right to parallel their path. We crested a small rise, and the sticks were once more set up. It took a few moments to locate the kudus among the scattered bush. When I did, they moved off once more. Again, we tracked along behind and to the side. Finally we climbed the grade of a larger hill, and Wil froze on top. I was far enough back I couldn't see what he was looking at on the other side. He studied the area for some time with naked eyes and his field glasses. Then he planted the sticks and signaled me forward.

I quickly set up and looked into another brushy depression ahead. I could see nothing but mopani and thornbushes.

"Where?" I said.

"There!" Impatient. Irritated.

The bulls took off again and climbed the next rise, pausing to look back in a stand of small trees. This time I had them dead to rights.

"On the left," Wil hissed.

I placed the crosshairs midway up the chest and a few inches behind the shoulder of the big bull on the left, careful to hold my breath, steady my aim, and squeeze smoothly. When the recoil had subsided and I was able to look over the rifle once again, the second bull was gone but the first was lying on his belly in the long, dark grass among the trees on the knoll top. He was down hard, and only his head was bobbing slightly.

"Hit him again," Wil said. "Sometimes they get up."

The long grass came to nearly the top of the animal's back. I had to guess where the front shoulder would be and fire through the dense, brown stems. The big kudu, beautiful with thick, soaring, spiraling horns, flopped onto his side and never moved again. It was all over in seconds.

We all rushed to the fallen kudu. My first shot had struck him a little higher than intended, through the top portion of the ribcage and below the spine. It was clear the massive and powerful .375 magnum round had penetrated high through both lungs and expanded enough to stun the bottom of the backbone, causing the bull to collapse on the spot. A certain kill shot. My second had passed through the grass, entering low and barely behind the shoulder, then crossing slightly forward through the chest and heart, and finally exiting the shoulder on the far side. Death had followed instantaneously.

Everyone was grinning and shaking my hand. Nickie was with us.

"Oh my God, he's beautiful!"

"Excellent shot!" Gibson said in his slow, measured English.

I looked back. "Where were we when I fired?" Everything looked the same, and with the adrenaline pumping I had made little note of our shooting position.

"Way back where the grass is lighter yellow on that hilltop," Gibson said. "Well over a hundred meters."

Levitt was standing next to me, admiring the kudu. "What is it in your language?" I asked him.

He looked at me in confusion. He didn't understand.

"The word for kudu in Shona," I said slowly.

"Nhoro," he said, rolling the *r*. "Kudu."

"Nhoro," I repeated.

The animal was beautiful and huge and elegant. The light was fading toward evening, but even in the dusk his hues of gray perfectly matched the mopanes. His horns were long and very dark and thick at the bases. They rose high in graceful, wide spirals leading to sharp ivory-colored tips.

"The gray ghost of the Chewore," I said aloud.

"He's a good one," Wil said. "A very old boy. His breeding days were behind him. He was ready."

I heard the groan of the engine as Marusi worked the truck in. There would be more congratulations back at camp and medium-rare kudu loin chops, broiled to perfection for dinner this evening.

I looked at the fallen animal a final time before the men winched him aboard the truck, and couldn't help but think the kudu bull could only be created by the mind of God and rendered on the canvas of nature in the African bush. My day was complete, and now there was one final trophy to go.

Eight – The Widow-Maker

"There's simply something addictive about buffalo hunting," Sharon had said to me during our meal one evening. "Our clients come to take an elephant, a leopard, or a lion only once. But they come *back* for buffalo."

And for me it was true. Few words can describe the drama, the anticipation of stalking the dense bush and thick, dry jesse willows, hearing the impossibly close snorts and short, strong, invisible bellows, or catching the faintest glimpse of black moving close among the thick brush, all the time aware of the betraying potential of a shifting afternoon breeze or cracking twig beneath one's foot. These thoughts occupy the buffalo hunter's idle time, are the stuff of his dreams while drifting into sleep each night. I had taken my buffalo many times in my imagination, shot him through a narrow gap among the jesse while he was facing me only yards away. Or running right-to-left across my field of view, me taking the perfect lead on the front of his shoulder and nailing him cleanly through the heart and lungs, often breaking the opposite shoulder with a through-and-through shot in the process. Then following up, stopping his wounded charge as he exploded at point-blank range from a dense tangle, dropping him in his tracks with cool nerves and a perfectly placed center-chest shot. Followed by handshakes all around. Of course, reality never matches fantasy, as I would soon learn.

We actually saw buffalo most days of the safari beginning on the very first when I had badly missed my impala and redeemed myself with a perfect one-hundred-ten-yard frontal shot late in the day on the elegant tsoma, the lovely bushbuck. But we always saw a group of buffalo only once on any particular day—not every day—and always in the late afternoon or early evening.

On our first day we had scouted the hills in the morning, stopping to check what proved to be old spoor and scat, noting the lion tracks shadowing the buffalo, finally working down to a huge, tiered floodplain along a bending stretch of the dry M'Kunga River. Buffalo sign, some of it quite fresh, was everywhere and so were the tracks of our pride of hunting lions. Wil had stopped the truck to investigate on foot and we walked the open savannah of the plain with its widely scattered small trees and assorted bushy scrub. Taller mopanes and spreading acacias lined the riverbank itself. The plain was gently rolling with small knolls and ridges we climbed to have a better look at the vast area. Buffalo dung and prints dotted the landscape. But there were no animals.

"There was quite the herd here recently," Wil said after we had walked the area for close to an hour. "But they're being pushed by these lions. That keeps them constantly on the alert and moving. And the other side of the river is the Dande concession where we're not allowed to hunt. It's likely they've moved over there."

"Maybe we can check back here later," I said, excited to see promising sign. We had been searching for buffalo since before dawn. It was getting close to noon, and this was the most intriguing, by far the largest and freshest area of buffalo evidence we had yet seen.

"We'll walk the riverbed for a mile or two before breaking for lunch," Wil said. "Perhaps we'll catch them at a seep, or come upon a few stray dagga-boy stragglers. One thing, though. If we get into a large herd, we'll need to be quite careful about picking the right animal to shoot. It can be a bit chaotic."

His words would later—on the final day of buffalo hunting—prove to be as ironic as they were prophetic.

It was late on that first day of hunting when, with the bushbuck stowed in the bed of the truck, we made our way back toward camp as the sun was dropping down to barely touch the tops of the higher, most distant hills. The Toyota banged along the rough track and up-and-down steep gullies. Finally Wil brought it to a stop on hard, white bedrock that formed a natural bridge of sorts among a chain of large, still and clear pools in a stream bottom.

"No shooting here," Wil said. "But we'll have our look for sign. It's a favorite watering spot. If we see something interesting, we can come back and follow up in the morning."

Wil and Levitt walked the edges of the pools in one direction while Favor and Gibson set off in the other. Nickie, our driver Marusi, and I waited with the truck on the smooth sheet of rock separating two large pools. The banks above the pools were lined with huge, green-leafed mahogany and mopane trees, and the hills, rising sharply up and away from the streambed, were thick with varied dry underbrush below a forest of bare-limbed, tall mopanes.

The two scouting parties had been gone about twenty minutes when Favor hurried back and past us, continuing in the direction taken by Wil and Levitt. After a few minutes they all returned to the truck.

"The guys spotted some very fresh, large tracks by one of the pools downstream. Could be nice bulls. Wait here while we go down there to investigate. We're going to try and see where they've gone and check if there's any fresh dung along their track. If it's promising, we'll call for you." Wil sounded excited.

Wil, Levitt, Favor, and Gibson headed out of sight around a bend in the stream. Nickie, Marusi, and I waited at the truck. After only fifteen minutes Favor came rushing back.

"Wil say you come." He retrieved my rifle from the back of the truck, and I chambered a round.

Nickie and I quickly followed Favor along a game trail that meandered variously up and across the high hill that rose above the stream with its chain of pools. After ten minutes we caught up with the group. Levitt and Gibson, now joined by Favor, were sorting the intersecting and diverging game trails, picking out the path taken by the buffalos. I moved up by Wil.

"Two big ones are traveling along here," he said. "The dung is still hot. They couldn't be but minutes ahead. We must have arrived at the pools just moments after they left."

We followed Wil and the trackers. They became very cautious in the stalk, stopping, crouching, and peering ahead at intervals before proceeding slowly again. Favor soon fell back, and Wil motioned me up close behind him. Levitt tracked carefully in the lead, creeping and pausing frequently. Suddenly Levitt froze, bent down low, and pointed up the hill with his entire hand. Wil looked in the direction Levitt had indicated for only an instant before setting up the sticks and urgently signaling me forward. I rested my rifle in the crook. The sun was well behind the hill, and it was becoming quite dark. Upon seeing my gun go up, Levitt—in front—dropped face-down, flat on the trail. Wil was directly beside me. My peripheral vision revealed Favor, Gibson, and Nickie dropping into a low, almost sitting squat behind us. Immediately to the front some ninety yards up and ahead, two massive, compact and muscular black buffalos sorted their way through the brush just before the crest of the hill. I put the crosshairs of the scope on each of their chests in turn as they made their way toward the top. They looked identical.

Wil was studying them with his field glasses.

"Junk," he said.

I didn't understand. The animals were huge.

"Scrum caps."

I thought he had said *scum* and was more confused than before.

"Which one?" I asked, meaning *"Which animal should I shoot?"*

"Both," he said. "They're both junk."

"I don't understand *scum caps*." I was becoming even more confused.

"*Scrum* caps! Like the helmets the football players wear. In the rugby scrums. Both of them have broken horns on each side. The inside intact fragments run tight down along the sides of their heads, looking something like a rugby helmet. The part where they'd normally curl out then up is completely broken away. Happens sometimes when bulls are very old and deteriorated. They're both junk as trophies. Quite big, ancient bulls, though. What are the odds they'd both be scrum caps? I've never encountered that before."

By the time we got back to the truck and were on our way toward camp once more, it had become completely dark. I was aware of an odd mix of elation at stalking up on two huge old dagga-boys we had encountered suddenly and unexpectedly at last light, and disappointment at having to pass on what would have been a thrilling shot.

"That was exciting," I said to Wil. "I couldn't believe how quickly we got on those two big m'bogos." I had learned the word from my reading, Hemingway, Ruark, Capstick.

"*M'bogo* is a term they use in the far east of Africa, in Kenya, Tanzania, and eastern Mozambique. Where Swahili is the base of the languages. Here in southern-central Africa, with its Bantu culture and family of languages, the natives call them *nyati*. Or in English, The Black Death. We whites often say 'Widow Maker'. All well-deserved terms. They're the deadliest animals hunters face by far."

"I know they can be dangerous," I said. "But I'd have thought crocs, lions, or snakes take more people."

"Despite the stories, lion attacks really aren't all that common. It's true villagers using rivers for water are often killed by crocs or hippos. Or black mambas looking for rodents among the dense crops while the farmers weed and harvest. And elephants raiding fields can get aggressive and kill or injure the workers. But those aren't hunting situations. Far and away, more hunters—clients or their PHs—are killed by buffalo above all other game combined."

"Have there been problems here in the Chewore?" I asked, as titillated by the idea of the risk as I was uneasy.

"Hunting is inherently dangerous," Wil said, "and trouble assumes many forms out here. Just this season another PH, chap named Edwins, had a client shoot his own toes off. Seems the client was hunting buffalo with a new, expensive .458 double. He lacked practice and experience, not to mention ability. Butchered his shot on the buff. Edwins and his client followed up, but he—the client—continued to shoot badly until he announced he was out of ammunition. Edwins had to finish the buffalo."

"It didn't end there or well, I assume."

"Lucky they weren't both gored. Back at the truck, the client rested the muzzle of the double on his boot tip, apparently to keep it out of the dirt, and snapped the trigger to release the tension on the firing pin spring. A strange and unnecessary move to say the least."

"I can imagine what happened next," I said. "I've been deer hunting with novices more than once who pulled the trigger on an 'empty' chamber, only to have the gun go off."

"Blew three of the fellow's toes off and bloodied Edwins and the trackers with the exploding debris of gravel, boot leather, and bone. They had to air-medivac the client out."

"A classic case of more money than brains, it sounds like," I said.

"Over in Dande, a client shot the arm off an apprentice PH last year. The appy is back now and a fully certified if one armed professional. One must admire his perseverance if not his good sense."

"And buffalo attacks?" I said. "You know, 'the most dangerous game.' "

"Each year there are hunters or PHs injured or killed by buffs throughout Africa. Buffalo have a tremendous capacity to absorb damage and keep going. A lung or heart shot would drop other game, including lion or elephants, in moments. But a buff shot like that can run off some distance and hide for quite a time. They'll be dead at some point, but in the meantime, feeling sick and weak, they'll go into the thickest stuff they can find and wait. When the hunters follow up, the animals seem to sense they don't have the strength to escape and, no doubt feeling cornered and out of options, can summon the reserves to mount a terrific, desperate last charge. They're big and strong enough to kill a man straight away."

"Has it happened here?"

"Last season a colleague, a PH named Owain Lewis, was killed out here by the charge of a wounded buffalo. A nice fellow, a farmer like me whose land had been seized. He turned to professional hunting to eke out some sort of living. Quite a well respected hunter. Anyway, his client had wounded the animal and it took a while to get back on it. Lewis and his apprentice found it in impossibly thick jesse three days later. It was so dense, the animal charged from only feet away, goring and tossing the PH, who broke his neck in the fall. It happened in seconds. No one had a chance to fire. The apprentice couldn't get a shot off until Owain was clear and then killed the buffalo clean enough. By then it was all over for the PH, though."

"The widow-maker," I said.

"Indeed. The most apt name of them all. Professional hunters came from all over Zimbabwe to attend the funeral. A tragic but too familiar loss."

"I suppose it goes without saying one must be extraordinarily careful."

"To be sure. The key is to be certain of your first shot. No *shoot-and-hope*. Then put more lead in him in any manner you can. If I think a wounded buffalo is escaping, I'll shoot, too. And I'll be in front of you for the follow-up. It's for everyone's safety, especially the trackers who must search in the lead. And we certainly don't want an inexperienced client—any client— positioned alone out front with the prospect of a wounded, angry buffalo hidden in the nearest jesse stand. "

Those words would prove telling on our final day as well.

The following morning, the beginning of the second day of our hunt, was much like the first. We scouted the back-trails, walked ridgelines and dry riverbeds, and hiked back into the bush to little-known wet spots tucked in the odd crevice or gully. Wil's knowledge of the Chewore was truly impressive.

We returned to the big floodplain along the M'Kunga we had visited the first morning with the extensive buffalo spoor and scat. Little had changed there, and we saw no new sign. We made our way along the bank of the river, coming upon only a few impala and waterbuck cows with calves. Troops of baboons barked at us occasionally from the wooded hilltops that rose beyond the riverbank. But no buffalo.

It was late in the morning and getting hot as we drove a faint trail through a pass between heavily treed hills. Just as Wil said, "There's a little spring near here worth checking..." a tracker tapped on the roof of the cab. Wil pulled over and we all piled out.

Wil and the trackers, Levitt and Favor, carefully studied the sandy stretch behind the truck. They talked quietly among themselves in what I assume was Shona. I could see buffalo tracks and piles of brown dung along the road. Finally Wil walked casually over to me.

"A fairly large group of buffalo crossed the road here a few hours ago. Sometime earlier this morning. The skin on the dung is still thin and the center is light and moist. Some of the tracks are good sized and may be bulls."

"Do you think they're still close?" I felt a tingle of excitement.

"It's hard to tell. We're entering the hottest part of the day when they don't move a lot. In the early afternoon heat they often bed down in the jesse. It's impossible to get up on them then. The wind is light, and with the buffs not moving to feed or travel to water, the bush is dead quiet. And they're constantly alert, eyes everywhere when they're bedded. I've talked with the guys and we believe it's best to have our lunch break and begin a stalk back here later in the afternoon when it's cooled a bit and the wind has started rustling the trees again. A long shot, but it's our most promising chance."

I was stunned. Our first real sign of a truly huntable buffalo herd, and we were going to have lunch! It seemed completely counterintuitive, unlikely the animals would simply wait for us to return. I knew a man walking at an average pace would cover about three miles an hour. If the tracks were, say, three hours old, and we came back in another three hours—assuming the herd moved only at the pace of a walking man—they would be eighteen miles away by then if they didn't stop to rest. It seemed improbable, but I was paying for Wil's experience and expertise, and decided to go along with his strategy without argument. He had certainly demonstrated a strong work ethic and an impressive knowledge of the area and its animals.

We had a leisurely lunch followed by a siesta in the cool shade of trees and tall brush high on the bank of a sandy river overlooking a tiny waterhole only a few feet across. A parade of baboons, impala, and duiker visited the water, nervously and briefly, as we watched from above. I supposed the prey animals somehow understood their need to visit that isolated bit of water would be known to a lurking leopard or lion as well, and it would be unwise to linger.

It was past three in the afternoon and still hot when we returned to the spot where the buffalo herd had crossed the road. The two trackers took the lead into the bush, followed by Wil then me. Marusi stayed with the truck. Nickie was behind me, and the game ranger, Gibson, took up the very rear as always.

The trackers picked their way slowly through the dry grass and brushy scrub. The trail immediately led at an angle across and up a big hill. It was obvious they were having difficulty keeping the track as they paused frequently, combing the ground with their eyes for long periods and casting to the side or back before continuing on again. Even though we were moving slowly, the steep climb and rough terrain were punishing. Wil was lean and fit, and our entire crew, other than Nickie and me, was tireless. These treks through the hilly bush seemed to be merely another day at the office for them. Levitt must have noticed me struggling with the hike as he walked back and held out his hand.

"Gun, Boss," he said, taking my rifle from me and then assuming the lead once more.

I never asked for help, but he was to do this frequently during long, steep climbs throughout the safari. My loaded rifle with sling and scope weighed well over ten pounds. It made things more bearable, particularly in the suffocating heat, and I truly appreciated his unsolicited consideration.

After about an hour we paused on the backbone of a high, heavily treed ridge. Everyone seemed to mill around, looking here and there in a manner I thought to be aimless. The heat was oppressive, and swarms of tiny mopani flies buzzed about our eyes and nostrils. Like summertime gnats back home, they had no bite but clustered around the face until you swatted them away in frustration. It was clear we were off the track and had little means to pick it up again. My earlier anticipation had given way to disappointment, and I was tired and irritated. Wil, as usual, had said nothing.

We stood around for another several minutes, taking what was obviously a break in the absence of any action or apparent plan. Levitt and Favor finally began talking softly and then approached Wil. After exchanging a few short, quiet words with him, Wil walked over to Nickie and me.

"The guys think they heard something down below in the jesse opposite the back side of this ridge. We'll have a walk down there and take a look. Levitt will go with us, but everyone else is to stay here."

We worked carefully down the brushy hillside. A little swale of dry, brown grass sat at the bottom with a large area of leafless but seemingly impenetrable jesse on the next hillside. This time Wil led, followed by Levitt then me.

As we reached the bottom and approached the edge of the grassy area, I heard a short, loud bellow from the jesse, sounding very close. Then I spotted a few movements of black patches between the jesse branches no more than fifty yards ahead. Everyone stopped and dropped low near the ground, knees bent and heads erect. Wil finally motioned me forward, signaling to stay down and move quietly. Levitt handed my rifle to me, then crept back behind. I had already chambered a round when we left the truck area.

"It's a big herd," Wil whispered. "Sit down on your bum and be ready."

I slowly sat on the ground, legs crossed. I was able to rest my elbows on the knees of my crossed legs, providing quite a bit of support to steady the rifle. I adjusted my angle so the weapon came up quickly and naturally to a position aimed at the closest jesse. I set the scope at 2-power and practiced looking through it to be sure the lenses were clear and my sight-picture steady. The buffalo were still occasionally snorting and bellowing. Several times I saw animals walk between and behind the nearest bushes, but the branches were too dense to get a close enough look to tell if they were cows, calves, or bulls. *This could be it*, I thought.

I felt the wind on my face blowing from ahead and my right, favorable for keeping our scent away from the browsing herd. But occasionally I could feel a breeze on my right or left cheeks, or the back of my neck. Still in the heat of the mid-afternoon, it was becoming variable. I knew Cape buffalo had notoriously sensitive noses and could wind a man at considerably over a hundred yards.

All at once, a loud, rushing noise arose from the jesse. It sounded for all the world like a Chicago elevated train barreling through a station without stopping. The tops of the high jesse bushes vibrated visibly over a surprisingly large area due to the obvious stampede. The buffalo were gone just that quickly!

Wil jumped to his feet and looked up the hill behind us.

"Nickie is fanning her face with her hat!" he hissed. "She spooked those buffalo. They were feeding toward us and would have drifted out of the jesse in another few minutes." He was furious.

"The wind was shifting," I said in a feeble attempt to defend her. "I could feel it on the back of my neck. I'm surprised they didn't take off sooner." I had no idea what caused them to run, but it sounded good to me.

Wil looked up the hill at Nickie and the others. He waved his arms back and forth across his face in the universal sign for *NO—STOP*. Then he pantomimed removing his hat and waving it across his face, shaking his head back and forth to indicate *NO—DON'T DO THIS*.

I have to confess I found his hysterical dramatics hilarious. I, too, was disappointed the herd had stampeded off, but was more caught up in the comedy of the situation. I couldn't wait until he confronted Nickie.

"She can't come on our buffalo stalks anymore," Wil said. "She can remain at the truck with Marusi from now on."

I knew that would be fine with Nickie. She was not athletic and was struggling as much as I with the hundred-degree-plus heat and exertion. She had suggested several times she remain at camp or with the truck, but I had prevailed upon

217

her to join me in the field to share the experience and be our official photographer of sorts.

"Just let me know when you're going to tell her," I said, struggling to suppress a smile. "I want to be far away."

Hell hath no fury like a woman scorned, I thought.

Wil was not amused. He stomped back up the hill, Levitt and I intentionally lagging well behind.

"You waving that hat across your face stampeded the herd." Wil was calmer only by a degree than when he had sounded off to me down below. "They can detect any movement. They were about to feed out of the jesse into the grassy area we had set up on."

"The flies were swarming my face," Nickie said unapologetically. "Everyone was shooing them away. And it's *hot*. I couldn't see a single animal so they certainly couldn't see me." She was civil but defiant.

Wil walked angrily away.

Of course, rather than his irate display of charades and condescending rebuke, he might have simply said, "*Madam Nickie, I know how important it is to John and you to get a buffalo. We were very close a moment ago. I know each of us gets tired and uncomfortable out here amongst the heat and insects, but our chances depend upon everyone remaining absolutely still when game is near. I'm not sure what caused that stampede or if fanning your hat played any role, but we all want to do everything in our power to assure a successful outcome for this safari. I know you want to help in every way possible.*" But he didn't say that. Not Wil.

"The wind shifted," I said to her later, safely out of Wil's earshot, providing an excuse I didn't really believe. "I'm sure they couldn't see anything," I lied. "Did you see his tantrum?"

218

Now I couldn't suppress a grin. "They were ready to take off no matter what."

"I heard this roar," she said. "And all the bushes shook. I asked the men what it was, and Gibson said calmly, 'Buffalo stampeding.' " She was grinning, too.

This time I laughed out loud. "Wil says you're banned from our stalks," I said, still laughing.

We stood collecting ourselves for some time, letting Wil calm down. Several of us were looking in the direction the buffalo had run, to our front-right and up the next hill.

"There they are, right there!" Nickie said, pointing.

Halfway up the facing hill, perhaps a thousand yards distant, the unmistakable dark, black forms of buffalo drifted among the many little clear spots between jesse stands. The ridge upon which we stood was quite high, and the hill in front where the herd milled midway up was considerably higher yet. The whole area, as far as one could see, was hilly to the point of being mountainous in the fashion of the Appalachians or Smoky Mountains of the American South. But the largest by far were two different, very tall, heavily wooded foothills directly to our right—just slightly behind—and several miles distant. And they were to figure into the day's remaining events.

I walked over to Wil. "That wind was mostly from our right," I said. "We could hike half way up the hill straight ahead, then cut directly into the wind and come up behind that herd again. It doesn't look all that far, and the cover would be really good."

He was silent for a long time, looking away. Finally he said, "I don't think so. It's a bigger climb than it looks, and the sun's starting to go down. We should start back for the truck."

I didn't know if he was genuinely concerned, still pouting, or had rejected the notion simply because I, not he, had suggested it. But we quickly got organized and took off down the backside of our ridge in the direction from which we had originally approached.

After several miles, perhaps two-thirds of the way back toward the truck, we found ourselves at the base of the extraordinarily high hill, the tallest that could be seen, the one I had noted earlier. Wil abruptly turned, saying nothing, and led our party directly up the face. When I had suggested before that we climb the lesser grade where we had seen our stampeded buffalo herd stop and begin feeding again, he had said, "*No. It's a bigger climb than it looks and the sun's starting to go down. We should start back for the truck.*" Apparently that didn't hold anymore.

The climb was punishing. Not only was the mountain face long and steep, but the terrain was irregular, undulating with intervening ridges and dips. We had to traverse stone shelves, jump fallen logs, and scale down into steep, rocky depressions before resuming our ascent among more stones and boulders on the far side. Whenever we descended an extreme down-slope, I felt my toes jam forward painfully against the front of my boot. That evening I would find a toenail had loosened and blackened, engorged with blood beneath. A day or two later it would come off completely. My many foot blisters would have the skin peeled painfully back and ooze runny, pink lymph and blood. But for now we carried on.

It must have taken forty-five minutes to reach the top of a secondary summit, positioned about two hundred yards from the absolute pinnacle.

"Wait here," Wil said, the first words he had uttered since we left the ridge where we had heard and later seen our buffalo herd. He, Levitt, and Favor set off for the highest point of the hilltop, which rose just ahead.

Nickie and I sat down to rest, exhausted and demoralized. We watched as Wil and the two trackers reached the wooded peak and stopped, peering off into the distance. Then they stooped low among the brush, craning carefully for a better look. Wil used his field glasses briefly. After a few moments of this, Favor returned and told us to follow him forward.

We formed a line behind Favor, making our way along a narrow, precarious game trail that in places was barely etched along the steep side of the summit. The drop down the mountain was no more than twenty degrees from the vertical for at least several hundred feet before the grade shallowed a bit after that. The rolling hills of the Chewore we had driven for two days now stretched out below as far as we could see. They looked tiny compared with their high, imposing appearance when we had been navigating them.

Nickie progressed tenuously, gripping the handholds provided by any sapling or bush as she went. Game ranger Gibson, AK47 in tow, was behind her, holding her elbow and reaching in front to clear brush from her path with his arm as she went.

"Oh, thank you," she said to him at one point.

"Your welfare is my duty, Madam," he replied.

She smiled broadly.

We all paused at one point to admire the beautiful vista.

Nickie stared into the distance. "There's a buffalo herd on that plain way out there."

Even on our evening nature drives back in Michigan, she was always the first to spot game.

"That is in Dande, the other side of the M'Kunga," Gibson said. "More than five kilometers distant."

The animals in the huge herd looked like black dots, no larger than the mopani gnats that continued to harry our faces. Brief segments of the sandy M'Kunga bed appeared between the solid forested stretches as tiny, beige lines etched on the landscape.

We approached the highest point of the final summit where Wil and Levitt waited. Wil held up his hand traffic-cop style to halt the group about twenty yards back, then pointed to me and waved me forward. I could see the sticks had been set up.

I bent low and crept forward the final few feet. Levitt had my rifle and handed it to me. I looked over the edge ahead at a herd of about twenty buffalo slowly crossing a saddle between ours and the next rise, only sixty yards away. The buffalo were all cows, juveniles, and calves meandering slowly, clearly unaware of our presence.

We watched for about ten minutes.

"No bulls," Wil said. "Come."

He took off across the back face of the summit just slightly below the peak, working his way to the opposite side. There we saw yet another group, the advance element of the first, no doubt, beginning a descent from the pass. They were perhaps ninety yards away, easily within shooting range. Again, no bulls.

Damn! I thought, feeling a surge of admiration. *How could Wil have known they'd be up here?* We had driven and searched for countless hours, for two days, checking sign and likely spots, without seeing much for most of that time. First, yesterday, we jumped two scrum cap dagga-boys near dusk by a spring Wil just had a feeling about. Then this afternoon he put us on two herds—three if one counts this last, forward element—within an hour with a cockamamie strategy of climbing the highest and most unlikely mountain imaginable. It's true they all may have been part of the first group we stampeded out of the jesse, but still...

This guy is amazing! I was becoming a believer.

It was nearly dark as we left the mountain and completely black when we arrived back at the truck.

"What made you think to climb that mountain and check the pass?" I asked Wil when we were back in the truck and underway again.

"That herd we jumped from the jesse was moving in the general direction of the only water around here," he said. "They can't go without water for very long, particularly at this time of the year. It didn't make sense to try and sneak up behind them. Once they've been startled, they're on the alert and always looking back. We'd have been bound to jump one unintentionally, likely a cow or calf, trying to move up through that thick brush. Stampede the whole herd again. And sorting a bull out of that mess would have been impossible. The only way to the water was over that fairly open pass. That's the direction they seemed to be headed."

I resolved not to question Wil's strategies again, even silently in the recesses of my own mind.

Nine — Fear and Death Above the M'Kunga

The next evening we came upon yet another buffalo herd, late, just after the setting sun had brought on dusk. We surprised them, and in a rarity, I was the first to spot them.

We had been driving generally alongside the dry M'Kunga River over a track across the very back of a broad, miles-long floodplain. The trail approached an area of dense jesse brush when I spotted a cow and calf dash across the cut the two-track made through the bush ahead, stop on the other side, then run back again.

"There!" I said. "Two buffalos came out of the jesse and onto the road headed toward the river, saw us, and went back."

Wil stopped the truck and we all got out. They were the only buffalos we had spotted since the group going through the mountain pass the evening before. Of course, for three days now we had been seeing and taking plenty of game—the bushbuck, impala ram, and our duiker—as well as coming upon the first of the kudus. Then there had been the eland stalks, the wild dogs, plenty of sow warthogs, baboons everywhere, and even a fat, scuttling black-and-white-and-gray honey badger. And we had seen buffalos up close, including these, each evening.

We grabbed our rifles. Wil looked all around us in an unhurried manner, then took off suddenly at a trot toward the

M'Kunga about a half mile distant. I followed close behind, trailed by Levitt and Gibson. The others remained at the truck.

We ran crouching through the open scrub and brown grass before dropping down into a shallow, sandy gully on the back side of a little raised dune that ran along the floodplain parallel to the river. We crept up the other side and peered over the top. A huge herd of buffalo stood in the dying light just before the riverbank nearest us, about two hundred yards away. Wil ducked down and led us to our left until we had placed thicker brush between the buffalos and us. Then we made our way over the dune and toward the herd using the heavy scrub for concealment. About seventy five yards from the river, we stopped again.

The buffalos had moved across and were nearly to the bank on the far side, about a hundred eighty yards ahead. They showed no sign of having seen us. It had grown so dark they looked like a swarming, moving shadow against the lighter background of the river-bottom sand.

"They're going into Dande now," Wil said. "Too bad. There's a nice bull in there."

I put my rifle to my shoulder to take a look through the scope. "I'm not going to shoot, just check them out." I could distinguish the individual animals, but with the darkness, not clearly enough to see which was the bull. They were all moving away.

By the time we arrived back at the road, it had become nearly black. All at once we heard the distinct sounds of large animals—the loud rustling of brush and cracking of sticks— just off to one side in the bordering jesse thicket. Wil froze, as did everyone else. Visibility was limited to a few feet.

"Let's wait," he said. "I don't want to walk into that group of elephants in the dark."

I recalled the tusker silently coming for us earlier, ears flared and stare fixed, as we had made our way through his territory following the three kudu bulls. I imagined him moving toward us, invisible this time in the dark, and felt a surge of uneasiness.

Wil had taken his handheld radio from his belt and was talking. I was glad to see the lights of the truck approaching a few minutes later.

Over the next several days we continued our buffalo search but were to see no more for a while, although we were fully occupied taking my waterbuck, kudu bull, and that hapless old baboon. We spent the mornings sneaking into our hyena hide, and the hours prior to lunch and in the late evening checking the leopard baits, which by then numbered six. And of course we were always looking for Nyati. Nickie seemed to enjoy the African landscape. In our down moments she occupied herself photographing fish eagles, marabou storks, a host of other birds, and the landscape with its many beautiful flowers, trees, and shrubs. The Chewore vistas were as varied as they were magnificent and made fine photographic subjects.

It was well into our safari, days after last coming across buffalo on the floodplain of the M'Kunga, when we all had gathered around the fire pit back at Chenje in the early evening for snacks and a sundowner before cleaning up for dinner. Matt, our apprentice PH, had arrived in his safari vehicle late and joined our group just as we were getting ready to return to the tent to change before eating.

"I've checked all the baits this afternoon and pulled the game camera chips," he said excitedly.

"Activity?" asked Wil.

"Several have been fed on by leopards. Lions managed to pull one down and drag it off. I hung a fresh kudu leg on that one. And the one on the bank of the M'Kunga had been taken down by someone. The chain that secured it on the limb was missing."

"Lions hitting a bait isn't all bad," Wil said to me. "It masks human odor and makes things seem a bit more normal to the leopards. Happens all the time in the wild, lions steal-ing a leopard's meal like that. We may still see something interesting at that bait." He turned to Matt. "Have you checked the chips yet?"

"Not yet. Let's have a look." He placed one of the chips in a camera with a viewer he had brought with him.

The photos were time and date stamped. There were several shots of a gorgeous leopard feeding in the dark at one bait.

"A female," Wil said. "You can tell by her size. She's been coming in the middle of the night."

Another series revealed a female with a half-grown cub, most in the dark but one just as light was creeping across the sky. They were beautiful as well.

Then Matt scrolled to a heavy-bodied, thick-necked cat.

"A nice male!" Wil and Matt commented almost simultaneously.

"Look at that tom."

"Damn!" Mat said. "It's the set along the M'Kunga, the one where someone stole the chain and dropped the meat. It's doubtful the cat will be back soon now that everything has been disturbed." He had turned to me. "Wouldn't you know that's the only one hit by a shootable male. Bad luck."

"Go back in the morning," Wil said, "and hang some fresh bait. It's still worth a try."

Matt continued to advance the viewer through the re-maining photos.

"Hey," he said. "Here are the guys who did it."

230

There were several daylight photos of a small group of black Africans at the bait tree. The cameras, carefully hidden at each site, were motion activated and designed to operate silently, day or night, just like the ones we used to scout deer back in Michigan. There were clear pictures of the faces of three men, some smiling or laughing.

"I'm going to take these over to the wildlife department up by the Zambezi tomorrow," Matt said. "After I re-hang that bait in the morning and reset all the cameras. Maybe they'll recognize these guys or be able to track them down."

"Be sure to bring your radio," Wil said. "We'll plan to meet somewhere before lunch and you can bring us up to date on everything."

Dinner that evening was the delicious, elegantly prepared affair to which we had grown accustomed. After we had finished dessert and the conversation slowed to the point no one was talking, Sharon finally spoke again.

"It's such a shame your bait was disturbed," she said. "Particularly the only one being visited by a big tom."

"If that's the worst of what happens, I'm a happy man," I said. "This safari has been wonderful. I'm sure it will work out fine."

"There's so much petty theft and poaching," she said. "They try to stop it. The wildlife department patrols, and the safari operators pay rewards to locals for collecting snares or turning in violators. But the people are so poor, it's difficult to prevent."

"I can imagine there aren't many opportunities to earn money for these rural tribal people," I said.

"Oh, no. The average monthly income in all Zimbabwe is well under sixty dollars a month. And that includes the well-paid bureaucrats, the military, and police—government jobs handed out to the families and cronies of those in power. If one were to consider the incomes of only the others, it would be far, far below that number. We, as the safari operator in this concession, are one of the few sources of jobs for the villagers."

I had noticed shortly after our arrival the camp staff numbered eighteen—four whites consisting of Jerry, Sharon, Wil, and Matt—and fourteen blacks. Nickie and I were the only guests, our fees paying for them all.

"I see you employ a sizable staff," Nickie said. "And it pays off in the quality of the experience here. Everything has been wonderful."

"It goes beyond just this camp," Sharon said. "We employ scores of workers to maintain the hunting trails, especially after the summer rains wash out everything. Each camp has a full staff, and we retain a local watchman at each when there aren't guests in all of them, like now. Safari hunting is a major source of employment for these people. There are few other alternatives."

"How about photo safaris or eco-tourism?" I asked. "Isn't that a growing area of employment?"

"Not really. Most of that is around Victoria Falls. There is so much public land closed to hunting that goes completely unused. The Hwange and Matobo parks. Mana Pools is sparsely used by tourists and most are Zimbabweans there. No hunting, of course, in any of them. There are plenty of venues for the few tourists away from the falls. We have far more parks than interested tourists. You hunters are a completely different market. Without hunting, the incomes and lives of hundreds would be devastated."

"Everyone I've come in contact with works hard and does an amazing job. They are all competent, eager, and a pleasure to be with."

"Speaking of that," Sharon went on, "many of our guests want to leave a gratuity of some kind for the staff before they depart." It was nearing the end of the safari, and she was seeing to loose ends. "It's entirely voluntary and at the client's complete discretion, but it has become somewhat customary and is deeply appreciated by everyone who serves you. It's an important source of their income. I know our booking agent stateside provides guests with some written guidelines since it's frequently asked about. If that's something you feel you'd like to do, I can give you envelopes with the names of the staff members on your last full day here. It's up to you."

"By all means," I said. "The staff has been remarkable. We'd love to remember them with something."

We had excused ourselves and headed back toward our tent for the evening when Wil walked up beside me.

"If you decide to give the guys a tip, I know they'd appreciate it," he said.

I'm sure he knew I planned to do just that.

"But don't give a lot to Gibson. Those government game rangers are completely useless. Always have their hand out. Unfortunately, it's the law and we're stuck with them."

I recalled Gibson had been the one to pick up the track on my wounded baboon when the others lost it. And he'd been the first to spot my fallen waterbuck. He had found a lost track on other occasions, as well. It was he who had initially and enthusiastically congratulated me when I had been redeemed from abysmal shooting by my first trophy, the bushbuck. And he who had noted my marksmanship on the kudu bull at over a hundred ten yards. "Your welfare, Madam Nickie, is my duty," he had said as he helped and protected my wife making her way along the narrow game trail perched precariously on the side of a cliff atop the *Mountain of Doom*, as Nickie and I jokingly called it, the one we had painfully scaled behind Wil. Gibson—helpful, articulate, knowledgeable, and experienced.

"Haven't given it much thought at this point," I said to Wil. And I hadn't. "I suspect we'll stick pretty close to the written guidelines, though." But I knew Gibson would be treated every bit as well as any member of the field staff.

In our tent that evening I had difficulty falling asleep. I'm one who dreams often and vividly, but who seldom remembers even the clearest or most remarkable dream for more than a day. Still, over the last several years I recalled a kind of dream I had again and again, one not really recurring in the sense the same details are repeated time after time, but more a dream with an oddly common theme but varying circumstances. In it I would be going about my business, perhaps at home, at the shopping mall, or work, or taking a walk. But an animal would always be strangely present—on one occasion a bear, a wolf on another, and then a hyena. Intimidating animals by their nature, to be sure, but in the dream they never moved to harm or even threaten me. They simply were always there, facing me, whatever I did or whichever way I turned. Watching and waiting.

And lying on my bed that evening, trying to drop into sleep—half sleeping and half awake—in our dark, comfortable tent on the bank of the Chenje River, well into our safari and anxious to resume our buffalo hunt in the morning, I had such a dream. I was working in our yard back in Michigan. This time the animal was a Cape buffalo bull. Not huge, but muscular and fit, with elegant spreading and symmetrical upward-curling horns. His boss was distinctive and protruding. His tough, dark, dirty hide rippled from the massive bones and chiseled muscles contained beneath. As in all these dreams, the animal turned slowly to face and stare at me no matter where I moved. When I left the area, he would suddenly be there with me once more. His expression was not so much threatening as contemptuous and focused intensely on me. And I couldn't possibly have imagined that this time, with this dream, I would face that very buffalo in much the same setting the next afternoon.

In the morning we set off again through the hills and across the savannahs of the Chewore searching for buffalo sign. The sun just beginning to creep over the horizon was a dull burnt orange, the sky a line of pink just above and extending to each side. The air in the faint dawn light appeared to shimmer.

"There'll be a hunter's sky today," Wil commented absently as we drove along.

I looked at him quizzically.

"When the heat haze is so thick the rising sun looks dark orange and the morning sky an odd red like this. It means it's going to be bloody hot. The game will lay up much longer in the heat of this kind of day but will then have to move to water in the late afternoon when it starts to yield a bit. More likely to ambush something going for their drink just before evening under a hunter's sky."

Even though we had only a few days of hunting left, I was more excited than concerned about getting my buffalo. We had, after all, come upon them with some regularity. And the safari overall had been anything but uneventful. I had already taken six animals, most of them impressive trophies, and we had seen many more. If anything, I was overwhelmed by the action.

It was getting hot and close to noon when Wil picked up his handheld radio and spoke into it.

"Matt's on his way back from the wildlife department camp. We're going to meet him on the trail up ahead beyond where he just finished fixing that leopard bait on the M'Kunga. The one visited by the tom and then disturbed by our chain thieves."

About twenty minutes later Matt came rumbling down the track toward us in his safari vehicle. Two camp staffers were in the back. Each vehicle squeezed to a different side until they stopped with the cabs close beside one another.

"We hung some kudu ribs and reset the cameras. No sign of new leopard tracks, though. I'm doubtful."

"I thought as much," Wil said. "Worth a go, anyway."

"Showed our pictures to the rangers at the wildlife service," Matt said. "They don't recognize the fellows, but I'll join their poaching patrol this afternoon. See if we can't track them back to their village. The chief ranger said if we come upon them armed in the Chewore, we're to shoot to kill."

Wil nodded. Just then one of our trackers leaned around from the back and said something to Wil in African.

"We'll see you this evening," he said to Matt. He put the truck in gear, and we continued slowly down the two-track.

"The trackers said they thought they heard something up ahead in the brush. We'll move up a ways and check."

After only a hundred yards we stopped and got out in a small clearing. Elsewhere the jesse was thick and bare-limbed on both sides of the trail. Wil and the trackers moved off cautiously to one side of the little road and I followed at the rear. We had walked only some forty yards from the truck when everyone stopped and dropped to a squat. They ducked low to look under the willow limbs and listened carefully. I saw and heard nothing. After a few minutes, we returned quietly to the truck.

Another dead end, I thought before Wil spoke.

"Definitely buffs in that jesse. They weren't moving and in all likelihood will bed in this insufferable midday heat. It would be folly to walk in there now. We'll have our lunch and come back around three. They should have started feeding again by then. There're a few damp elephant digs in the shade of the high cut banks of the M'Kunga at the base of these hills, some with little puddles still in their bottoms—the only water around here. They'll need to feed down toward that before evening on this kind of day. Is that all right?"

It was the first time Wil had asked my opinion on anything during the entire safari.

The thought of simply walking away from buffalo, particularly with only a few hunting days left, was difficult. But I recalled his unlikely-seeming strategies over the past days that had always put us on game in the end.

"Sure," I said. "Just about everything you've suggested has worked for us. Let's do it."

We drove several miles through and down the hills, over the riverbank, and back up through the dry, soft sand of the M'Kunga river bottom for another mile. Then we turned up into a narrow, tree-lined dry creek bed and stopped in the shade about seventy yards upstream from where it had joined the river. A nice breeze blew across the riverbed and directly up the creek, providing some level of relief from the heat. The staff set up folding canvas camp chairs for Nickie and me and spread our lunch on the tops of coolers before us. Wil, Nickie, and I ate together, but as always the black field staff had leftovers off by themselves, down where the creek joined the river, watching for game as they rested and waited. After lunch Nickie and I took brief naps in our camp chairs as best we could. At one point, a parade of guinea fowl marched from the woods, across the creek mouth, and out into the M'Kunga where they strutted back and forth in the sand. I was aware those buffalos were likely still up above in the hills, and the waiting was difficult.

Nickie was wearing her watch, so I knew it was just after three when the staff began gathering everything and stowing it in the back of our truck. We took our rifles, and I loaded a round, safety *on*, as Wil, Levitt, me, Favor, and Gibson—in that order—set off down the little creek, across the wide, scorching hot bed of the M'Kunga, and toward the sharply rising, sun-baked hillside above its opposite bank. Nickie and Marusi remained with the truck in the relative coolness of the little tree-lined streambed. Each day that we had lunch at one of the camps, I checked the thermometers that sat in the shade before setting out for the afternoon hunt. The most extreme reading had been one hundred six, but it was far hotter today. The sun was high, the air above the sand of the riverbed wavered dream-like under the oppressive temperature below the hunter's sky.

The climb up the hill was steep and tiring in the heat, through a mixture of big mopanes, scruffy mopani bushes, thornbush, and jesse. We hiked uphill at a brisk if measured pace for at least a mile before stopping in a small clearing by a hunting road. I recognized it as the spot we had checked out before lunch to scout the buffalo the trackers had heard in the jesse. Everyone paused, stooped, craned, and peered.

Then Wil, saying nothing as usual, took off at a fast trot away from the jesse thicket that spread roughly parallel to the M'Kunga, the river now out of sight far below, and across the two-track, moving away from where we had found the herd in the morning and deeper into the bush. After ten minutes he turned hard left to parallel the road and river, both invisible to us now. We continued for another half mile before he turned back again in the direction of the road and jesse.

As he approached the trail and brush, he became cautious once more, searching carefully. Levitt was with him and I bent low a few yards behind. It was obvious they were looking at or listening to something, but I saw and heard nothing. Then they scuttled in a low squat back toward me before standing and heading off at a good pace away from the road and jesse once more. We repeated the paralleling, moving up, searching, and retreating maneuver once again. The third time, as we had moved back across the road and to the edge of the heavier bush I imagined held the buffalos, Wil continued looking for a long time. I knew there was something promising out there as he put his field glasses to his eyes. Then he set the sticks and waved me up with his fingers.

"There's a good bull near the front," he said. "They're milling a bit, but it's about the third animal from the lead."

It was the first I had heard him speak to anyone since leaving the creek bed more than an hour and a half earlier.

We had been squatting, but I rose slowly and placed the forestock of my rifle in the pocket formed by the crossing of the three sticks near the top. I adjusted their height to a steadier shooting position, as I had learned to do after missing the first impala ram. A herd of buffalo stretched from left to right before me. There was less jesse here and more mixed brush with scattered big mopanes. Broad open areas between the trees and bushes provided a good view of the animals as they grazed across my field of view, moving to my right.

I looked at the lead buffalo, a big, full-horned cow without a boss, and counted two then three back. The third and fourth were a cow and calf passing other animals. I checked through my scope to be sure. The fifth back was a juvenile, a half-grown cow. The next few animals were mostly obscured by brush. The herd was moving as it grazed, buffalos shifting positions as some stopped to eat while others moved forward. They seemed completely unaware of our presence.

"Between the two trees," Wil said, realizing I hadn't seen the bull yet. There were trees and buffalos everywhere.

I looked at the next animal on the left, the next one back. It was the closest, directly in front, and was stopped, facing toward us. It stood motionless between two mopane trees about seventy yards to our front.

It was staring exactly as in my dream the night before. Big, thick, protruding bosses crowned its forehead. Its head was held high, the very top roughly level with its big, long back. The horns dropped down, then curled out and up in perfect symmetry, ending in sharp, shiny and inward-turning points. The ears were partially up and out to its sides in the alert position, not drooping as were those of the big cows. The tips of the ears ended well before the upward rise of the outermost portion of its horns. The bull was quartering toward me, facing almost head-on but with enough of a cant in its position to expose its back flank and reveal a penis near the rear of his underbelly. His muscles were full and chiseled beneath the dark hide.

It's been famously said a bull buffalo looks at you like you owe him money, and that was true enough with this one. His stare revealed neither fright nor hostility, but appeared more as a superior and surly glower, the animal seeming unthreatened but confident in its ability to handle any trouble this small, pathetic intruder might bring. His gaze was unsettling, as it had been in my dream.

I picked up the center of the buffalo's chest in the crosshairs. Still, Wil had said the third one from the front and this one was only slightly farther back in the shifting herd. I wasn't sure.

"The one I'm looking at is directly in front. Between the two trees," I said.

"Yes, the bull between the trees," Wil said urgently.

"The one closest to us. He's looking straight at us."

"No," Wil said. "He's looking forward, and his head is partially behind that...no, wait. Yes, I see, he's looking at us now."

"Closest, the bull looking at us, standing between two trees. I can see his bosses and penis."

"Yes," Wil said impatiently. "It's the only bull in the herd. Between the trees, looking at us."

"I'm sure it's a bull," I said. "Should I shoot?"

All the other animals had stopped and were now staring in our direction. I was certain they were about to bolt.

"Yes. That's it. *Shoot!*"

With the bull's quartering stance, I realized a center-chest hold, if pulled accidentally only slightly to my right, would risk angling between the brisket and away-shoulder, mostly missing the heart and lungs and raising the chances of a dangerously wounded Cape buffalo. I moved the crosshairs over a few inches, between the brisket and shoulder positioned more forward and to my left, steadied the rifle, exhaled, drew a half-breath and held it, then smoothly squeezed off a shot.

As the magnum jumped and roared, I lost sight of the bull and most everything else. When the rifle came down a half second later and I could again see over the top, all the animals were running to my right in a black, surging jumble. It was impossible to pick out the bull at which I had fired. As they stampeded across the face of the hill and just slightly down toward the M'Kunga, they compressed into a dense, shifting black gob. All the buffalos were gone in seconds, and it was strangely serene once again.

Everyone was oddly quiet for several moments.

"It didn't look hit," Wil said.

"I had a pretty solid hold on his chest," I said.

"I didn't hear the bullet impact. Are you sure you hit it?"

"Pretty sure." *How could I possibly miss a standing Cape buffalo bull at seventy yards shooting at my seventh trophy in a week—all previous ones smaller and most at longer ranges—from perfectly aligned sticks?* I didn't realize at the time my rifle was a few inches high, as I would learn after the hunt had ended, but that would not be enough to ruin a shot on a buffalo presenting as huge and stable a target as did this one.

We all moved down to the area where the herd had been. The trackers—everyone—searched the ground methodically. No blood or hair. No sign of a hit of any kind.

Levitt and Favor led us along the track the buffalos had taken. Their compressed hoof prints and the trampled ground were obvious. We worked along their trail for about twenty minutes, about three hundred fifty yards or roughly a quarter mile by my estimate. The trackers would cast to the left or right occasionally to see if an animal had straggled or stumbled on the edge of the herd. The bush had thinned, but there was thicker jesse just ahead as we paused to consider our next move.

"You're sure you hit something," Wil said, more as a statement seeking a reassuring response than a question. "We can't find anything."

I was beginning to doubt myself.

"Wait here," he said. "The guys and I will double back to be sure an animal didn't cut off to the side back there. They do that sometimes if they're wounded, break away from the rest of the herd. We checked that while moving down here, but we need to be certain."

The junior tracker, Favor, waited with me, unarmed. All the others disappeared back up the hill. I knew I couldn't have missed that buffalo, and was struck by the fact I was alone but for the young, inexperienced, gunless tracker—with every possibility there was a wounded bull Cape buffalo hidden and seething in the dense jesse that stretched ahead. *Don't want an inexperienced client—any client—alone out front with a wounded buff in the jesse*, Wil had said a few days earlier. And there I was, imagining his charge from the brush and what I would do. I had reloaded after my shot and now brought my rifle to the front, finger on the trigger and thumb on the safety. I waited.

About fifteen minutes had passed when Wil and the others returned.

"We didn't find anything back there."

Everyone was just standing around, waiting. Wil lit a cigarette. No one made eye contact with me.

It was Gibson, the despised game ranger, who moved forward toward the leading edge of the thick jesse stand that stretched as far as one could see. Gibson, the optimist, thinking outside the box, with his positive attitude and friendly disposition. Gibson, who liked and generally wished to help people. Who liked and helped me.

He moved up about thirty yards and a few yards to our left, then stooped to better see beneath the overhanging jesse bows. He stretched his neck and head forward, paused, and pointed with his finger.

We all rushed over. I squatted and looked beneath the jesse in the direction he was pointing. There, some eighty odd yards ahead, lay the unmistakable black carcass of a Cape buffalo.

We quickly moved up through the jesse stand, stopping about thirty feet from the big animal lying lifeless on his side. Wil approached the downed buffalo carefully and nudged his head with the barrel of his rifle.

"He's a bull all right, but not the one I wanted you to shoot. He's a younger one."

I surprised myself with the overwhelming feelings of joy and accomplishment that swept through me. I was ecstatic, beaming I'm sure from ear to ear. I walked up near the animal to admire him. He was as magnificent in death as he had been staring sullenly at me up near the crest of the hill a few minutes before. He had gone perhaps four hundred yards before collapsing in the thick brush. I knew an average human track runner could cover a hundred yards in just over ten seconds. With the speed at which that herd took off at my shot, it couldn't have been over forty-five seconds, well under a minute, for my buffalo to run down here and die in this jesse stand. I was glad it had been quick.

"Nickie's going to go crazy." I meant to say it to myself but realized I had said it aloud.

I moved closer to the bull and inspected him carefully. My shot had hit very near my precise point of aim, slightly above by only a few inches and perhaps an inch, if that, to the left. The bloody wound on his chest between the brisket and the animal's right shoulder displayed the track of the bullet on his hide. It had entered from the front, angling in such a way it would travel through its body back and across to the organs behind on the other side. It was clear the right lung had been raked from front to back, the crossing bullet probably hitting the rearward portion of the left lung as well, and going on deep into the body through its liver and beyond. There was no exit wound. I doubt the bull ever really knew what hit him.

My spirits were soaring, the adrenalin doing its work more so than during the stalk or the shot. I had thought upon our arrival in Africa taking a buffalo was secondary to experiencing the bush and its animals. But I understood then I had been wrong. This was the thrilling and fulfilling culmination that had turned our safari into an unforgettable experience.

"We try not to shoot the younger ones," Wil said in his scolding tone.

"Look, Wil," I said, grinning. I was not about to allow his condescension to dampen my moment. "Shit happens. I know shooting old animals is important to you. And it's good with me, too. But I described what I was looking at in detail three times so you'd understand. And I asked for your permission to shoot."

"I was talking about the older one between the tree and the bush."

This was the first he had mentioned *bush*. It had been "between the two trees."

"You said it was the only bull in the herd. I saw the bosses and penis sheath on this one right away."

"The older bull was farther forward, behind the brush. He's the one I wanted you to take."

"You might have said as much, Wil. I'd have been glad to do it. But I didn't see any animal in that herd larger than this one. And this one was clearly a bull."

"The older ones aren't necessarily always bigger."

"For my money, I shot the bull I wanted—the one I described in detail and you cleared me to shoot. If there was a miscommunication...well...you need to be more careful next time. But I'm here to tell you I couldn't be happier. This is what I came for." I think I was close to laughing, not at Wil but purely from joy and excitement. "I'm sorry if you're upset, but I'm the happiest man in Africa."

At that moment a visible change came over Wil. A smile spread across his face, something that had not previously occurred while we took game together. He spontaneously clasped my shoulder, another first.

"You came here to take your buffalo and you did it," he blurted, no longer measuring his words. "You kept pace during our climb and while we maneuvered in on that herd. It wasn't an easy thing, especially for a man who has reached seventy and has had health issues. And your shot was spot on. It was quite the achievement."

He was grinning the whole time, his demeanor all at once joyful and spontaneous, like mine. It was as if the death of that nyati in the thick jesse in the hills above the M'Kunga had caused something in Wil and me to die along with it. For

246

Wil, it seemed to be the awful weight of command, the fear of failure, purged by my joy at taking my buffalo bull. A perfect completion of our safari. It was as if the anger and discontent that seemed to simmer beneath Wil's surface had died along with that animal.

And for me the thing that died on the hillside was the fear that I, battling cancer and reaching seventy, had passed a tipping point. That I no longer could do the things I loved or achieve the things I once had. I felt redeemed and resurrected by the sacrifice of my beautiful Cape buffalo bull. And I somehow knew my strange dreams had become a thing of the past.

"It was an exciting kill," Wil grinned, "with its twists and turns."

"Fear and death in the hills above the M'Kunga," I laughed. Perhaps I should have phrased it ... *the death of fear*.

Wil lifted his radio to call in Marusi with Nickie and the truck. I couldn't wait for her to arrive.

Ten — The End of a Thing

The next day everyone was more relaxed and cheerful.   Wil's underlying edge appeared to have
evaporated.   The field staff riding behind in the truck bed
seemed happier as well.

"You've had your way with the game in the Chewore,"
Wil smiled as we set out a little later in the morning following
a more leisurely breakfast.

I had taken my bushbuck, a nice impala ram, the truly
impressive waterbuck, such a noble kudu bull, an elegant little
duiker, and the crowning achievement, a beautiful Cape buffalo bull. The sad old baboon and the missed opportunity on a
warthog boar had been afterthoughts. Hyena and leopard had
been added after the safari began at Wil's suggestion and were
never my goal, although baiting and hunting them had added a
fascinating dimension. And driving up to meet Matt by the
disturbed tom-leopard bait had ironically led to our discovery
of the buffalo in the jesse and my kill later that afternoon. The
Chewore had already exceeded all my expectations and hopes.

"Would you care to try for a zebra? There aren't a lot,
but we do come across them, and they make an impressive
trophy."

We hadn't seen zebra at all, but the idea seemed exotic.
"Sure."

We spent the day driving and scouting the more open
savannahs, avoiding the thick bush, river bottoms, and springs
tucked back in the hidden gullies. At one point we stopped

near a towering baobab tree—the "tree of life"—with its massively thick, smooth and soaring trunk topped by a spreading cluster of huge, crooked branches.

"The locals use the fruit," Wil offered. "The pulp can be eaten outright, made into porridge, or used as a thickener in other dishes." He sent Favor to climb up and bring back the football-like, dark green pod. Wil broke it open and Nickie and I sampled the bland but slightly sweet white, pulpy contents.

Lunch back at the Chenje Camp was more drawn out than usual and followed by a nap. In the evening we drove the open floodplains along the M'Kunga, seeing plenty of impala, kudu,waterbuck cows with their calves, and warthog sows bouncing along with piglets in parade. As dusk was arriving, we stopped on the riverbank.

"Thought you may want to have a look at one of the tribal villages in the Dande communal area," Wil said. "There are hundreds scattered throughout. Favor is from one much like this very near here."

On a small, grassy plain above the far bank, only two hundred yards off, sat the village of five crude structures. The small, round living huts were made of mud walls and thatch roofs. A little, square animal stockade of vertical sticks enclosed a tiny thatched barn of sorts in its center. A band of five goats browsed uncontained in the low grass and brush between the dwellings and the river. A single clothesline held a few white and some brightly colored items. Three or four black natives stood staring across the river at these odd, suspicious intruders. No power lines, roads, wells, or vehicles of any kind—not even a wheelbarrow or bicycle—were anywhere to be seen. Once again I was reminded of the poverty and resilience of these native African people. I felt grateful for their contribution to my magnificent safari experience and hoped they benefitted in turn.

"We'll only hunt a half-day tomorrow," Wil said on the way back to camp.

Tomorrow would be our last day before leaving early the following morning for our charter to Victoria Falls and some traditional sightseeing.

"Paperwork to complete in the afternoon. All your trophies must be listed for export, tax forms, fee statements filled out and the like. You'll need to review and sign everything. Takes some time. And it's poor form to hunt the last afternoon in any event. I've seen game wounded late in the final day near dark, with the client leaving the next morning and not available to properly recover it. Causes all kinds of havoc."

The last morning of hunting was spent in a relaxed, unhurried search for zebra. Wil stopped the truck at one point on a ridge looking out over a vast, scenic savannah with the wall of the Great Escarpment marking its southern border in the far distance.

We walked to the crest to better see its base. At that moment a group of five eland exploded from the thin bush below and ran at a frantic trot directly away. Wil set up the sticks but said nothing.

I watched as the eland put several hundred yards between us, climbed the face of the next ridge, and turned ninety degrees to our right, running broadside across the ridge top in the distance.

"At least three hundred yards out," Wil said.

I placed my rifle on the sticks as I had done so many times before over the last ten days. The four lead animals were cows, but the fifth and last was a huge bull.

"They're bigger than buffalo," Wil said. "That bull is over two thousand pounds."

I recalled some of the ballistics information I had learned about my .375 magnum. For a rifle properly zeroed at one hundred yards, the bullet drop at two-hundred was about six inches and fifteen inches at three hundred give or take. And I knew the required lead on a running animal was substantial at the range and the speed with which those eland were moving. Still, the bull offered a huge target.

I pulled the crosshairs up and forward until they were centered on the top of the big eland's forehead, several feet in front of his shoulder and a like distance above the sweet spot at mid-chest level. The rifle was swinging smoothly to keep pace with the moving antelope, the largest kind in the world. My sight picture was steady. I placed my finger on the trigger and continued to swing. I knew I could make the shot.

But I never moved my finger to push the safety *off*. After a few moments, all the eland ran down the end of the ridge, disappearing from view behind it. Wil was smiling, seeming to know what I had been thinking. He said nothing. And as I write these finishing words on this journal, several months after our return from Africa, my only regret of the entire safari was deliberately foregoing that shot at the eland bull. With my safari finally concluded, we headed back to camp.

Eleven — A New Beginning

After lunch back at camp, Nickie and I relaxed, read a little, and socialized with camp manager Sharon. Our hunting was through, and Wil busied himself with the paperwork.

It was mid-afternoon when the skinners brought the fleshed and boiled skulls of our trophies with horns attached and arranged them in a display on the lawn against the backdrop of the Chenje. The men stood proudly at parade rest behind the array, feet spread and hands clasped low behind their backs. The skulls were brilliant white as if they had been baking under the sun of some desert for years, and the horns were dark black and cleaned of the dirt from the bush. The skinners—rugged, scruffy appearing men compared with our starched and pressed waiters—wore wrinkled shorts and stained T-shirts. Still it was an impressive sight and a statement on the tough, strong people of the Zambezi Valley. We snapped some photos, then Nickie and I posed with the trophies while Sharon took a few more.

We had an early dinner, a fine and fitting feast for our last night in camp. We were to leave early the next morning to meet our pilot, Ahmad, at the Chenje airstrip and board the Centurion for our flight to Victoria Falls. Nickie and I went to our tent immediately following our meal to finish packing.

Nickie was efficiently fitting our belongings into our duffel bags as only she can. I had finished cleaning my rifle and was stowing it and the supplies in a hard, secure travel case.

"It's still unbelievable how well we did," I said. "The entire thing was just outstanding."

"It was a fine safari. I'm so glad it was successful for you."

"Did you really have a great time? You seem sort of lukewarm."

"Everything we saw and experienced was wonderful. It's just that it was a little hard on me physically."

"Seeing that lion hunched on the riverbank only yards away was a highpoint," I said. "I'm sorry it was rugged at times. I know it's not the Ritz. Thanks for putting up."

"The heat was oppressive, and the walking before I was banished. The worst was being crushed in the middle of that truck bench seat between you and Wil. It wasn't built for three. And when I sat in the open, up in the back, I was always getting swatted by low-hanging brush. The pounding for hours on those excuses for roads may have actually been the worst. My back is still sore."

"I know. I'm still nursing my blisters and missing toe-nail."

"And Wil was insufferable. He talks to himself, you know. I could see his lips moving and hear the whispers as we were driving around."

I hadn't noticed, but still had to laugh.

"And he was so rude out in the bush. Charming and talkative back at camp, but a different man when we were hunting. I didn't like the way he treated us at all. I hope you're not going to give him a tip."

"It got better near the end," I said. "Sort of. And I can't believe his knowledge and work ethic. He's the most focused and goal-oriented soul I've ever met. The results were incredible. What a safari!"

"Still … I think he was unprofessional. We were paying him, not the other way around. I don't think he should get anything more from us."

"Honestly, Wil was part of the challenge and excitement. For me, it made everything all the more satisfying. His peculiarities were beyond interesting and added to the uniqueness of the entire experience. And with his background—the heir apparent to a profitable farm, the boss man even as a teen—I'm sure I couldn't help being a little bitter myself if all that was taken through no fault of mine. His behavior in the field is simply all he knows."

"Well … just so *you* know, this is my last hunting trip," Nickie said. "It was wonderful and all. But like we talked about when I agreed to come with you, next time we'll go to an all-inclusive resort in the Caribbean for our vacation."

"We had talked about an Alaska bear hunt instead of coming here. There's always that still out there."

"*Pleeeeeze…*"

"I'm just saying."

"It was either-or, never both."

I recalled what Sharon had said a few days ago at dinner. *Our clients come to take an elephant, a leopard, or a lion only once. But they come back for buffalo.* There was that to think about, too. Maybe … just maybe …

Nickie continued packing, and I made up the envelopes for the gratuities. I expressed my appreciation by giving no less than the already generous amounts recommended by our booking agent. There was Levitt, the middle-aged and getting-thick-in-the-waist tracker, tireless and skilled, the man who could not do enough for me. "*Gun, Boss …*" holding out his hand to relieve me of my burden during a particularly long and hard trek. I placed something extra in his envelope. And, of course, the game ranger, Gibson. Then there were Sharon and Jerry, who had made our stay wonderful in every way, who had become genuine friends. The kitchen staff—waiters, cooks, clean-up—the outstanding meals, they all received something extra. And Wil? I placed the full recommended amount in his envelope, but no more in his case. His talents had resulted in a remarkable take of game, but his poor communications skills, rudely critical behavior, and absence of coaching cost him what would otherwise have been an additional several hundred dollars, not a small sum in the austere Zimbabwean economy.

As Nickie was going through her nightly ritual of preparing for bed, I had a chance to reflect on the entire safari experience. I'd heard it said Africa could be life changing for a Westerner. I hadn't truly understood the import of those words, but I did now. It's a simple concept that everything has a beginning and an end. And the end of a thing, especially if it was good, marks a beginning for something else. It's the most basic of ideas, but one that is fully grasped only by humans, and it is the basis of all religions, for man's unique capacity to plan and design, for our dominion over the world's animals, and for civilization itself. And I saw in that moment, at the end of our safari, I was a changed man. The African bush and its animals had transfigured and resurrected me. I knew, going forward, the end of this safari would mark the beginning of a new and better chapter in my life—in our lives. And I understood that Africa had awarded me another chance at wholeness, however brief or enduring it may prove to be.

Nickie had completed her preparations, performing a few final tasks before getting into bed. She was cheerfully humming a familiar popular tune, one I recognized well. I could tell she was feeling happy and carefree, too.

"Are you going to be coming to bed?" she asked. "They'll be shutting off the generator anytime."

I liked to act silly with her when we were both feeling lighthearted. I liked to make her smile. I stood in front of her and placed my hands on her shoulders.

"Today, while the blossom still clings to the vine ..." It was what she had been humming. *"I'll taste your strawberries, I'll drink your sweet wine."* I sang in my awful monotone, exaggerating it to be comical.

"You didn't give Wil a tip, did you?"

"What I did is invited him to come visit over Thanksgiving," I said. I liked to rattle her chain a bit.

"You're not the least bit amusing."

"He'll only stay through New Year's. Or Easter at the latest."

"You think you're funny, but you're not."

"I'll be a dandy and I'll be a rover," I droned. *"I'll feast at your table...I'll sleep in your clover..."* I could never hit a note or carry a melody.

"Aren't you the flirty one, though." She got in bed and put out the side-table light. The overhead controlled only by the generator was still lit. I crawled in beside her.

"It's really been a fine experience." She changed the subject. "I truly mean that. I'm glad we did this."

I continued my little song, singing the refrain once more, teasing her, lying close beside her, turning on one side to face her. *"Today while the blossom still clings to the vine ... I'll taste your strawberries, I'll drink your sweet wine."*

"Don't you be getting any big ideas, Buster. The staff is still going about their business just outside."

"For the love of God, don't be ridiculous. I'm seventy and still not over my last surgery. Come on!" I didn't mention the end of our safari heralded yet a new beginning. I'd tell her about that later.

The generator spun down and died with a rough cough. The faint illumination from the hanging light faded away with it. I turned on my elbow, my face above hers only inches away. It was dark inside the tent, with not even the light from a moon just beginning its rise or perhaps only forming the slightest crescent yet visible.

"*I can't be contented with yesterday's glory.*" I barely whispered it, not even trying to sing. "*Today is my moment and now is my story.*" I hadn't realized I remembered so much of the lyrics.

"I can't wait to see Victoria Falls," she said, ignoring my shenanigans.

"It'll be great. And, maybe when we're home, we can at least talk about the Alaska thing again." I knew I was pushing it, but her mood was fine.

"PUH-leeeeze!"

She was lying on her back, the sheet pulled to her chin. I knew her eyes were open, but in the dark of our tent I couldn't make out any colors at all. Yet I remembered from long experience their dazzling, unique hazel with little flecks of green, bronze, and brilliant gold. Even in the dark, I could see their colors in my mind's eye. And I could sense the warmth radiating from her face and the moistness of her mouth, as any man does when very near a woman to whom he is deeply drawn.

"*A million tomorrows shall all pass away ...*" I was singing softly once again. Barely audibly. Nickie was still.

"*... 'ere we forget ...*" I moved close to see that she was still awake, then kissed her on the lips. Once again, only fleetingly, I considered our safari, our shared experience, and the new beginning I was sure it portended.

"... all the joys ... that are ours ..... today ....."

THE FIGHT of the CENTURY

No fiction here, this story is true to the most minute detail.
At least according to my recollection.

Boxing historians say it was one of the Joe Louis-Max Schmeling rubber matches of the '30s, with the Nazi-era German white hope Schmeling KOing the Brown Bomber in twelve the first time, only to be mercilessly destroyed by Joe in the first round of the rematch. The second fight between Ali and Smokin' Joe Fraser, the Thrilla in Manila, is still touted by fans as the most memorable of an era. Bitterly contested, it ended in the fourteenth with a TKO of Joe, but only after punishment had been heaped upon Mohammad. My personal best Ali fight was the Rumble in the Jungle when unbeaten, powerful, and overwhelmingly favored George Foreman, an Olympic gold medal winner and reigning world heavyweight champion, at the time in his absolute prime, was knocked reeling across the ring, clutching at the air for nonexistent support before crashing slow-motion-style to the canvas in the eighth. He didn't get up.

But for my money none of those qualifies as the fight of the century. That occurred in 1956 at the Catholic Youth Center, the CYC, in the old, quiet and treed, the idyllic close-in St. Louis suburb of Webster Groves, Missouri. I was one of the combatants.

That year marked an era apart from the twenty-first century world of today. The nation was heady in the glory of our righteous and still fresh triumph over power and evil in

World War II. The GI bill had given thousands of vets a previously unthinkable opportunity to attend college. Jobs were abundant; tract houses sprang like new June corn from recently vacant, rag-and-milkweed-choked lots just on the outskirts of cities and towns. General Eisenhower, the war's conquering hero, gray and steady, wise and strong, was our president. Crews constructed new and awe inspiring expressways across the nation, while families bought cars and appliances they had seen advertised on television, back then still regarded as an innovative and amazing new technology. *Lucy & Ricky* mugged, Jackie Gleason and his *Honeymooners* clowned, and Elvis made his appearance wailing and gyrating to *Hound Dog* while he wooed hysterical teen girls down Lonely Street to the *Heartbreak Hotel*. And I was a twelve-year-old, seventh-grade student at the local Webster Catholic elementary school, Holy Redeemer, unsuspecting that I was about to have the fight of my life.

Father Kaletta, a young and hip priest, wavy haired, good looking and energetic, was the assistant pastor—today he would be called a *youth pastor*. It was he who would come to our school classroom across the parking lot from the church to talk to the students about religion or some activity or event being planned. Father Ernst, the old and serious and gray-headed pastor, stayed secluded in the rectory. As far as we children knew, he concerned himself with Sunday sermons, grumbled about parish finances, and in general dealt with the adult parishioners, with our parents, on serious and mysterious matters beyond the understanding of mere kids.

And I believed then Father Kaletta hated me.

As a prepubescent seventh grader, I was boney-ribbed skinny, small for my age, and only an average student on my best day. And I was painfully shy to the point of being withdrawn. Girls, of course, a world apart from mine in those days, absolutely terrified me.

I hung out enough with other boys from school or in the neighborhood, though, but recoiled from any group attention, particularly so if the audience contained adults or other, especially older, kids I didn't know. Reciting lessons in class among students I knew well was one thing. It caused a little nervousness but was something I managed through. But the thought of participating in a school-wide play in front of *everyone* or being asked to say something to a collection of parents caused me to tremble in panic. Occasionally students would be enlisted to take part in a church service, leading a prayer or reading from a Gospel. Naturally, I would shrink away from anything that horrifying.

So it was that I, slight and pale-skinned, freckled and redheaded, quiet, unsure and unaccomplished, would hang back in safe obscurity when Father Kaletta came to recruit kids for his latest activity.

But I think the final straw for the good Father was when I shirked—*rejected* might be the better word—the normally prized opportunity to become one of his altar boys.

Father Kaletta was in charge of the *servers* program, the boys who assisted the priests while conducting mass. And it was considered a high honor and rite of passage by most of the boys. Traditionally performed by eighth-grade males, the new corps was selected and trained from the crop of those just completing the seventh grade, to be called into full service at the beginning of the following school year, although there would be an earlier trial run. It required learning Latin, used in most of the mass in those days, as well as the rituals and intricate actions of the priest. An altar boy had to openly respond in Latin to the priest's prayers and chants during the service as well as be ready with certain equipment at the precisely correct times. And they were required to wear black and white vestments—layered robes—adorned as a sort of toned down *mini-me* of the presiding priest. Even the thought sent waves of humiliation through me.

Of course, the prospect of performing in such a way before an entire Sunday congregation—hundreds of men, women, and children—was beyond simply frightening. To make matters worse, I was, I now realize, a touch dyslexic and therefore terrible at memorizing anything. I was more than dismayed at the prospect of needing to learn the lengthy and obscure Latin liturgy of the Catholic mass.

In keeping with all of this, Father Kaletta addressed the boys near the end of our seventh-grade year.

"You've all been provided handouts with the priest's words and your responses," he said, looking down at his copy of the material. "As you know by now, it also contains instructions for the things you'll need to retrieve and provide during the service. What, when, and where."

He shuffled through his papers. Everyone was silent.

I had received this material, as had the other boys, weeks earlier, but had barely glanced at it before setting it aside. I stared at the floor, head hanging, avoiding eye contact with Father Kaletta or anyone else.

"You've had plenty of time to memorize everything as you were instructed to do. So we'll have a full rehearsal tomorrow afternoon, Saturday, and then you boys will begin serving your first mass according to this schedule, which I'll post in the back of the church." He looked down at the eight-by-eleven sheet of lined writing stock he held in his hand. "Your first mass, your trial run for your duties as eighth graders next year, will begin with the six o'clock evening service immediately following tomorrow's rehearsal. The first boys on the schedule are Bascom and Dwyer."

He turned and walked from the classroom.

Me. Bascom. Scheduled to *serve* at mass tomorrow. The first one. I was rocked and traumatized by his announcement. I hadn't memorized anything and was not about to perform some impossibly intricate ritual, preposterously attired, under the scathing eyes of adults in any event. No way.

Needless to say, I never mentioned a thing to my parents. I simply didn't show and later stammered a lying excuse about having taken ill. Father Kaletta never mentioned the incident again, and it was accepted by all I was not to be an altar boy. Ever.

If he had been aloof with me before, his demeanor was icy after that.

We were required to attend confession occasionally, and, of course, Kaletta was usually the priest hearing it. The penance doled to me seemed to get tougher.

"What did you get?" I asked my best friend, Bruce, after we had both been to confession with Father Kaletta one afternoon.

"Three 'Our Fathers' and three 'Hail Marys.' "

Pretty standard.

"Jeeze," I said. "I got six 'Our Fathers', six 'Hail Marys', a rosary and the 'stations of the cross.' "

"What the hell did you *do,* anyway?" Bruce said.

I didn't answer, but what I confessed was *I talked back to my mother. And I teased my little brother. I lit a prayer candle in the front of church for my sick grandmother, then found out I didn't have the money. But I brought it next time.* Six Our Fathers, six Hail Marys, a rosary and the stations. The handwriting was on the wall. Father Kaletta hated me.

But that evidence alone was insufficient, only circumstantial. No, the nail in the coffin confirming that priest's hatred of me came from the fight of the century.

Sister Mary-Alvin, clad as they all were in her heavy, white, full-length Dominican order gown, her diminutive, lined old face squeezed tight by surrounding white muslin headgear beneath an encapsulating stiff, long black veil, had walked to the door and spoken briefly with Father Kaletta before ushering him into the classroom. She assumed her standard position in the right front corner—the place all nuns occupied when a priest had entered to address the class—while Father stood behind the desk centered at the front.

"We're going to be holding a boxing exhibition for the seventh-grade boys," he announced.

I had attended Holy Redeemer since third grade. Nothing like this had happened before.

"For those interested, come to the CYC after school today for sign-ups. You'll get all the information there. We'll need a note from your parents before the matches, which will be in two weeks. You'll have all the necessary equipment, some basic instruction, and the opportunity to train before your bout. See you there."

Now, I was no athlete. And normally I would have just ignored such an invitation from Father Kaletta. But, honestly, I was oddly drawn to boxing and felt titillated at the prospect of participating in such a contest.

Neither was my father athletic. Thin and at five-nine shorter than I would eventually be, bespectacled with barely gray-tinged, tightly wavy brown hair just beginning to reveal a bald spot that would grow to define him later, I never saw him do anything truly physical. Yet he considered himself a student of all sports. It was one thing to enjoy a baseball game, but my dad would analyze it.

"Look at Musial's stance," he would say of the Cardinal star. "Feet together, balanced on the balls, bat out front high

266

and ready to swing. *That's* why he's leading the National League in hits."

And my father loved boxing. We would watch the *Friday Night Fights* on the *Gillette Cavalcade of Sports* on our black and white, round-screened, massively cased nineteen-inch Sylvania TV together. *"To LOOK sharp, and be on the ballll..."* the opening jingle would go. *"To FEEL sharp, tah dah da da dahhh...to BE sharp...get Gillette—BLUE— BLAAAAADES..."* Sugar Ray Robinson would bob and weave effortlessly across the ring, landing a blinding array of deadly accurate blows. "The best fighter pound-for-pound in the history of the sport," my father would yell, watching the Sugar Man destroy Rocky Graziano. Or Archie Moore, the Old Mongoose left-jabbing to victory over Bobo Olson. *"That's* how a jab is supposed to be used!" Dad would say. "To wear the man down, set him up for the right. It's a science, not brute strength." My father, the thinking man.

Watching the fights or *Gunsmoke* or a few of the other popular shows then were some of the rare things we did together. A traveling salesman, he was away much of the time and really wasn't one to do a lot with the kids when he was home. Dad rarely showed emotion, much less affection. He seldom hugged or kissed or complimented his children, not because he was angry or disapproving. It simply wasn't his nature. Of course, he could be a harsh disciplinarian when, rarely, his anger was aroused. Looking back, the word that first comes to mind in describing our relationship is *cordial*, as odd as that is. But I now realize I valued the little time we spent together, and sharing an interest in boxing, in the *Friday Night Fights*, was one of the things that piqued my fascination with the sport.

And I admit I was the consummate daydreamer, especially in school. Walter Mitty, the infamous daydreaming character created in 1939 by humorist James Thurber, was a rank amateur of the art compared to me. While Sister Mary-Alvin was explaining the intricacies of multiplying dissimilar fractions or calculating a vexing lowest common denominator, I was expert at feigning concentration while in reality hitting a home run in the final, tied inning of the World Series, or leading my troops to victory in a famous battle where bumblers like Robert E. Lee or Ulysses Grant had failed miserably. And as often as not, my exploits played out in fanciful boxing rings. I would, for instance, throw a savage left hook to the body, my unsuspecting opponent wincing in pain and lowering an arm to cover his battered ribs, opening the very opportunity I had foreseen to follow with a thundering overhand right to the jaw, dropping the bigger and heavily favored man to the canvas for the count. While undeniably heroic, it was really all quite easy.

So on a warm spring Friday afternoon in May, the lure of actually participating in my beloved boxing foremost in my mind, my shyness at least temporarily pushed into the recesses, I headed from our school down the few blocks to the aging, Quonset-like structure of the Catholic Youth Center on Lockwood Avenue near Big Bend Road in the little commercial district of suburban Webster Groves everyone referred to as Old Orchard.

Father Kaletta had seen to everything. A canvas-floored, roped ring was set up in the center of the gym. Around the periphery sat training equipment of every description. A little speed bag hung from a fixture, the kind fighters pummel in a hand-over-hand staccato to hone quickness and timing. A large, heavy, stuffed body bag, simulating, I suppose, the torso of an opponent, dangled low from a chain attached to the ceiling. It was used to pound an imaginary foe into submission, building the trainee's ability to land a series of coordinated, crushing blows in the process. A skip-rope was available to improve endurance and footwork. Weighted pulleys and dumbbells were there to increase arm strength. Padded leather headgear was available to protect us during sparring sessions and for the actual bout that lay ahead. Fat, overstuffed leather boxing gloves gave a look of realism to us would-be brawlers while assuring none of the blows would be too damaging. Thrilled and eager to begin, I signed up immediately and visited the CYC daily after school and on weekends to train. I was pumped.

Getting the note from my parents was easy enough. In those days, we were seldom denied permission to do anything. And I think my father was more excited than I was.

"It's all about balance and form," he explained, demonstrating the proper stance and footwork. Dad said that about every sport. "Extend the left foot and remain absolutely balanced. The left hand should be raised to protect your face, and be ready to jab. If your jab lands cleanly, follow with a hard, straight right, but never lead with it. That would leave you open and vulnerable." He poked at the air with his left, followed by swooping rights directed at an invisible target as he bounced in and out on his carefully positioned feet. I did likewise.

My grandfather, Carl, my mother's father, had dropped by to see what all the excitement was about. A compact and robust looking, self-made, fourth-grade-educated German immigrant, he had achieved a measure of fame and admiration in our family for his street honed wits, toughness, and success as the owner of a lucrative small business renting jukeboxes and pinball machines to bars. His father had died when Carl was only fourteen and my grandfather had been educated and hardened on the mean, turn-of-the-century streets of the German enclave of South St. Louis. Outgoing and always confident, he had an opinion on everything and seemed to be loved or at least admired by just about everyone. Those things that would be faults in others were, in Carl and especially to me, remarkable qualities. His well-known history as a bootlegger early in the Depression only made him loom larger than life in my mind. And he was a master of profanity, effortlessly slipping the most vivid and vulgar curse words seamlessly into his everyday conversation—language no one else in our buttoned-down family ever used. While lesser men would have been shunned as boorish for such behavior, it seemed only to add to Carl's raw charisma. He was legendary for his late night drinking and gambling, but to my knowledge was never judged negatively for it. It was, after all, Carl.

And unlike my own father, he seemed to relish and seek out my company, taking me on fishing trips and along on his rounds of visiting bar clients as part of his business, day-long excursions he called "going bumming." Calling me "butsie," a German slang term of endearment for a young boy. He drank like a fish during those outings, patrons and barkeeps who were delighted to see him buying drinks at each stop while I, having red cream soda pop, played his pinball and bumper pool games with nickels he gave me. I idolized Carl.

"All that science stuff is crap!" Carl boomed in response to the instructions given to me by my father, still standing right there. Dad just smiled. Everyone loved Carl.

"Just wail the hell out of him," Carl advised regarding my as yet unknown opponent. "The guy what lands the most punches wins. Forget that other s--t..."

And Carl would know. One of his most memorable features was a prominent, jagged scar angling all the way down and slightly across his left cheek. When I had asked him, years earlier, how he got it, he simply said, "In a bar fight. Guy whacked me with a broken pool cue." Carl never said who won, but I knew. He grew larger and larger in my boyish esteem.

A few days before the contest Father Kaletta halted the training session that was in progress and called all the boys together in one corner of the youth center.

"There are sixteen fighters," he said. "Eight matches. As you know, it'll be this Saturday at eight. I'll post the matchups on the wall here. Keep up your training and good luck."

All the boys crowded around the paper taped to the wall. I looked down the list for my name. Finally, there it was at the very bottom, the last bout of the event. Bascom— Winfrey. I was stunned.

I stared at the paper, disbelieving, as if pondering a fact from an alternate universe that would be quite impossible in this one. Most of the parents and students recognized at least the names of the kids in my class. But *everyone* was well familiar with Bob Winfrey, the most notorious and feared student in the entire school.

The nuns, in the peculiar ways that are only theirs, lined all the kids up when filing in or out of class by order of height. Two lines, one for boys and the other for girls. There were some thirty of us in the seventh-grade boys' line. As one of the shortest in the class, I was only third in line behind midget-like Larry Dillon and short, wiry, cocky Tom Shenkenberg. Then came me, followed by twenty-seven taller boys. Near the very back of the line, where the early maturing, soaring kids resided, was Bob Winfrey.

It was not just a matter of height. I was slightly built, my shoulders narrow and upper arms barely bigger than my wrists. My flesh was straight and even and smooth, my muscles, if one could detect any, completely absent of definition. Had the class members been stripped naked but for a pair of shorts on each of us, my torso would have been barely distinguishable from that of the average slow-blooming girl in the class. Only a year later, at the end of eighth grade, a grand and confusing awakening would occur. I would be noticeably taller, the shape of muscles beginning to be revealed. A prominent Adam's apple would emerge and my voice would crack occasionally, to the derisive glee of my older sister. Peach fuzz would emerge on my chin, and girls would welcome my approach, leaning against me and subtly touching my developing arms and chest while we danced close to slow music, the female scent of hair and makeup and perfume of the greatest interest and a source of mysterious motivation. I would have and enjoy my first romantic kiss with a blossoming girl, its memory still clear and delicious today nearly sixty years later. But in 1956 as a seventh grader, all that was beyond my wildest imagination.

Not so with the surly and glowering Bob Winfrey. He sported long, oiled hair with a greasy fall hanging over his forehead. Shoulders broad and bulging, the shape of his upper arms were becoming ripped and cut by developing muscles beneath. Winfrey was big and well built without even a hint of fat. His belly was hard, his hands were large, at least compared to mine. And Bob had a *reputation*.

Schoolyard brawls were his stock-in-trade. I had not been in a scuffle since third grade. Bob Winfrey got in trouble for them all the time, picking the fights and to my knowledge always winning them. He challenged the authority of the nuns with an arrogant, upper-lip-curled sneer, something none of the other kids would even consider doing. A constant visitor to the principal's office, occasionally the police would be called to quell one of his rampages. On one occasion, with the nuns unable to control him, his father was called to the school. He was taken by his dad—a huge, grim appearing man—into the boys' room, emerging a few minutes later sullen and reddened. The rumor was he had been soundly beaten. In short, he was the school bad-boy, one of the toughest, roughest kids, big, angry, and physically precocious. And my opponent—Bascom, the thin, shy boy at the front of the line—the greatest mis-match of all time. Finally there could be no doubt. Father Kaletta hated me.

Now, as odd as it seems, I actually didn't mind the thought of receiving a thorough beating from Bob Winfrey. After all, most of the boys had at one time or another, and I told myself it was simply a matter of when. But in front of all my friends? In front of *their* parents, my parents and grand-parents, my sister's friends! I imagined I understood how the sacrificial slaves and condemned prisoners felt in the Roman Coliseum, their lives, hopes and fears counting for nothing more than fleeting entertainment for the audience as their flesh was torn to shreds by gladiators or lions. Such was the metaphorical fate I saw for myself.

My parents stared unbelieving as I told them.

"My Lord above," my mother said. "That doesn't seem right. What could they be thinking?"

"You'll have protection, right?" my father chimed in. "A cup, headgear, the large gloves. It's just an exhibition. For the love of God, nothing's going to happen."

"You don't have to participate if you don't want," Mom said. "No one can force you."

"Don't be silly," Dad countered, seeing rightly running away would be worse than the beating. "The bigger they are, the harder they fall." He tried to sound jaunty and confident. It came off hollow. I was inconsolable.

With only days until the fight, I redoubled my training, going afternoons to the CYC and working out at home each evening. At that point it was mostly about damage control. I fashioned my own body bag from an old drawstring-topped duffel bag, stuffing it with rags and crumpled newspaper, hanging it from a rafter in the basement with tripled-up twine. I poked at it each evening with all the ferocity I could muster, my scrawny arms and little hands barely moving the bag. I shadowboxed in front of the bathroom mirror, door locked to avoid the embarrassment of discovery, carefully monitoring my stance, pose, and movements as my father had instructed. Snapping phantom jabs darted through empty air at my imaginary opponent, at Bob Winfrey, followed by what I hoped and believed were vicious straight rights. I delivered what were, in my mind, punishing left-right hooking combinations to his invisible body, followed by a jab and slamming right upstairs to his head. I told myself I had a reasonable chance of giving a good accounting, of avoiding a complete, humiliating public thrashing. By Saturday night I was sore, exhausted, and ready for whatever fate would deliver.

Winfrey and I, the last bout on the schedule, stood together in the door of the locker room watching the matches. Boys batted frantically at one another, no one doing any damage. There was actually quite a crowd present. Each bout was followed by polite applause and an occasional soft, audible "good job" from some contestant's parent. My father and Carl had come to watch, seated near the back of the rings of folding metal chairs that surrounded the boxing area. My mother had not shown, unable, I now know, to face what was to come.

When our match, the final bout of the evening, approached, Bruce helped lace my gloves and secure the headgear. Winfrey and I walked to the ring and climbed through the ropes, each taking an opposing corner as we had seen the others do. Father Kaletta was the referee. He said a few words—I don't recall a single one—and when the bell clanged, he motioned us out into the center, our gloves raised in the classic fighting position.

I clearly recall the odd state of feeling absolutely no emotion, my mind completely fixed only on what was happening in the ring. I felt neither fear nor confidence, nervousness nor calm. I simply concentrated on what I needed to do next like some robot. Winfrey and I closed, came together, and exchanged a flurry of pattering pushes and slaps as we had seen all the other boys do. I focused on the things my father had advised, on stance and balance and coordination. But also on the advice Carl had offered—*the guy what throws the most punches wins.* I gave not a thought to defense or avoidance or protecting myself, but only to the next punch. And the next and the next and the next.

I doubt Winfrey had given the fight a moment's thought, had prepared in any way. He was, after all, fighting the little Bascom kid. He had whipped the likes of me time and again in the schoolyard. This must have seemed just another day at the office for him. But I sensed after thirty seconds or so of raining tiny blows on him with increasing intensity, of advancing continuously forward, he was surprised and taken aback.

Suddenly there was a brief opening as he allowed his hands to drop from in front of his head to his chest. I snapped a clean jab through the gap, feeling it land solidly on the center of his face. Winfrey seemed to slowly lean back at the blow and then sit hard on the canvas floor, his arms extended behind to keep his body from falling all the way on his back. Unbelievably, he was *down*. He looked up at me uncomprehending, sitting on the canvas, glaring glassy-eyed up at the small and introverted Bascom boy, my fists still raised and ready. I think I was as surprised as he must have been. *This can't be happening*, I recall thinking. His thoughts must have been similar.

"I tripped!" Winfrey was still looking up at me.

There may have been a grain of truth, but I felt the solid impact against my fist when it struck his face. And I clearly recall thinking *I'm glad I'm the one standing up here listening to the explanation, rather than the one down there giving it.*

Father Kaletta directed me to a far corner, then went back, helped Winfrey to his feet, and checked his condition. After a moment he motioned us to resume the fight.

Again, there was the flurry of largely ineffective punches. Winfrey did seem a bit more tentative, but maybe it was my imagination. Again, in a carbon copy of the first encounter, I saw an opening between his gloves and launched another jab. Flush on the center of his face. Once again he leaned back and sat down hard on the canvas, arms supporting him from falling completely back. Again he looked blankly up at me. But this time he said nothing. There had been no knockdowns in the previous seven bouts, but a minute and a half into this one there had been two.

Kaletta again checked Bob and motioned for the fight to continue. Everything had taken time, and there was only a little left to go. Winfrey spent the rest of the bout backing away, bobbing and ducking while I rained a stream of little-boy blows on him. I can't remember him throwing another single punch.

I'm certain everyone in the audience knew all about Bob Winfrey. The whole community did. And the initial mismatch between us had been obvious enough. At the end of each previous bout, there had been a brief moment of the muted, required applause accompanied by the occasional mumbled word of praise. But when the bell sounded the end of our fight, the place erupted in a roar. I think they were mostly struck by the incongruity of it all. Bob and I climbed from the ring and started back to the locker room.

"Great fight, kid," a middle-aged man I had never seen before shouted at me enthusiastically.

"Way to go, Bascom," floated from the audience, from whom I don't know. People were still clapping and an excited murmur rumbled through the crowd. Other words of congratulations were directed toward me. It was as if the audience

276

had come alive. No one spoke to Bob. Then I saw my dad and grandfather seated in the back row. My father, who spent little time with me, who never praised or hugged or kissed me, was beaming from ear to ear, as if unable to contain some primal, internal joy. I felt ten feet tall. My grandfather, Carl, was grinning too. Later, intoxicated with the excitement and elation of the evening, each would claim I had adopted his recommended strategy and forsaken the other one's advice. I let them each believe it.

Winfrey and I never spoke of that night, all through that summer, through eighth grade and our graduation from Holy Redeemer the following year, after which I never saw him again. Mutual friends later told me Bob claimed I had repeatedly tripped him, that he had handled me with dispatch. There might have been some truth. We were both clumsy kids in that ring after all, and I'm sure my recall is through my own personal filter of the events. But it was clear no one there that night believed his version, and I certainly didn't. I came to understand our fight wasn't about Bob Winfrey losing, but more about my own ability to summon reserves and strengths—physical, mental, and emotional—I hadn't understood I possessed.

Honestly, Bob had never bothered me in any way before or after that evening. In fact, we had been occasional pals at times, he living only three short blocks from my home. We would hang out now and again, in earlier years, in the hot, humid Mississippi Valley summers of St. Louis, looking for something to do, Bob usually getting us into some kind of trouble with his mischief. Me the follower, Bob the leader. The time we snuck into the farmer's barnyard and caught his chickens, hauling them up on a shed roof then throwing them off to see them fly, the farmer rushing out—short, fat, and balding, his baggy jeans sagging—shouting with clenched hands and swollen neck veins, "...you boys get the hell off my farm..." Or Bob casually throwing a rock at the picture window glass of a neighbor's house, me wanting to run like a scared rabbit, Bob shrugging and saying "Don't worry...I know them and they ain't even home...they're out of town..." After graduation I heard he had stolen a car armed with a loaded German luger pistol, the police chasing and finally catching him, Bob going into a youth detention center, *reform school* it was called when our parents threatened us with it. I lost track until Bruce told me a few years ago Winfrey had died, long sick and disabled. I imagined his life had been grim, but really I don't know. Truth be told, despite his transgressions, his *reputation*, I always liked and felt a bit sorry for Bob Winfrey. God rest his soul.

The euphoria following the fight gradually died down in our house, and the event seemed to be quickly forgotten. I'd like to tell you it marked a turning point in my relationship with my father. Alas, it is not so. Things gradually returned to pretty much what they had been. The fight was more of a single, obscure milepost in my life, one of many on a long, twisting journey. Growth, while occurring with occasional little spurts, is by its nature slow and steady, healing even more so.

Into adulthood, my shyness gradually yielded to outgoing confidence. Eventually I would complete college and then advanced degrees, become an executive in both large and small businesses, participate in the leadership of community organizations, serving on their governing committees and boards of trustees. I would appear several times on television touted as a business expert, be quoted liberally in the *Wall Street Journal*, give talks at national banking conventions, teach advanced college business courses, and write a full-page op-ed piece for the largest daily newspaper in Detroit. My photo and biography would appear with some regularity in the popular and business press. At one point I was invited as a financial industry expert to address the U.S. Senate Banking Committee in the Rayburn Office Building in Washington, DC. It was nationally televised, albeit on C-Span. I would achieve a satisfying degree of financial security for my family. My paltry accomplishments, I fully realize, would be rightly judged by an independent observer or when juxtaposed with those of a truly successful man as pedestrian at best. So I recite these things not with self impressed braggadocio, but more with a sense of the embarrassed and acknowledged hubris necessary to draw a contrast between my ordinary adult life today and the timid, scrawny and scared boy fighting his heart out in the steamy CYC in Old Orchard, Webster Groves that Saturday night in late May, 1956.

I had gone on to establish a career in Detroit. My parents eventually retired to San Diego County where I saw them perhaps once a year. My relationship with my father continued as *cordial*, but lacking the edge of disappointment and resentment I felt as a child. Pain fades under the great anesthetic of time. When his time finally came in 1986 at age seventy-six with a diagnosis of metastasized bowel cancer, I went to see him a few weeks before the end. We always greeted or said goodbye to one another with a shake of hands. But as I was leaving to return to my wife and family in Detroit, he hugged me for the first time in memory and said, "I love you." I said the same.

Shortly after that I sat down to write him, knowing it would be the last letter he would receive from me. I pondered his life and mine. By all conventional measures his was unremarkable. A private in the army, a salesman rising eventually only to middle management. He never assumed a leadership role in any group, was never singled out for any recognition to my knowledge. But what I remembered then was a man who overcame a Depression-era absence of an opportunity for an education—he had never completed high school, going to work instead as others were forced to do—to build the middle-class life of the American dream for his family. A father earning a modest income who still made sure his children had well beyond a basic public education. A man who, when he lost a job, was steadfast and confident, never spreading the fear and assault on his self-confidence to his family, calmly going about finding another while keeping the home ship on a steady course. I knew he had been an infantryman, only a buck-private manning a light BAR machine gun, fighting the Nazis in Italy during World War II. Of course he never spoke to me about it. But my mother had confided, out of his earshot, he had been wounded twice and returned to his unit both times, had been shelled mercilessly and watched his best friend randomly blown to pieces in the foxhole next to him, had been in a close man-to-man firefight in the very final days of the war, machine gunning to death a charging young German at point-blank range. My father, lacking rank or recognition, simply doing what he needed to do without question. Soldiering on, as always.

And even with death he was strong. "I'm not afraid to die," my mother told me he said after receiving his diagnosis. "Everyone has to some time. I've gone through life knowing I'll spend eternity with God in heaven. I believe it still and am ready for that."

In my letter I said to him true things I never had the strength to say in person. "Your courage and resolve have always been an inspiration to me...I've spent a lifetime trying to equal them but have never been able to achieve that, yet every day I try again...your example and what you've meant to me will always be a part of me, will never die so long as I'm alive..." I never saw my father cry, but my mother told me tears ran along his cheeks as he read it sitting on the living room couch. He was dead a few weeks later.

I think in a strange way my ability to finally say to my father those things I had felt and believed for so many years began that Saturday night in May in Webster Groves. When, with the crowd buzzing at the unlikely turn of expectations that had just unfolded in the ring, I saw my father's euphoria, his pride and exuberance with the accomplishment of his oldest son, burst uncontained in that spontaneous, heartfelt grin. That sweltering night when I walked head high back to the locker room, past my beaming, proud father, striding victoriously in front of vanquished Bob Winfrey, his eyes downcast and expression beaten, the boy I liked and felt so terribly sorry for. That Saturday night in late May at the Catholic Youth Center with Father Kaletta as the referee. The night of the epic, the undisputed *Fight of the Century.*

This story is dedicated to my youngest daughter, Molly, who asked that I write a personal childhood memoir of a sort so that she might become familiar with relatives she never had a chance to know well or at all. Here you go, Beans...

...and to the memories of Monsignor Robert F. Kaletta (1925-1995), the assistant pastor in 1956 (I'm quite sure he never hated me or anyone else, but it seemed so back then) who led an unblemished and distinguished life of spiritual service; and Robert (Bob) Winfrey (1943-2001) for whom—and for reasons I can't quite articulate—I harbor the fondest memories and deepest affection....

...and finally and most important, to the memory of my late father, John Gay Bascom Sr. (1910-1986) whom I love dearly and painfully miss, and to whom I owe so much. RIP. Thanks, Dad.

AUTHOR'S NOTE

This is a dramatized memoir recounted as a literary device through the eyes, and with the voice and biased perceptions of a twelve-year-old boy. It was created solely for entertainment value. It is not intended as an accurate or objective depiction of any actual individual or any organization. Any resulting negative perceptions of real people, living or dead, or organizations drawn by a reader would be wrong. It is only a story.

THE HUNDREDTH LION

I've thought of it every day since, but still am not sure exactly what really happened, or why. After all, who could possibly know? Other than maybe me.

One who hunts Africa for a living develops an eerie sense of intuition. As when following up on a poorly shot nyati in an impenetrable jesse thicket and it is oddly quiet or somehow the breeze is too still or there is that faint, ambiguous aroma. Yet the seasoned professional hunter, hammered by experience against the anvil that is Africa, inexplicably knows an instant before it happens—the black explosion of the dying buffalo from the thick brush, the terrifying, grunting rush, the breath-sucking close, lowered and twisting horns of the gigantic animal that stood impossibly hidden seconds before only feet away. When the PH anticipates, not the details, but the foreboding sense of the kind of trouble that is about to be thrust upon him. And it is just such an edgy sixth sense of impending though ill-defined mayhem that one experiences when first meeting the rare train wreck of a very bad client.

"Brian Cassidy." He stood close and said it loudly, showing his big, professionally whitened teeth in an open-mouthed smile. His right arm dangled at his side while his left hand touched the hefty digital camera that hung from a strap around his neck. "So this is the Chewore," he said with neither admiration nor amazement, but more as if assessing a situation that required his evaluation.

"Ian Lentos." I held out my hand. "I'll be your PH for the safari."

The charter pilot had already popped the luggage compartment hatch and began unloading the gear. A slightly built young blonde woman pushed the copilot seat forward and slid unaided from the Centurion's cramped back seat, cautiously taking the long step onto the footpad attached to the landing gear strut. She lowered herself to the ground with all the grace she could muster.

I see this one's not waiting for his buffalo or lion, but has brought his own trophy, I thought. The wife was easily more than a decade younger than the mid-forties client. Unlike the makeup-and-hairspray-sculpted wives of some clients, with their carefully crafted good looks, this woman possessed a windblown, bare-skinned natural beauty that was impossible to ignore.

She moved to the left and a half step behind her husband, literally in his shadow cast by the high, hot August Zambezi Valley sun.

"I'm Emily Cassidy." She smiled softly while extending her right hand. Her blue eyes met and held mine in a way that was warm and friendly and nothing more.

"Ian Lentos, Madam Cassidy. Welcome to Chewore." I took her right hand lightly in mine.

"Emily, please..." she said.

We loaded everything in the back of the bush-lorry and headed down the dust-billowing two-track toward the Chenje River tent camp, my client, Cassidy, riding in the cab with me, and his wife up on the padded seat above the open truck bed for the view.

Back at camp the clients settled in before Cassidy and I drove to the range to sight his rifle.

"Take a look at this baby," he said, handing me his perfectly engraved, choice-stocked double safari rifle.

I hefted and examined it with feigned interest. Almost every client during my twelve-odd years of professional hunting has insisted for some reason on showing me his weapon to admire. I'd seen them all time and again, and the only thing remarkable about his was its pristine, barely used condition as if it had just come from the box.

"Nice," I said. "Have you gotten comfortable with it?"

"I had it custom made for me by Blaser. It's chambered in .458 Lott. A classic. None of those peashooter loads. The stock and engraving are their imperial grade."

"How does it shoot?" I was more worried about his marksmanship and experience than the aesthetics of the rifle.

"If you have to ask how much it costs, you can't afford it," he laughed.

"I'm only too aware of the cost of these doubles," I said. "That's why I've had my beat-up Winchester 70 standard bolt action for a dozen years. All I can afford."

"I'll guarantee it's more than your house. When you get to a hundred thousand, just keep going."

"How well do you shoot it?" I asked. The rifle was short and massive, well over twelve pounds. The usual iron express sights on these old-school doubles were topped on his with a long, variable Swarovski scope that cost more than a brand new version of my rifle.

"I've been shooting since I was a boy. I just got this one and have only had it to the range once. But I know well enough what I'm doing."

His three-shot group at a hundred meters was barely passable but not a cause for concern.

"We'll start in the morning by collecting bait for your lion. We've scouted some nice tracks along the banks of the M'Kunga and Maura. A few cats were following buffalo spoor up in the hills as well. We can start after your nyati straight off and use the carcass if we're lucky for meat at a few likely lion spots. Pick up some impala and chance plains game we come across. Can't have too much bait."

We left camp an hour before dawn the next morning, Cassidy and me up front as before with my tracker Levitt and all-around man Marusi back in the truck bed. It didn't take long for my misgivings about this client to be realized.

We rounded a bend in the track among scattered mopani and thornbush when I saw a very nice warthog boar hurrying stiff-legged and tail erect through the brush. It was perhaps seventy meters off the trail. I stopped abruptly and we hopped out. Levitt handed the big double down to Cassidy.

"Not much meat for lions, but it'll give us some nice meals back at camp," I said. I set up the shooting sticks and motioned Cassidy forward. "Take it when you're comfortable."

The hog trotted another ten meters and stopped to look back just as the client fired. The animal dropped immediately and lay kicking wildly.

We rushed forward. The shot had struck mid-body behind the ribs, leaving an ugly gut exit wound. The warthog continued to thrash on the ground.

"Put another in him," I said.

The client stood there grinning. "Would you look at that..." He was bouncing from foot to foot.

"We need to finish him," I said.

Cassidy handed me his camera.

"It's set on video. Take a few seconds of me with the boar before it dies. This'll be great."

I pushed it back at him.

"Uraya i ne banga rako," I said to Levitt in Shona.

He took a folding knife from his pocket, opened it, and carefully slid the long, thin blade deep into the downed animal's chest low just behind its exposed shoulder. The warthog shuddered momentarily, then was absolutely still.

"Why'd you do that?" Cassidy frowned.

"We take game as quickly and painlessly as possible," I said calmly. I thought he might just be simple-minded, but deep down I knew it wasn't true. "It's just the way it's done. An unspoken code of conduct here. It's not only about everyone's safety, but respect for our game animals as well." I walked quickly back to the lorry without waiting for Cassidy or his reply.

We spent the remainder of the day taking a few impala and a nice waterbuck bull without further incident. We used the carcasses to bait several sites where lion tracks had been spotted before the client's arrival.

That evening at camp we enjoyed choice roasted warthog loin chops with a good red South African wine. We adjourned to the fire pit on the patio to have a final sundowner before retiring for the evening.

Cassidy was regaling everyone—his wife, our camp manager, Sharon and her husband, Jerry, and me—with his exploits of the day. I noticed when he poured his third vodka and tonic, two-thirds of it alcohol, into a very tall water tumbler. I was still nursing my lone three fingers of scotch over two cubes, the ice just about completely gone. The client's pretty, young wife, Emily, sat back from the fire reading a book, seemingly oblivious to her husband's ranting.

"Get a load of the little princess," he said sarcastically after he realized she was ignoring him. "Too good for this crowd. As long as she has her designer jeans and credit cards, she wouldn't know if she were in Africa or Cincinnati."

She carefully laid the book on the table next to her, then turned slowly toward her husband and forced a smile. "You've had quite the productive day," she said. "I knew you would."

I could tell she was self-conscious.

"My biggest fan when I prod her," he grinned. "She's pretty and well behaved when reminded, even if not too smart." He laughed out loud. "Just the way I like them."

Emily said nothing for several seconds then rose from her chair to leave. "I believe I'll freshen up before bed." She turned and walked into the dark toward their tent with that mesmerizing body motion shared by every magnificent woman.

The camp managers and I shifted uneasily in our seats. The silence was obvious and awkward.

"We should all probably turn in," I said at last. "We'll have an early start tomorrow and try and follow up on that fresh buffalo sign we came across near the second bait site."

Cassidy drained his drink and headed toward his tent. Sharon looked at me with rolling eyes and a shaking head before she and Jerry walked off.

I had remained by the fire alone for at least an hour when Emily emerged from the darkness and walked over to the place she had been sitting.

"I'm not going to be able to sleep for a bit," she said. "A touch of jet lag. I came to collect my book. Reading in bed always helps me drift off, it seems."

"Of course. It works for me as well."

"You two will doubtless have another big day tomorrow. You'll want to get your sleep, too, I'm sure."

"Are you all right?" I'm not sure why I said it and was embarrassed as soon as the words left my mouth.

"Oh, yes..." she laughed unconvincingly. "He just gets a tad wound up when he's had his drinks. It's nothing."

I got up and walked across the patio. We both waited for the longest moment, not talking but neither making a move to leave.

"You're such a lovely woman," I said slowly, "...with so much going for you. I'm sure you know you're remarkably beautiful with an engaging manner. And in the short time I—the staff here—have spent with you, obviously intelligent and educated. Why...?" I stopped myself before completing the thought.

"He's much different in his element back home," she said, answering my unfinished question. "He's smart, dynamic, a leader. He started a company years ago that has grown to be one of the most successful business software developers in America."

I couldn't tell if she was more impressed with or intimidated by him.

"Just amazingly driven and capable. Brian has been featured in *Fortune* and is a sought-after speaker nationally."

"So that's enough?"

"We've travelled the world. He provides everything I need or even want. And he's very good to me."

"Most of the time?" I said it with intentional irony.

"Honestly, he drinks like that rarely. He's just so very excited about all this."

"Forgive me, but I assume this isn't his first marriage." I suppose my three fingers of scotch were having their effect.

"For me it is, but Brian's first didn't work out. Then we met—before he became successful in business, actually. It was simply lovers' magnetism between us, I suppose." She had a soft, lilting laugh. "But almost as soon as we met, it was obvious he was deeply in love."

"With you," I said, "or with himself?" The scotch was definitely doing its work. I was way out of line.

She turned and again walked slowly into the darkness.

After a few steps she paused and looked back over her shoulder. "Goodnight," she said without even the slightest hint of irritation. I thought her soft lips suggested the faintest smile, but maybe it was my imagination.

The next morning Cassidy and I drove the forested hills and riverbanks looking for buffalo sign, but staying far from the areas we had baited with game taken the day before.

"We're after more lion bait right now," I said. "We'll go for a trophy later. An old bull with broken horns or even a fat, barren cow will do."

After several hours of scouting, Levitt, in the back, tapped the roof of the truck. We all hopped out and examined the cluster of tracks across the sand road.

"These are quite fresh," I told Cassidy after conferring with the Africans. "And there look to be some big ones in this herd. I suggest we follow up on these."

The buffalo spoor led us through low swales between the hills, up on the ridge backs, down into stretches of brushy savannahs, and over hills again. The going was hot and draining, but Cassidy—fit, muscular, and motivated—kept up the hard pace. A few times we heard bellowing or saw splotches of black drifting well ahead through the jesse willows, but the animals always moved on before we could get a good look. Finally we worked up close on the herd grazing along more or less in an open area between two jesse stands.

"There's quite a nice bull in there," I said, looking at the buffalos stretched out before us. "He's better than simply a bait animal. It's an old boy and the horns spread beyond forty inches. The bosses are large and have a lot of character."

"I see him," Cassidy said excitedly.

The animal was no more than fifty yards out and facing us, although clearly unaware of our presence behind a stand of brush.

"Take him when he turns broadside, low, directly in the shoulder. Your first shot has to be good, so take your time and make it count." I set up the sticks.

Cassidy laid his big double .458 in the pocket formed by the crossing tops of the tripod of sticks, aimed carefully, and fired with the massive bull buffalo still facing us. The animal pivoted at the shot and took off directly away from us. I was surprised the hunter had not waited for the buff to turn sideways as instructed, but with a huge, stationery target at only fifty yards it shouldn't have mattered much.

" A chete atekeshura i."

"Levitt says it was barely wounded," I said to Cassidy.

"Yeah," he replied. "I intentionally hit it just inside the shoulder so we'd get to stalk a wounded buff, and maybe get him to charge."

I could barely comprehend what I was hearing. Still, we had a dangerously injured buffalo to deal with, and there was no time for discussion. We all rushed forward and Levitt picked up blood spoor immediately. We trailed the animal for a half hour, carefully picking our way through the jesse thickets into which it had run. Finally we came upon him standing behind a dense clump of willows, only thirty yards ahead.

"Hit him in the shoulder cleanly," I said, "or I will."

Cassidy fired from the sticks and again the bull wheeled and ran. It was a good shot this time. I followed in the lead with Levitt then the client behind. After only a few minutes we heard a loud, low, and long bellow.

"He's down!" I said.

We spotted the buffalo on the ground, lying on its side in an opening between jesse stands. It was down hard but still moving. We ran to a position where the prone animal's back was in front of us. I raised my rifle as a precaution but waited for my client to finish him.

"Shoot between the shoulder blades," I told Cassidy.

"I want to stand closer while he's moving and have you video me making the kill shot." His grin was gaping and obnoxious. He had uncased his camera and once again was pushing it toward me.

"Shoot him or I'm going to, even with you in front of me," I commanded.

Cassidy scowled at me in disgust, turned, and fired into the buffalo's back. It jerked hard and never moved again.

"For the love of God, did you hear nothing we talked about yesterday?" I yelled.

"That was exciting."

"You could have gotten any one of us killed!"

"I was hoping he'd charge. THAT would have been something. I wasn't worried with my double and all, and you behind me. What an experience."

Marusi brought the lorry in, and we winched the huge old bull aboard. On our way back toward camp, we came upon and collected two old calfless kudu cows, Cassidy taking them with an uncharacteristic clean, single shot each. I dared to hope things were changing for the better.

Back at camp the skinners quartered the buffalo and kudus. The Africans and I headed out again with the meat to check all our sites for activity and bait several more lion hides. Cassidy remained at camp to avoid the menial and unpleasant tasks. We drove the bush truck back toward the Chenje River compound well after the sun had set.

I missed the sundowners before dinner, but joined everyone around the fire pit afterwards just so the camp managers wouldn't be stuck alone with Cassidy. He was hitting the vodka even harder than the previous evening.

"There's some news, Brian," I said cheerily, wanting to confirm the next day's hunting plans before he became too alcohol soaked to remember them. "Levitt and Marusi went with me to check all the baits while heading out with the fresh meat earlier."

Cassidy looked expectantly at me but said nothing.

"There's clear sign of lions hitting that one beneath the big acacia on the high bank above the Angwa. A few very large tracks, too. I suggest we give it a go first thing. The boys set up a proper blind atop the little rise about eighty-odd meters out. But we'll have to sneak in early, at least an hour before first shooting light, if we're to have a chance. Are you up for that?"

I took his glare to mean "yes." He seemed to still be pouting from the words we exchanged about the manner in which he took the buffalo.

"Mr. Lentos," Emily said after a lengthy, uncomfortable pause in the conversation, "your speech betrays you as a fellow American. How long have you been here in Zimbabwe? There must be a story there."

I think she simply wanted to distract things from her husband's dismal mood display.

"Everyone calls me Ian. And I came here as a very young man in my mid-twenties to have some adventure. Over a dozen years ago. I was fortunate to be taken under the wing of a greatly respected professional hunter and never looked back. One doesn't get rich, but it's a rewarding life in many other ways."

"And have you a family, Ian?" she asked.

"I married a wonderful third-generation English-Zimbabwean girl nearly a decade ago. We have three children, ages eight to four. She came from a European immigrant line of farmers here, but that's all over now. We have a little home on a very tiny ten-acre plot in the southern lowveld area not far up-country from the Limpopo River. Just a vegetable garden and a few sheep. A very modest place, really, but we love it."

"Your *Ian*," Cassidy cut in, drawing out my name in a way clearly intended to be derisive, "the *Great White Hunter*, gave me a proper scolding out there today. Seems I don't shoot fast and straight enough for his standards."

I turned toward him. "The biggest part of my job is keeping everyone safe, and that includes correcting practices that aren't up to snuff. That and making sure the hunt is conducted lawfully and ethically. It's for everyone's benefit, especially the client's. It's never intended as a personal affront and mustn't be taken that way." I was not about to apologize.

"I'm sure his manly display of superiority only adds to his raw charisma. Isn't that right, Emily?"

"Brian, is this necessary?"

No one made eye contact with him. Cassidy was obviously quite drunk. He stood unsteadily. "I believe I'll hit the sack so I'll be fresh for our lion hunt tomorrow. You two," he nodded at Emily and me, ignoring the camp managers, "enjoy your little conversation." He walked off from the patio area swaying as he went.

We sat for a time in an uneasy silence. The camp managers finally excused themselves and headed toward their quarters. Emily and I were alone.

"I'm so sorry, Ian."

"It comes with the territory. It's not the first time I've been set straight by a tipsy and irritated client. I expected it, actually."

296

I doubt she wanted to go to her tent while he was still awake, and I was nowhere near ready for sleep. We talked by the fire for what must have been an hour or more, her lovely blue eyes reflecting the last flickering light of the dying mopane flames. About our families, growing up, Africa and a dozen other things, until the conversation faded to silence. Until I felt embarrassed in her presence, quite sure the intensity with which I was drawn to her was all too obvious. Was emblazoned like a neon sign across my forehead.

Another hour passed before we finally turned in for the evening. An hour during which our bond blossomed and my attraction became something very much deeper.

In the morning my hunter and I drove in the moonless darkness toward our setup by the Angwa River. Cassidy seemed to feel absolutely no ill effects from his binge the night before and acted at first as if nothing out of the ordinary at all had occurred. I couldn't help but admire his recuperative powers.

"This safari couldn't be going more perfectly," he said with apparent sincerity. "It's been incredible. And I'm beginning to see your point about not only what game gets taken, but *how*."

"Africa has a way of renewing one's soul," I said warily. "I suppose it's why I stayed."

"I've been the difficult client, I know. A thorn in your side. Let's agree we're both turning a new leaf, and not look back."

"Everything's good," I said with false enthusiasm.

"Honestly, I've had a bellyful of that bitch wife of mine, though." He looked out his window as he spoke, at the blackness that revealed nothing.

Somehow I had known his positive mood wouldn't last.

"She seems pleasant enough to me." I could feel myself blush and was glad it was dark inside the cab.

"She gave me quite the tongue-lashing when she finally came to bed, you know. She'll pay for that and everything else when we're home." He turned and looked directly at me. "And I gave her a little taste last night of what's to come."

"Right now we've got our lion to think about," I said. "The sign looked very good last evening." I was anxious to change the subject.

"I want one with a huge head and bushy black mane. I'm having a trophy room built. Can't wait to pop the first really big boy we see."

"We're very selective about the cats we take here—to preserve them for future generations. Fortunately we have a healthy, huntable population now. Still, they're ecologically quite fragile, despite their strength and ferocity."

"Wouldn't it be something if one charged!"

"We take only mature males, and never pride lions. If the dominant pride sire is killed, there is often a disastrous domino effect on the entire group. The females and adolescents are incapable of protecting the others from hyenas, or the cubs from leopards. And any new male moving in will kill the cubs and drive the young males away, often to die. If a young lioness resists, say to protect her cubs, she may be severely or even fatally injured. It could spell the end of the entire pride. So we're looking for a big male alone or in a bachelor group. For an old one that's already been forced out by younger and more fit rivals, or one not dominant enough to take over or establish his own pride."

"Have you had one attack?"

"Most dangerous game, including lions, will run from humans at the first hint. But as with any creatures, they do not all behave precisely the same. Occasionally, for reasons I really can't quite explain, the odd lion will charge when threatened or wounded. It's quite rare, though. Never happened to me. But the old-timers say one percent—one in a hundred—will do the unexpected. I'm sure we'll be fine. If we get on lion, just listen carefully and do precisely as I say. It's your best chance of taking a nice cat and staying safe."

We parked our safari truck some two miles downwind of the hide and crept in with stocking feet. The blind was about six feet square and five feet high constructed from a grid of straight mopane limbs lashed together with vines. Long, dry yellow hard-grass harvested the afternoon before with machetes from a well-distant glade among the mopanes covered the stick frame. A door of sticks and grass swung outward in back. There was a shooting hole eighteen inches square in the front-center, positioned at the level of an aimed gun held by a man sitting on the low log the Africans had put in place. I sat to Cassidy's right in the corner on a higher log and looked from a properly located peephole at the baits chained to the acacia tree some eighty meters away. Levitt was behind me and could pop his head through an opening in the roof put there for that purpose. Marusi had remained back at the lorry. The wind was perfect and it was completely silent. We waited for the lions to return.

The far horizon was just showing the first line of faint light when Levitt pulled his head into the blind through his observation hole in the roof and hissed, "Shumba ri kuuya."

Beyond the acacia tree, the first few cubs rushed clumsily and unconcerned toward the well-fed-on impala baits chained to its base. Then the big lionesses appeared, as if magically, from the darkness with their cautious, halting, eyes-searching movements. When they reached the carcasses, they paused and looked carefully about. The largest one began tearing hunks of meat from an impala. There was no sound.

There was no mistaking the huge and majestic form of the male as it emerged from the brush and began its lumbering, swaggering walk toward the others, its head swaying, feet padding heel to toe silently, its big shoulder blades moving up and down piston-like as it came confidently forward. *The king of the jungle,* I thought.

Even in the dark, its head looked impressively wide, its mane thick and protruding and black. The lion continued to within ten feet of the feeding pride, paused as though completely bored, and lay down on its belly with front feet extended forward, its rear feet folded beneath its huge hindquarters as if in a crouch.

I looked away from my peephole and over at Cassidy, who had his gun shouldered and pointed through his shooting port. His cheek lay along the stock, and he was looking through the rifle's scope. I could see his hand supporting the forearm trembling.

"It's a pride male," I whispered. "No go. We'll wait 'til these feed out. Another subservient one may be waiting safely behind. We might still get a shot this morning."

At that point the massive lion rose suddenly to his feet and stood glaring at the blind. His muscles were visibly taut, attention riveted, his weight well forward over his front legs as if preparing to advance. It was clear he had seen us.

An earsplitting blast shook the blind. As I glanced reflexively toward the source of the explosion next to me, the recoil from Cassidy's big-bore .458 jolted him noticeably backward. From the corner of my eye positioned beside my viewing hole, I caught the motion of the great lion jerking back hard from the impact of the bullet and slamming down oddly in roughly the same position he had assumed a moment earlier, this time both front and back legs extended straight out from his body. His shaggy mane hung down covering his chest, but even in the predawn I could see a smear of dark liquid just off center. His eyes were wide-open, alert, and still fixed intently on us.

I've seen big animals charge time and again. A huge bull elephant crashing forward, fast and nimble, through a young mopane stand. A trapped hippo accelerating from a clump of riverine scrub toward his tormentors, or the iconic wounded, broad, ton-heavy Cape buffalo bursting from jesse willows, propelling his monstrous wide and hulking and long frame from a standing-still start to incredible blinding speed in less than the blink of an eye.

But nothing I had seen before prepared me for the charge of that chest-shot male lion. It rose in an incomprehensible instant from prone on its belly to a blurred, legs churning streak as it closed the hundred yards to our blind in mere seconds with amazing speed and agility and purpose.

I'm told many people, when confronted with a life-or-death threat, experience what I did when that lion charged. A complete focus only on the menace to the exclusion of the outside world. And despite the speed at which the horrible event plays out, a weird sense of viewing things in slow motion, where every step in the unfolding sequence, every movement is clearly seen and later vividly remembered. I recall his legs driving beneath his body, the wind generated by his rush blowing his mane and whiskers back, his head extended and focused on the shooting port—the spot occupied by Brian Cassidy—and, most vividly of all, that rumbling, raw snarl.

The lion hit squarely in the center of the shooting window, his back legs propelling him in a powerful, final airbornee vault, his front legs fully extended with claws spread. His claws entered the blind an instant before his face smashed through the opening, exploding the front of the rickety structure in a shower of grass and sticks. Cassidy fired his second barrel wildly into the air, above the lion's head, just as it crashed through the port and into him.

Contrary to what's seen in the movies and read in popular literature, a lion does not roar when attacking game. That would only serve to alert then terrify the prey, giving it the motivation and opportunity to effect an early escape. No, the lion is still and stealthy when taking down its meal.

But attacking an enemy is another thing altogether. The roar serves to give voice to the beast's rage, to stir the fighting instinct in his soul, to intimidate and overwhelm his foe. And as this huge cat gripped and clawed and ripped the back, chest, and shoulders of the hapless and helpless client, of Brian Cassidy—the soon-to-be *late* Brian Cassidy—as it prepared, mouth open, to seize its victim's face, the booming roar shook what remained of the blind every bit as mightily as had the animal's initial impact.

When a client prepares to take dangerous game, I always stand ready with my own rifle shouldered and centered on the animal, safety *off*, to take a follow-on shot if necessary. But here, I had not expected Cassidy to fire, and my own weapon, while loaded, was at my side, the safety *on*. With the speed at which the lion closed on us, there had been no time to ready the gun and aim through my little viewing window.

As the lion savaged Brian Cassidy, I thumbed the safety *off* and somehow managed to raise my Winchester 70 near my shoulder in the shattered and still-collapsing blind. From the edge of my eye, I glimpsed Levitt ejecting himself through the ceiling hatch in the back corner where he had been sitting, ripping it apart as he exited. The blind was distorted and leaning. The lion had one claw behind Cassidy's head, the other behind his back in a terrible, tight bear hug as it raked his flesh in frenzied strokes. With the man and lion intertwined while rolling about there was no way for me to fire without the bullet clearly going through them both. I watched, rifle ready, as they tumbled as one until all at once Cassidy was on his back on the ground with the lion straddling him from above. I had an unobstructed side view of the lion without my client in the line of fire. I raised the rifle, placing the muzzle directly against the animal's neck in the close, twisted quarters of the wrecked blind. A round was chambered and the safety *off* in the firing position.

How long I waited and watched, or even why, I still don't know. It couldn't have been more than another second or two. But most deliberately and without any reason I can offer, I held my fire. At that point a shot would not have hit Cassidy. In the incredibly brief time I willfully hesitated, the lion placed his gaping mouth over Cassidy's skull and bit down hard. I distinctly heard the cracking of bone. Cassidy gave out a sharp, low moan just as his head was crushed in the huge jaws. I fired into the lion's neck, and it instantly changed from a powerful, magnificent, attacking beast—the *king of the beasts,* long live the king—to a pile of limp and lifeless tissue.

I yelled to Levitt to go to the lorry, have Marusi bring it up, on the way in to notify camp with the radio in the truck there had been an accident. Notify Sharon and Jerry to call for a medivac plane, to meet us at the airport. I pulled Cassidy from beneath the lion and out the back door, by then deformed and ajar. I used the towel in my kitbag to wipe blood from his face, to apply pressure. The most serious wounds were to the head where a tourniquet would be of no use.

"AHhhhh, gaaawwwwd," he managed a low, gurgling moan. It was perhaps the most chilling sound I have ever heard.

We put him in the truck bed while Marusi drove, Levitt and I attending the horribly injured man as best we could. The camp lorry was waiting for us at the dirt airstrip. Sharon and Jerry had brought some first-aid supplies, some bandages, sterile antiseptic wash, morphine, and antibiotic powder. We cleaned and medicated and bandaged Cassidy with our limited supplies and modest abilities. At first, there was an unbelievable amount of blood, not in spurts or from a single source, but flowing liberally from his entire head down and beneath his body like one of those fountains at a mall where water flows continuously along a stone face. By the time the plane arrived and he was loaded aboard, the bleeding had mostly stopped, and he was silent and still. About an hour later we received word he had been pronounced dead on arrival at the hospital in Harare.

The inspectors arrived the next day for their investigation. I filled out a detailed report, writing that the client surprised me by firing even though told not to, that I had shot as soon as I had been able, but by then it was too late. That everything had been done to save him. Levitt had leaped through the roof hole just as the lion hit and saw nothing of what occurred after. His oral account that the Chief Inspector dutifully recorded was completely consistent with mine. Marusi testified to the client's defiant and unpredictable behavior in the field, while Sharon and Jerry reported his unstable outbursts at camp. I'm not sure of Emily's account, but it must have supported ours as the death was immediately ruled an *Act of God* complicated by the client's own mistakes.

During the investigation I had not seen Emily, although I heard her crying whenever passing near her tent. Driving her to the airstrip that final day she looked only at the floor and wept.

"I'm so, so sorry," I said.

"Puh-lee-lee-leeze, God..." She could barely be heard through her heaving sobs. "Please...tell me this had nothing to do with me..."

Her beautiful, previously clear and bright blue eyes were dulled and reddened and swollen. Tears streamed from them. Her lovely, smooth face was contorted in pain.

"It was a horrible accident," I said. "I'm just so sorry." And honestly, I was.

We merely touched hands as she boarded the Centurion, her crying silent once more.

I was scheduled with another client in a few weeks, but cancelled after a fellow professional agreed to fill in. Back home the rainy season was approaching and I had plenty of chores with which to busy myself. During the humid, hot summer months I reroofed the house, repaired the stock fences, and hand drove a new borehole for watering our sheep at a field tank. Summer gave way to fall with a numbing slowness. I spent plenty of time with my wife, Sheila, and our three children. The approach of April heralded the retreat of the rains and the upcoming Easter holiday.

As a Catholic, I was expected by tradition to go to confession at least once each year, during the Easter season. When I visited the aging white frame church in the little European-settled town near our farmstead, the old German priest slid the divider in the confessional open as he had so many times before. I gave him a brief account of what had happened on the last day of Cassidy's life, on some of the events that had led up to it.

"Zo, vot den iss der sin you vish to confess?" the old man asked at the end.

I thought I had made it clear. "I failed to protect my client," I said, probably with obvious impatience in my voice.

"I zee...und vot off der vooman?"

In the Catholic faith, the very act of concealing a serious sin during confession is a greater offense than the suppressed sin itself. I knew that well. Still, I said, "Nothing. She went home. She was very upset. My sin is failing in my duty to her husband. I had a responsibility to be more diligent. I knew he was unreliable and should have taken that into account. And I failed to do it. That is what I am here to confess."

The month dragged on. Near the end of April, I went to town to buy a few supplies and stopped by the post office as usual for our mail. I knew it was from her before I read the return address. The words on the thick, beige, personal-sized envelope were handwritten in blue ink. The letters were elegantly formed with feminine, flowing strokes and swirls. I had never seen her writing, but it was unmistakably from her. And while I had not expected it, had never thought I'd see or hear from her again, I was somehow not surprised.

That evening I sat before the hearth with the last of its mopane fire we built each evening even in the hot rainy season to drive the humidity out. The kids were asleep, and Sheila was in the bedroom getting ready for bed. Sheila with her thick, lustrous brunette hair, those beautiful blue English eyes, and soft, white skin. With her perfectly proportioned, seductively rounded, inviting form. My best friend, the mother of my children. Sheila, my confidante, partner, and bedmate.

"Are you coming?" she called to me. "I'm about to switch off the light."

"In a moment," I answered. "I just want to damp the fire."

I took the unopened letter from my pocket and stared at it for the longest time. I touched it to my nose and lips. My thoughts were of Emily and the brief time we shared. The scent of her hair and glistening moistness of her lips were brought back.

"...and what of the woman?" the priest had said.

I knew I'd be going back to his confessional soon, long before next Easter. I slipped the still-sealed envelope into the hottest part of the remaining flames and watched as it disappeared. Then I closed the damper.

"I'm coming," I called to Sheila.

THE CHURCH OF THE EPIPHANY

"In war there are no unwounded soldiers"
José Narosky, Argentine author

My wife, she likes our family to call her "Mother," was in the front passenger seat next to me, talking on her cell. Our son and my mother-in-law, Mawmaw, rode in the backseat.

"We certainly hope you can join us for Rory's welcome home celebration," Mother spoke loudly into her phone. "It's at Epiphany. Yes. They have the loveliest churchyard with a big gazebo in case it rains. I'm having the food and refreshments brought in. And Rory is *so* excited to see everyone." She turned her head to smile at him in back. "Oh my, yes. That church has been such a part of our lives since I was a little girl. We lived near there back when it was still a decent neighborhood. It's so nice being involved, they're like family. I'm heading the ladies' auxiliary, and John is on the lay committee. Honestly, that church is the center of our lives."

I merged onto Jefferson headed down toward Spalding, the way she liked me to take. That would intersect the ramp to I-74, then twenty minutes on the divided, walled, sterile freeway northwest, safely past the blight that is now downtown Peoria, and home to Charter Oaks.

"Yes, we just stopped by the church for a few last-minute arrangements on our way back from the airport," she continued. "His flight got in from Baltimore only an hour ago. It's wonderful to have him back with us. He had to be checked over at Walter Reed briefly before coming home, just as a formality. He saw a lot of action in Afghanistan."

"It was the psych ward, not a physical exam." Rory said it to me in a loud voice, but it was clear it was intended for Mother. "And I was *treated*, not checked."

"It's The Church of the Epiphany," Mother said into the phone. "One-one-five Alexander, the corner of Madison and Alexander. Peoria, Illinois. Right near downtown. We'll certainly look forward to seeing you there." She disconnected the call and put the phone in her purse.

"You know Walter Reed was just so much bureaucratic procedure." She had turned her head and was facing Rory in the back. "There's absolutely nothing wrong with you at all. I'm sure it's simply a precaution they take with just about everyone. We're so very proud and just glad to have you home."

" 'f you say so," Rory mumbled.

"I'll bet you're glad to see your wonderful Mawmaw again," Mother said to him, acknowledging my mother-in-law with a shift of her eyes and nod of her head. "You two were always so close. You'll have some catching up to do."

"He never called me that," Mawmaw said.

"Why, he most certainly did," Mother said.

"It was you who gave me that name and wanted him to use it. But he didn't."

"You know very well that isn't true," Mother said. "He couldn't say 'grandma,' pronouncing it 'mawmaw' ever since he was a toddler. It was so cute. And it stuck."

"Said it once about two and never used it again," Mawmaw said. "It was you called me that whenever he was around."

"I only said 'Grandma Leli,' " Rory said to Mother. "I remember just you saying she was Mawmaw and nobody else."

I could see Mother's face reddening as it did every time she was about to descend into one of her tizzies. It would be only seconds before she turned her pique on me. Ahead were orange traffic cones and backed-up cars at the construction where Jefferson and Spalding intersected. I made a quick, hard right onto Green to bypass the gridlock, into the bad area of boarded-up businesses and ramshackle tenements with their grassless, litter-strewn yards, shirtless black men sitting on porches beside their barely dressed women, and carefree kids playing in the street. I knew she wouldn't like it, but really it wasn't as much a shortcut as a way to distract her from the *Mawmaw* debate. A lesser evil.

"You know I don't like to go this way!" Mother was almost shouting.

"There was a backup at Jefferson and Spalding."

"There's so much crime and ugliness in these neighborhoods now days," Mother said. "It's so upsetting. I just don't like to see it."

"Can we stop at a drugstore?" Rory said. "I need to get my zannies refilled, bad."

Children were playing at the curb. I saw them, slowed, and edged toward the opposite side of the street to safely pass by them.

"Oh my God! You could have hit one of those children. Or they could have opened the door and jumped in. I *told* you not to go this way. God knows what would have happened..."

Mother was reddening again. I was no longer sure the detour had been such a good idea.

"Oh my Lord. Would you look at all the lil' picaninnies." Mawmaw was looking at the black children. "Awn't they dawling." She affected a southern drawl, smiling. She normally spoke plain Midwestern English the way we all did.

"We used to sing the loveliest little children's song to keep time while skipping rope," Mawmaw said. She sang...

"Ah's a lil' picaninny
Work'n on a cotton-ginny
One-two-three-four
Bales-a cotton I ken score"

"That's horrible," Mother said. "Reverend Jackson says those people deserve our respect no matter."

"We sang it to count our jumps when I was a chile on the plantation in Alabama. And to see who could do the most of 'em."

"You know very well you were born and always lived right here in Peoria. Except when you were away at college."

"Up'n the hollars above the river, all we had when not chorin' was skippin' rope...

"Tall 'n skinny
Work fer a penny
Black as coal
Still got me a soul
Five-six-seven-eight
Love is best 'stead-'a hate"

It was obvious Mawmaw was trying to needle Mother.

"Everyone knows you were an English teacher," Mother said, "and taught young girls piano and elocution in your spare time. Your feigned accent and misplaced humor aren't amusing in the least, and it's as rude as it is odd."

At least her scolding of Mawmaw took her displeasure from me and my detour.

312

I turned left on Glendale to intercept the entrance to the expressway. As we passed the dilapidated old St. Anne's Catholic Church, Mawmaw pointed to it.

"Oh my, there's John's church," she said. "I haven't seen that for ages."

"John goes to Epiphany now," Mother said as if I weren't sitting right there next to her. "You know that. He hasn't gone to that horrible Catholic church for years. Since we were married."

"I always liked the Catholics," Mawmaw said. "Their services have so much more character, with the incense and Latin and fancy robes."

"Why, they pray to statues. And charge money to light candles so prayers will reach up to heaven. They believe priests, not God, can forgive sins. It's little short of black magic or witchdoctory. John is so glad he saw the light and got out of that." She looked over at me. I didn't react. No sense stirring up a hornets' nest.

"I've always wanted to confess to a priest," Mawmaw said. "I believe I'll try it sometime. Maybe you should do it too, Daughter. Cleans the soul. Perhaps I'll convert to Catholicism. John, you can go with me on Sundays. Would you?"

I suppressed a smile. I always enjoyed Mawmaw. "I'm at Epiphany now."

"And he loves everything about it," Mother said, answering for me as she did on all important questions. "No more of the Catholic nonsense. He's completely devoted to Epiphany. Involved in every aspect. He even makes his own unscheduled visits to meditate or pray, like when he can't sleep at night. He's one of the most devout and active members of the church."

"Are you, now?" Mawmaw said. She raised an eyebrow.

As usual, I didn't answer.

313

I saw the heavy steel sewer cover in the street off-center and tilted up above the manhole slightly at one edge too late to avoid it. The left front wheel must have caught the raised side because it banged suddenly and loudly as I drove over it.

Everyone jumped at the sharp *clang*, even me, although I had seen it coming an instant before.

"Jesus-crise!" Rory screamed from the backseat. I could see him punch the ceiling with a clenched fist in the rearview mirror. "Gah-dam summva-bitch!" His face was contorted in what looked like both rage and pain.

Mother turned to look at him. "Are you all right?" she said haltingly.

"It was just a manhole cover," I said slowly and calmly. "I didn't see it in time. Everything's okay now."

"I *told* you not to go this way," Mother said.

"You have no idea," Rory buried his face in his hands and began to sob. He cried softly for what seemed a long time but could only have been thirty seconds or so. "Please...stop so I can get my Xanax. Please."

"There's nothing right here," I said. "I'll find someplace when we get off near Charter Oaks. It'll only be a few more minutes now."

"If you could, please." Rory was calmer but still crying intermittently. "You just have no idea. The things that happened over there."

"Are ya a cryin'," Mawmaw said again in her put-on accent, "about what they done ta you-all...?" She paused for a long time. "Or about what you done to them."

I slowed for the exit ramp onto Charter Oaks Road. There had been an awkward silence for the past fifteen minutes. Mother broke it.

314

"You know, your father here saw and did things in Vietnam," she said to Rory in a soothing voice. "Everything, the uncomfortable things, they all pass eventually. You just have to be patient."

No one else spoke.

"He came home, adjusted, and has had a wonderful life. The two of us together. Your father working with Grandpa in the family business. Managing the second store and later all six of them after my father retired, before we sold out. It simply couldn't have been better."

I knew there was a pharmacy in the corner strip mall ahead and just off Charter Oaks. I slowed and eased into the left lane.

"Your father saw lots of combat, too, like you. He even won decorations. But eventually he was able to put all the ugliness behind him."

"Like you do the ugliness of turned neighborhoods in the city?" Mawmaw said. She was at it again.

"You will, too. In time," Mother said to Rory, ignoring Mawmaw.

Rory seemed to have regained his composure. "What decorations, Dad? I never really knew."

"Nothing much," I said.

"The Air Commendation Medal," Mother said. "And later, the Bronze Star. The point is, he got past it all and didn't let his service experience drag down his life. If he can do it, anyone can. You are certainly capable of the very same thing. Everything will be fine. I promise."

Rory had taken his medicine and was much calmer after we arrived home. He put his things away in his old bedroom upstairs that Mother had insisted we keep for him unchanged and unused even after he had turned thirty. The master bedroom, the one Mother occupied, was across the hall

315

from Rory's. Downstairs on the main level Mawmaw slept in the little guestroom by the short corridor before the garage. I now used the tiny former study as my bedroom, just off the living room, the study with its lone little window onto the backyard and a twin bed, more of a cot, pushed up against one wall.

Mawmaw sat dozing intermittently in the big, over-stuffed living room chair, her walker parked next to it. Rory and I were in the smaller chairs while Mother paced while checking with the prospective guests she had not yet heard from.

"It's tomorrow, Sunday, after the morning service," she spoke into the phone. She said the exact same thing to every invited friend, acquaintance, or family member who was not well familiar with our community: "At The Church of the Epiphany. One-one-five Alexander, the corner of Madison and Alexander. Peoria, Illinois. Right near downtown. We'll certainly look forward to seeing you there."

"When you think about it, it's a funny name for a church," Rory commented to Mawmaw and me, Mother distracted with her phone conversation. "*Epiphany.* I wonder why they call it that."

"The Bible story of *the epiphany,*" Mawmaw said in her precise, eloquent way of speaking, with Mother temporarily not part of the conversation. In her beautiful manner of speaking, intelligent and perfectly crafted without sounding pretentious in the least. With her distinctive and thoughtful use of words, as I knew and remembered for the forty plus years I had known her.

"Story of the epiphany?" Rory said.

"When the three Magi visited the infant Jesus in the manger in Bethlehem, and all at once realized he was more than a prince. That he was indeed divine. A realization of the true nature of a previously obscured reality. That's what an epiphany is."

"They should call it *The Church of Faith*. It sounds more religious than *epiphany*."

I didn't know whether it was the medicine or being home, but it was good to hear Rory making small talk, engaging the family in conversation again like the old days.

"Mark Twain said faith is an abiding belief in something we know is not true." Mawmaw drew her lips in a playful little smile as she said it. "I think I like *epiphany* better. Don't you, John?" She looked over at me.

Mother had put down her phone at last. "I'm going to run up to the florist and pick up the flowers, then a few other things for Rory's party tomorrow." She pulled her car keys from her purse. "I'll be back in an hour. I'll fix something special for dinner." She smiled at Rory.

Mawmaw rose haltingly from the big chair and staggered behind her walker down the hall toward her bedroom. Rory and I remained alone in the living room.

"Honestly, Dad, it's good to be home."

"We're glad to have you back. I'm really sorry it was rough."

"I'll be fine. It's just an adjustment. You must know, with Vietnam and all."

"It's so long ago."

"I never knew much about you being over there. About your medals and all. What happened?"

I took his question as a positive sign. That he was ready to talk about things.

"The medals? Not much, really. The Commendation one was for some of the close support we flew for our grunts. There was a lot of rough terrain and ground fire. I guess someone thought it was a big deal."

"And the Bronze Star?"

"That one...one of our units was being hit by the gooches. We had to maneuver our Phantoms in between some hills held by Charlie. After we dumped our two-hundred-fifty pounders on 'em and emptied our twenty-millimeters, they were still coming, so we flew into them at treetop, kicking in our burners right over them to disrupt things. Later the Marine ground commander claimed we kept his battalion from being overrun. Like I said, not much, really."

Rory looked at me expectantly without saying anything. It seemed like he still wanted to talk.

"I made it back, but all shot up. One engine out, a fuel leak, and the hydraulics just about gone. No way I could make it all the way to the ship. Had to dead stick in and land on a foamed runway at Da Nang, gear stuck up. I guess they thought it was bronze-worthy."

"Your wingman, too?"

"Yeah, but posthumously. He didn't make it all the way back. A good guy, my closest friend over there. He wanted me to be his best man when we got home."

"And you served a full tour? The bronze one must have been the toughest."

"Honestly, I only flew ninety-nine. A hundred missions was a tour. And that last one, the ninety-ninth, was the roughest in its own way."

Rory had slumped back in his chair looking relaxed. Hearing me talk about what I experienced seemed somehow cathartic for him.

"How so, that last one being the worst after the others?"

"It was routine enough to start, like dozens of others before it. We were assigned to hit a Viet Cong concentration in a little village in the sector we were to cover that day, Binh Long Province. I still remember the name of the village, Tan Loi. The maps we carried had a number for each sector, and a series of left-right, up-down coordinates on a grid to guide us to a precise spot. For some odd reason, I can still remember the forward control guy's exact words over the radio: 'Sector 173, Binh Long, C-13 East, V-27 South, Tan Loi.'"

"Why was it the roughest?"

"It wasn't, at first. We rolled in on the village a few miles out, dropping down to five thousand like always. I picked it up at about a mile with a unit of Charlies around a little pagoda off a few dozen meters from the collection of hootches that was Tan Loi. But as I got ready to release, something looked odd. Familiar. Out of place. It made me hesitate. I dropped my ordnance, though, and pulled up. After my wingman unloaded, we came back around for damage assessment. The pagoda was wrecked and there were bodies all over the place. Like clockwork. Another day at the office, I thought. Then we headed back to the carrier for debrief and downtime. That was pretty much it."

"It doesn't sound that bad. Compared to the others."

"Not until that night. I had felt funny all evening but couldn't put my finger on anything. I stayed up late and had trouble falling asleep. I remember the dull, rumbling throb of the carrier's engines before I drifted off. And the rolling and pitching from the wave action of the sea.

"Then I dreamed about that mission, about coming in on Tan Loi, the people, and the pagoda. But it wasn't a pagoda in the dream. It was the gazebo in the Epiphany churchyard where your mother took me when we were dating. And the people were our friends and neighbors. I tried to pull up, stunned, but the Phantom just kept barreling in no matter how hard I hauled back on the stick. I was looking through the bombsite, which was backlit in a kind of weird green light in those days. The harder I pulled, the more the plane shook until chunks of metal began flying off. The vibration of the plane resisting my pull-up got harder and louder. It sounded in the dream for some reason like the crescendo of an acid rock drum solo, like Jimi Hendrix's drummer, Mitch Mitchell used to do. All banging and noise. The plane was controlling me, not me it, everything bathed in green bombsite light, shaking and pounding and drumming, barreling closer and closer to the gazebo and my neighbors. Until it was just a speeding, green-glowing metal skeleton of an airplane, shaking so hard and closing with the ground so fast, with the people, I could no longer make anything out at all."

"Jesus Christ!" Rory said. "What the hell happened then?"

"I woke up suddenly and gasped in a big breath. I guess I realized I hadn't been breathing for a few seconds. I bolted upright in my bunk so fast and hard I banged my head on the steel frame above. I knew I couldn't sleep and just went out on deck, to the fantail where I looked at the black, churning sea beneath the moon-and-starless overcast. I stayed there for the rest of the night. I know it sounds odd. It's hard to explain. I had other missions that were far harder. But that dream really hit me for some reason."

I felt upset all over again just telling it...and awkward having said it to Rory. I didn't want him to think less of me, I suppose, and was afraid it would drag him down. But he only wanted to hear more.

"How do you process, deal with something like that?" he remarked more than asked.

"We were scheduled to fly the next morning. It would have been the final mission of my tour. But I checked into sickbay complaining of dizziness. To this day I don't know if it was true or I made it up. My heart just wasn't in it anymore. But I was given an 'unfit to fly' medical report and sent home with my unit. I mustered out and came straight back to Peoria and your mother."

"Did you ever talk to anyone about it, like one of the docs at Reed?"

"We didn't do that back then. I've never told anyone about it, ever. Not a doctor, my priest, your mother. No one. Until now."

"Wow. And then you went to work for Grandpa in the shoe store? I thought you had an engineering degree or something. What was that all about?"

"Architectural engineering from U of I over in Champaign, just before going in the service. Everyone had to serve back then."

"The engineering sounds way more interesting than running a shoe store."

"Yeah. I was going to Chicago to build bridges and harbors, airports and skyscrapers. Monuments to my talent that would last centuries after I was gone," I laughed. "But I guess 'Nam took the wind out of my sails. I told myself the store was temporary, only 'til I got my feet back under me. Then I married your mother. 'Temporary' just seemed to drag on and on. Mother was happy in Peoria and wanted nothing to do with the big city, but I can't blame it on her, really. I guess it was easier to go with the flow, to not rock our little boat for a while. Until it was too late."

My story seemed to trigger something in Rory, opened a floodgate. He talked on and on about being in Afghanistan, his experiences, the friends he made and the ones who didn't come home. About nights in remote outposts not knowing when the mortars would begin to fall again. How they attacked little mud-walled, ramshackle compounds in the desert, places from which they had taken fire, only to find traumatized, wounded, and dead women, children, and elders when they finally stormed the place. About sleepless nights and *his* nightmares. By the time Mother pulled into the garage, our conversation had already begun to slow.

That evening after everyone else had gone to bed, I made a final check of the doors before turning in. As I passed the hallway to the guest room, Mawmaw called out to me.

"John, would you mind terribly bringing me a glass of water. I'm in bed and it's such a chore to get up again, with my aches and pains and unsteadiness."

I brought the water to her bedside. "Here you are, Lelia, I'm glad to do it. I was just going back through the kitchen anyway."

She took a long, careful drink. "I know where you go," she said. "On your visits at night."

"I know you do," I said.

"I wish I could go with you."

"You wouldn't like it."

"It's better than this hellhole," she said. "But I suppose you wouldn't want a crazy old lady along."

"You're the sanest one in the family," I said. "Sometimes I wish you wouldn't bait her like that, though." I rested my hand on her scrawny arm, skin draped like discolored, blotched cellophane over brittle, protruding bones and raised, thick, blue-green veins.

"It's the only way to get noticed. To be part of the conversation. Lately she's been threatening to take me to the home."

"She won't do it."

"It would be better than here. Dying would be better. It can't come soon enough."

"You're too tough to die," I smiled. "Anyway, what would I do without you?"

"I do wish you'd take me."

"Goodnight, Lelia."

She began humming, then softly singing "Ah's a lil' picaninny, workin' at the cotton-ginny..."

"Don't let her hear you," I looked back over my shoulder as I left the room. "She *will* ship you to the home..."

In my makeshift bedroom I undressed for bed. The doors into the living room were thin double wooden affairs with slots in the upper half of each side to allow air circulation and some light to pass through. Even with the house dark, I could see the glow of ambient light from outside through the louvered slits, the light from cars driving by or neighbors' porch lamps across the street filtering through the living room window, through the slotted doors of the study. And if she was standing outside, listening or peering through the slots, I could sometimes see her shadow, her form traced by the interrupted glow of the light.

"A 'lil picaninny..." I sang softly. I didn't give a damn if she heard or not. To hell with Mother, at least for tonight. Still, I glanced at the door slits just to check. "Working on a cotton-ginny—jes a 'lil color girl—ain't got blond curls—five, six, seven, eight—love is better instead of..."

I lay on the bed in the dark and checked the door one more time. I made the sign of the cross—*In the name of the Father, the Son, and the Holy Ghost*—and began to pray. *I believe in God the Father almighty—creatorem caeli et terrae—et in Iesum Christum, Filium eius unicum—I believe in the Holy Ghost, the holy Catholic Church, the communion of saints, the forgiveness of sins, the resurrection of the body, and life everlasting.*

I closed my eyes and began to feel drowsy. I knew it almost immediately. The first thing was the familiar dim, green glow behind my eyes, in my mind, that soft, enveloping green light from within.

I confess to almighty God—beatae Mariae semper virgini, beato Michaeli archangelo, beato Joanni Baptistae—I

323

have sinned exceedingly in thought, word, and deed—mea culpa, mea culpa, mea maxima culpa...

I knew that tonight I would be making a visit. I found the soft, low rumble of the engines soothing. And the pitching and rolling of the waves. I would sit alone, as I had so many nights before, in my pew at Epiphany. The green light grew in intensity. Soon I would be in the cockpit once more. Yet tonight I understood, for the first time, there would be another visitor in the church. Rory would be there, by himself in a different pew, in his own place. But with me in his church, in our church, just the same. Rory, my son. My only son. The issue of my seed, the fruit of my loins. My savaged, wounded, suffering son.

Yes, tonight I knew I would be going on another of my visits. To The Church of the Epiphany. Sector 173 Binh Long, the intersection of C-13 East and V-27 South, Tan Loi. The people's democratic republic.

Vietnam.

.

THE MOTLEYTOWN BONEFISH EXTRAVAGANZA

"**W**hat would you like to do with your time off?" Laura asked. I had one unused week from my prior year's vacation allotment that would be lost if I didn't use it by the end of April. Time was running out.

"Honestly? What about bone fishing in the Bahamas. The weather is warm and sunny this time of year, and you'd love seeing the flats around Andros Island. Where Jack Verdon and I went."

"Is it nice there? Where would we stay?"

"Jack and I were at the Bonefish Club on the North Island. It's Spartan but clean and comfortable. Last time he went by himself, though, he tried a different place. Where the accommodations were more basic, but there's less fishing pressure and the action is better."

"But it's next week. Is it even possible?"

"Won't hurt to give it a try."

"If you say so," Laura said.

I Googled it and came up with a phone number. The basic website confirmed it was the one Jack had mentioned, on Littlesalt Cay by the south bite.

"Motleytown Deluxe Resort an' Bonefish Lodge. Lindsey Motley." A man's voice answered with the classic Bahamian dialect I had come to know during my visits there.

After identifying myself and exchanging a few pleasantries, I said, "Yeah. My wife and I are looking to come down there for a little bone fishing. Is that something we could set up with you?"

"Oh...ya, mon. Bonefish, dey be our specialty."

"I was thinking of a few days next week."

There was a long silence.

Finally, "No, Suh. We all full. Duh guess, dey mus book tree, usually six muns ahead. Sometime a year. No way nex week." His voice sounded both incredulous and irritated at my stupidity.

"Look," I said. "I'm only talking a night or two. And we're flexible. We could pop down anytime next week. Is there anything...?"

"Jus one minute, Suh..." I could hear him flipping pages in what I imagined was a reservation register.

After a few seconds he came back on the line. "We may put you in duh annex, Suh. Dey iz one vacancy dere. But yas mus come Tuesday and be gone by Tursday in duh mornin. Dot be okay?"

I was able to book a charter in a beat-up old four-passenger twin out of Fort Lauderdale, direct to Motleytown, Andros Island. I sat in front to the pilot's right, while Laura rode in one of the backseats. The upholstery was worn through with a few wads of remaining stuffing poking out. Black crankcase oil flowed in a little rivulet from a crack in the right engine cowling back and into the airstream. The paint, what was left of it, was faded, scratched, and worn through. Little bare-aluminum riveted repair patches dotted the metal skin. The radio the pilot used—apparently the only one working among the aging relics—was held in place beneath the instrument panel by nylon tie-wraps. Bundles of wires wound everywhere. We were out of sight of land.

"Is this safe," Laura said in a weak voice, more a concerned statement than a question.

Our final approach to the short and narrow crushed-shell airstrip was over a wet marsh. A wrecked Seneca II twin, much like one I had trained in back in the day, sat half-submerged a few hundred yards short of the runway, its engines gone and doors sprung unnaturally forward.

"Been there more'n twenty years," our pilot commented. "Longer'n I've been comin' here."

We hopped out and walked to the little open-sided wooden pavilion where a heavyset, squat and bald black Bahamian stood waiting. His red cap, peaked in front like those that elevator operators wore when there still were any, had the word *CUSTOMS* across the front. A wooden, crudely hand-lettered sign nailed crooked to a post announced, *WELCOME TO THE BAHHAMMAS*, the name of the country clearly misspelled.

We signed a form and showed our passports while the pilot offloaded our luggage. That pretty well completed our official reception.

"A cab was supposed to meet us," I said to the agent.

"Over dere, Suh," he said, pointing to a rusty, unmarked vintage car a few yards behind the pavilion. There was no one in it.

We carried our gear to the vehicle and looked around. The customs agent had followed. He opened the driver's side, slid behind the wheel, removed the *customs* hat, and donned a similar but yellow one that read *CAB* across the front. Laura and I looked at each other, loaded our luggage, and hopped in the back.

"I Lindsey Motley," the driver said as we pulled away. "Welcome ta Motleytown."

The Motleytown Deluxe Resort & Bonefish Lodge was an aging, two-story mortar structure like those of the bygone fifties-era motels one sees in the dying beach towns of mid-Florida's Atlantic coast. The once-whitewashed exterior was stained with gray streaks and blotches. Inside, the wooden floor was darkened and uneven. What served as a registration desk sat along one wall in the small combination lobby-bar.

After Lindsey checked us in, he said, "Ya care for a drink from duh bar before goin to yas room?" He motioned to the dark, old wooden bar along the opposite wall, its veneer warped and separating in places.

"Sure. I'll have a vodka and tonic."

"White wine, please," Laura said.

He walked behind the bar and placed a conch-colored baseball cap on his head that read *Motleytown Deluxe Resort,* and under it, *BARTENDER*, all in brown letters.

We sat on unsteady barstools and sipped the drinks that were particularly refreshing after our daylong travels.

"What ya like fer ya suppuh, and at what time ya eat?" Lindsey asked.

"Whenever and whatever your other guests are doing is fine with us," I said. "We'll go with the program."

"Ah...Suh...," he said. "Ya an duh Missus be duh only guess. Iz fer ya ta say."

Our quarters on the second floor were accessed by an exterior wooden stairway. There was a bedroom, sitting room, and bath, all surprisingly spacious. The floors were peeling linoleum tile squares, the walls stained plaster with a few holes punched here or there. The door jambs were all out of square. The toilet stool had gaps between its base and the tile, the plumbing visible in the floor below.

"Nice," Laura said, her sarcasm obvious enough.

"Lindsey said the fishing skiff will be across the street by the pier off the beach in the morning." I was trying to change the subject. "We'll meet our guide there, I guess, around eight sharp. After breakfast. I checked, and the weather should be fine."

She nodded glumly. It was a bad sign.

We arrived in the dining room for supper just off the lobby at the appointed time, seven in the evening. It was still bright outside.

Lindsey walked into the room wearing a French-style, high and puffed white chef's hat. Red lettering around the band said *Kiss the Cook*.

"What I fix ya fer tonight?" he said with a happy smile.

"So you're the cook, too!" I said. "Hope you're getting paid for all this."

"Da regla cook be from Arizona," he said. "Was in duh prison dere. He gun leff hare sudden lass night. Dey find him, I tink, he hadda go ver fass. I take care'ah yas, doe."

I hadn't seen a server, either. "You the waiter, too?"

"Waitress be duh girlfrien. Har goin wit dot mon, duh cook. I bring ya duh food, okay?"

"A lot for one fellow to do."

"My brudder, Umfry. He be over ta Nassau today, but gun come hare tonight. He duh big boss, duh owner. He help me out when he get hare."

"So Humphrey's the owner of the Motleytown Deluxe Resort?" I said more than asked, clearly pronouncing the "*H*".

"Umfry," Lindsey said. No "*H*".

"Humphrey?"

"It be *Umfry.*"

"How do you spell it?"

"Umfry," he repeated, not spelling out each letter.

"Okay, then," I said.

Dinner was a surprisingly nice, fresh yellowtail snapper with rice and beans. We enjoyed a good tossed salad with a cookie and coffee for desert.

The bed was lumpy but passable. Laura and I both read for a while, she dozing off and me getting up to use the bathroom. I opened the door from our bedroom to the main room and switched on the light. The biggest cockroach I'd ever seen scuttled away under the glare of the single bare bulb.

I swear I could have thrown a saddle over him and broke him right there. But I took the book I was carrying and hurled it down on him. It was a perfect hit, the book landing flat and hard directly on the squirrel-sized insect with a loud bang.

"Bingo!" I thought. "One roach down."

The thick hardcover novel bounced off the bug. It continued on unfazed, as if nothing had happened. I grabbed the book from the floor and gave chase, intending to administer another crushing blow. The cockroach scurried beneath the wide gap under the bathroom door. In fast pursuit, I threw it open in time to see him dive beneath the toilet base through the gap in the floor.

"Damn!" I said out loud. I used the toilet quickly, one eye on the opening, then returned to bed, careful to close the doors behind. I never said a word to Laura.

After breakfast Lindsey confirmed we were to take our things to the pier directly across the dirt main street, the harbor road of Motleytown.

"Umfry, he gun be hare dis night," Lindsey told us as we rose to go to our room and collect our gear.

"Fine," I said. I thought I remembered him saying last evening Umfry would be here this morning, but I really couldn't see what difference it made to us either way.

The beach was a heaping mound of broken, pink and white conch shells that stretched along the shore as far as one could see. A collection of aging wooden boats rode at anchor a few yards off the beach. Near the end of a sagging, twisted wooden pier sat a classic sixteen-foot or so bone fishing skiff with a forty-horse Johnson outboard, a level casting deck across the bow, and a poling platform extending on legs above the stern. There were three plastic bucket-type seats. No one was around.

We waited for ten minutes. With no guide in sight, we began loading our tackle and day-bags. "Maybe Umfry was supposed to be the guide," I said absently to Laura. Then I saw Lindsey ambling, big and awkward, down the pier. As he drew close, I could see the dark blue lettering on his white baseball cap. *GUIDE,* it read.

We took off across the harbor on a splendid, sunny Caribbean day, the water gin-clear but reflecting from the sky—from the varying depths and bottom-cover—lovely hues of blue, green, tan, or a mixture of different shades and intensities. The deeper trenches, channels, or holes in the bottom were well defined in very dark, sometimes midnight blue. The breeze was light and our mood fine.

About fifteen minutes out, a few miles from shore, a large, gray shadow floated across the shallow bottom fifty or so yards off our beam. "What's that fish?" I asked Lindsey.

"Dot be ver big hammerhead," he said. "Dey dangerous."

Perhaps a half mile beyond the hammerhead shark, I noticed a man standing in a small boat and waving his arms frantically. I pointed.

"Dot fella, he boat be broke. He want duh ride back home," Lindsey said. It was obvious he had seen the boat well before I had. He motored on, clearly intending to ignore the man and his plight.

"Go on over there," I said.

We pulled alongside the stranded skiff. Its outboard engine cover had been removed and was in the water, tied to a fraying length of old rope as some kind of makeshift sea anchor. The bay was shallow enough to see the sand bottom a dozen or so feet down. The interior of the old wooden boat held standing water. There was no spare gas can or oars to be seen.

The two Bahamians exchanged a few rapid, unintelligible words in their local, oddly cadenced dialect.

"He say he be stranded duh night," Lindsey explained. "Motor be broke. He come from duh fishin trawler out by duh deep ta go ta Motleytown, see duh girlfrein little while. Dot hammerhead, go roun dot boat all duh night. Want duh ride in. I say ta dot boi, no, I got duh clients, a meestuh an madam." He started the engine and began to pull away.

"Hold on," I said. "It's only fifteen minutes back. Tell him to hop in. We'll take him to the pier."

The stranded fellow beamed from ear to ear as he climbed into our boat.

"Tank you, tank you," he smiled, taking my hand in his and pumping it. "What kine-ah fish ya like. I bring ya some fer yas suppuh. Ta duh resort were ya be."

"Gotta love fresh grouper," I said.

"Sure...sure, duh grouper be good. Be dere fer ya dinner dis night. Tank you. Tank you."

Across the bay, our stranded sailor safely back at the pier, Lindsey cut the engine and poled the skiff slowly among the mangroves. We searched the shallow, clear water for any moving shadows that might signal bonefish.

"Dere, dere Meestuh Rob." Lindsey strained to bend at the waist to keep his profile low and set the pole. The boat twisted about the pivot point of the pole held into the bottom.

"Where?" The boat was turning. Finally I saw the three gray moving forms gliding beneath the surface forty yards to our right.

"Look there!" I said to Laura. "About one thirty, moving parallel to shore, toward us. Cast well in front of them so they won't spook and scatter."

Laura had one of my spinning rods with a pink lead-head jig, the hook baited with just of bit of crab Lindsey had brought, just enough to give the lure some scent and flavor. She tossed it only twenty yards out to the side. I doubt she saw the barely visible fish, but the jig landed right in their path.

"Let it sink and lie on the bottom. Don't move it, and stay low," I said. I could feel the excitement building.

The three bonefish moved to within a few feet of her motionless lure.

"Barely twitch it," I said.

She moved the tip of her rod slightly as one of the shadows approached the very spot where her bait had splashed into the water less than a minute earlier. Her rod bent sharply as the drag began to sing.

"Fish on!" I half shouted and laughed.

The fish made a hard fifty-yard run before stopping but still keeping Laura's rod tip bent well down.

"Work him back in," I said. "Lift the rod and reel as you lower it again. And keep the line tight."

About ten yards from the boat, the bone made another run, not as long this time. She repeated the process of pumping him in. The whole thing was repeated one more time. As she brought the fish alongside the final time, I reached in and scooped him up with a hand. He was about a three-pounder.

"I had no idea they were so strong." She was grinning and looking at her fish.

"He had a lot of fight in him for his size."

"Is he a big one?"

"Fairly good," I fibbed.

"He took so much line, I thought I'd run out."

"You did great."

"Let's take him back for dinner."

"I'm afraid catching them is just for fun. They're not good eating. Like the name suggests, too many bones."

I removed the jig hook and carefully slipped him into the water. He took just seconds to recover before swimming quickly away. Lindsey went back to poling the skiff, but after a few minutes, there was noisy splashing in the water near the shoreline where we had released the fish.

"Shark get him," Lindsey said. "Dey smell da blood an follow afta dem like duh houn-dog."

Lindsey's poling was lackadaisical. He stopped to rest and look around frequently. We moved between the mangroves and up a little tidal creek.

"What's this creek called?" I asked him.

"Dot be Freshwater Creek."

"It's the same name as the one on North Andros up near the Bonefish Club where I fished before."

"Ya, Meestuh Rob. Dey all be called dot cause duh water be fresh, not duh seawater."

Even with our slow pace and periods of inactivity, Laura and I each caught several more bonefish. She continued with her spinning rod and jig, while I used a sturdy saltwater fly rod I'd brought with a bulging-eyed pink shrimp imitation. At one point I spotted a very long shadow lying just below the surface over slightly deeper blue water.

"Is that a bone?"

"Barracuda," Lindsey said. "Dey like duh needlefish dot be on dis flat. Take dot rod dere and cass at him."

A sturdy spinning rod lay beside the seats along one freeboard. It was baited with a long, lime-green tube-lure made of colored rubber surgical tubing slipped over a wire leader. A lead weight capped one end of the tube, and three treble-hook gangs, attached to the wire leader beneath, protruded at intervals through the tubing along its length.

My cast was about a dozen yards beyond the cuda and a few yards in front of what I took to be the shape of his head.

"Reel fass, Meestuh Rob. Fass as ya can!"

I cranked with all the speed I could muster. As the lure approached the spot where I had last seen the fish, the water seemed to explode. The rod pulled parallel to the surface before I could haul it back and create the proper bend. I worked the fish to the boat, overcoming long runs, hard pulls, and lots of thrashing. Finally Lindsey used a gaff to bring him aboard in the stern beneath the poling platform.

"Our guess doan eat dese," he said. "But we boil dem ta get duh poison out. Den dey vere fine."

We had seen many rays and small sharks gliding over the bonefish flats. Big starfish lay along the bottom.

"What kind of sharks are these?" Laura asked at one point.

"Dey san sharks, Madam," Lindsey said.

"Do they bite?"

"Oh, no, Madam. Dey mosely eat duh crab or udder fish."

"Can we try to catch one?"

Lindsey lazily poled the skiff up a brackish creek with the tide flooding in. He anchored in the channel and baited the big spinning rod with a plain treble-hook and chunk of meat from the head of our barracuda. He handed the rig to Laura.

"Hole duh hook about tree feet above duh bottom, Madam."

It couldn't have been ten minutes before the rod bent double and the drag began to run out. Laura fought the fish for another twenty minutes or so, using our techniques for the cuda and bonefish. Finally she pulled the head of a nice sand shark just clear of the surface beside the boat. We could see through the clear water it was something over four feet in length.

"My gosh, look at that shark!" Laura said. She was squirming in her seat from excitement.

Lindsey had grabbed the gaff.

At that point the fish opened its mouth wide, lunged from the water, and bit hard. The braided steel line separated beneath its teeth like string. The shark fell back into the creek and disappeared, leaving the frayed, kinked end of the wire leader dangling in the breeze. I think Laura was more thrilled by the dramatic and violent escape than hooking her shark and bringing it boatside.

Lindsey brought in the anchor and poled the skiff a few yards to a sandbar on the edge of the creek. He beached the boat.

"I be goin get more crab back in duh mangroves," he said. "Yas rest here one minute an haf ya lunch." He disappeared.

"I guess he's a good guide," Laura said after he was safely out of earshot. "We've each got bonefish, there was your barracuda, and then my shark."

"He poles in slow motion." I measured my words, not wanting to throw cold water on the trip I had put together for us. "Rupert up at the Bonefish Club on North Andros works three times as hard. We cover way more ground and he spots lots of fish. I'm sure we missed a ton. And there are no rest stops with Rupert."

We enjoyed the sack lunches Lindsey had provided and took in the beautiful scenery. It was a half hour before he finally returned with no crabs.

We poled and waded flats for the balance of the afternoon, landing another bonefish each before returning sunburned and wind-drained to Motleytown. Dinner was more yellowtail snapper like the previous evening. It came as no surprise our rescued seaman hadn't shown with the promised grouper. Still, the evening was good.

"Umfry, he be hare in duh mornin," Lindsey said as we left the table and headed up to our room.

Laura and I just looked at each other. She rolled her eyes.

"Sure," I said to Lindsey.

In our room, we packed most of our things for our charter back in the morning. We read until well after dark. The only bar in town, a ramshackle place just next door with warped plywood over some of the broken-out windows, rang with talk and shouting and laughter. Soon the raucous group of locals spilled into the dirt street beneath our window.

"It may be a long night," I said.

"I'm so tired I'm sure I'll drift right off and sleep like a log," Laura said.

"Do you think there really is an Umfry?"

"Maybe he's Loa, the invisible voodoo spirit," she laughed.

"Or Lindsey's imaginary friend."

"Maybe Lindsey is Loa," she kidded.

"Or the real Umfry using an assumed identity. Maybe he's the fugitive cook from Arizona who has murdered the real Motleys."

"Honestly, though, even with everything it was spectacular out there. I never could have imagined."

"We actually did fairly well on the fish."

"It's one thing to see a place, like on a tour. But to actually be in it, participating in what it's all about, that's something altogether different."

"We'll remember this better than if we had been at a first class place like the Bonefish Club." Both of us broke out in laughter.

We had undressed and were sitting on the edge of the bed. I reached over and laid my hand on hers.

"I had such a wonderful time," she said. "With you. I'm so glad you arranged this, with the short notice and all."

"Speaking of which..." I said. "I'll have more vacation in a month."

"And just what would you like to do?" She arched her eyebrows.

"Actually, I've always dreamed of a hunt in Africa. And it's getting nice now. In May. The rainy season has ended."

"Are there decent accommodations? Where in the world would you have us stay?" She sounded skeptical, and I knew she was toying with me.

"If we're talking about next month, the good places are already booked. They're tied up a year, two years in advance. All right, sometimes three. But I heard about a new place. Pretty basic, but less well known and off the beaten path. A little rougher, really, but the hunting is supposed to be better."

"Is that even possible? To arrange something like that with so little time..." She lay down on her side and pulled the sheet up.

"Wouldn't hurt to give it a try. I'll call tomorrow night when we're home."

She raised up on an elbow, smiling, and kissed me lightly on the lips. "Nice try, but not a chance, Mister." Then she switched off the light.

From the Publisher

Now that you've finished, did you like our stories?

We certainly hope and expect you enjoyed them all. That's why we published them. Now could you take a moment to let us and others know what you think?

Please let the world in on your experience with a brief review on Amazon, Barnes & Noble, or maybe Google Plus. Then there's Goodreads.com. It's quicker and easier than you might imagine.

Or just post a comment on your Facebook page, Twitter, LinkedIn, YouTube, your e-mail list, or your favorite hunting and fishing blog. Better yet, try several of the above. We never tell readers what we want them to say: good or bad, it can be as brief as you wish and certainly in your own words.

We are a small publishing company with a modest marketing budget. Our ability to get our stories out and create more for your future enjoyment depends upon word of mouth.

And by all means, e-mail us at contact@cannichecove.com or write author John Bascom at jgbascom@ejourney.com. We'd love to hear from you.

Thanks for joining us on this walk *Beneath a Hunter's Sky*.

Canniche Cove Publishing
www.cannichecove.com

www.ingramcontent.com/pod-product-compliance
Lightning Source LLC
Chambersburg PA
CBHW070204260626
47160CB00002B/440